THE ELIXIR OF YOUTH

Further Titles by Gillian Bradshaw from Severn House

THE ALCHEMY OF FIRE
DANGEROUS NOTES
THE WRONG REFLECTION
THE SOMERS TREATMENT

THE ELIXIR
OF YOUTH

Gillian Bradshaw

This first world edition published in Great Britain 2006 by
SEVERN HOUSE PUBLISHERS LTD of
9–15 High Street, Sutton, Surrey SM1 1DF.
This first world edition published in the USA 2006 by
SEVERN HOUSE PUBLISHERS INC of
595 Madison Avenue, New York, N.Y. 10022.

British Library Cataloguing in Publication Data

Bradshaw, Gillian, 1956–
    The elixir of youth
    1. Pro-life movement - California - Fiction
    2. Molecular biologists - California - Fiction
    3. Fathers and daughters - Fiction
    4. Suspense fiction
    I. Title
    813.5'4 [F]

    ISBN-10: 0-7278-6308-8

Typeset by Palimpsest Book Production Ltd.,
Polmont, Stirlingshire, Scotland.
Printed and bound in Great Britain by
MPG Books Ltd., Bodmin, Cornwall.

One

I was poleaxed by jet lag when I arrived in L.A. It was one in the morning, English time, though in California it was only late afternoon. I hadn't slept well the night before I set off from Heathrow, and it had been a long flight. I shuffled into the queue for Immigration, stupid with fatigue.

The passport man eventually took my red EU passport, leafed through it, then gave me a look of suspicious disapproval. 'Alison Greenall?' he demanded. 'What's your purpose in visiting the United States?'

'I'm, uh, visiting a relative,' I told him, trying to sound as though it were something that happened all the time. 'My father.' It was the most natural thing in the world, after all, and perfectly true, too. Presumably my father was waiting out there in the airport arrivals hall now. Suddenly wide awake again, I wondered if I would recognize him. I only knew his face from old photographs.

The passport man grunted. 'And you're a student?'

'Umm . . . yes. That is, I just graduated.' The thought of my shiny new BA made me smile.

The passport man gave me a beady-eyed scowl. 'How long are you planning to remain in the United States?' he demanded, as if my new degree were just cause for suspecting that I was an illegal alien sneaking in to steal the job of some decent red-blooded American.

'Uh, th-three weeks!' I stammered, taken aback. 'I'm flying home on the sixteenth of August.'

1

He gave me another glower. 'Huh. What'd you graduate in?'

'Philosophy.'

This caused the usual blink and slightly blank look, and then the passport man evidently concluded that philosophers threatened no jobs, since nobody in his right mind would hire one. He lost all interest in me, stamped the passport, and let me through to claim my luggage.

There was a crowd of people around the relevant luggage carousel, but the belt was empty. I stood under the fluorescent lights with the rest of flight BA 236 from London, watching the conveyor creak around and around while a booming PA system made the occasional unintelligible announcement. I imagined my father looking impatiently at his watch. The image I had of his face came from one of my mother's wedding photos: a sharp, foxy face, with a wide forehead and pointy chin. He had been turned toward the camera with an insincere smile, his eyes fixed on something outside the frame. I pictured the same superior smile on his face as he greeted me, and felt queasy.

It had always annoyed me when my mother told me I looked like him. I'd hated it when she said that my brains or my ambition or my nasty argumentative disposition were 'just like your father'. I hadn't wanted to resemble the man who'd abandoned us. I didn't want to be just like my father; I wanted to be like . . . well, I'd had a series of adolescent idols, from Sigourney Weaver to Aung San Suu Kyi. If I was honest, though, I had to admit that I was not the least bit like any of them.

Maybe I *was* like my father. I was not a particularly nice person, I knew that. I *wanted* to be, but all the Ethical Philosophy in the world won't make up for an inherent lack of generosity and gentleness. I was much too fond of winning arguments, and not fond enough of people.

Perhaps, though, there was more to my father than I'd

heard about from Mum. Or perhaps he'd improved with age, and there was hope for me, too. He'd certainly been very keen on meeting me; he'd even said he was sorry he'd ignored my existence for such a long time. 'You should go,' Mum had said firmly, when I received the invitation. 'He's the only biological father you've got: you should at least *meet* him.' Then she'd smiled and added, 'At the very least it'll be a free holiday in California.'

I'd been a bit shocked by her attitude, actually. I'd expected her to be nervous about it, maybe even worried about losing the affections of her only daughter. Obviously not. Mum had remarried shortly before I started university. I liked Matt, her husband, and I was happy for her, but sometimes I felt that I'd been unceremoniously tipped out of the nest. I told myself that, firstly, she was entitled to her own life, and, secondly, she was quite right to feel confident of my loyalty. She knew, after all, that there was no way I was going to decide that my father had been *right* to walk out on us.

Luggage finally arrived on the carousel, first in dribs and drabs, then in clumps. I collected my suitcase and backpack, steered through Customs without too much trouble, and staggered out into the arrivals hall. A dozen human dramas were unfolding all around me: a thin, bottle-blonde grandmother tearfully embraced a plump young woman with a toddler; a middle-aged woman hurled herself into a man's arms; a large Chinese family thronged about a visiting matriarch; a group of black teenagers in base-ball caps cheered their returning school team. I paused at the end of the railing, looking around with a dry mouth and pounding heart. I couldn't see anyone who looked like my father.

Not far off was the business crowd, the group of men in suits or jackets who stand about at airport arrival gates holding cardboard placards with names on them. One of them had a placard that read 'ALISON GREENALL'. I stared at it, for a disappointed moment certain that my father had sent a taxi to collect me – and then the man holding it met my stare, and his eyes widened, and I saw that it was him.

He was a lot stouter than in the photographs – not exactly *fat*, but fleshy and soft where he'd been wiry and sharp. The hair which had been ginger was now mostly gray, and the fierce blue eyes were surrounded by wrinkles. He was dressed smart-casual, in pale trousers with a tailored cotton sports jacket over a pale blue shirt. My mother had married a hungry young outsider: this was a substantial member of the establishment.

I'd known that, of course. I'd known he'd grown rich and successful while Mum and I were poor and struggling. I just hadn't known how it had marked him. I knew his age was forty-six, but he looked older.

He lowered the placard and came over, hurrying at first, then hesitating and uncertain.

'Alison?' he asked breathlessly.

'Yeah,' I replied.

'It's me,' he said. 'Brian Greenall. Your father.'

We stood looking at one another for another long moment. He made a small movement of his arms, as though he wanted to hug me, and I hurriedly took a step back. He lowered his arms again, then tucked his placard under an arm, as though that was all he'd meant to do to begin with.

'Stupid thing,' he said of it, giving me a nervous smile. 'I just wasn't sure we'd recognize each other. The last time I saw you, you weren't even toddling.'

'Yeah,' I said again, and cleared my throat.

'I *would* have recognized you, though,' he went on, the smile still plastered across his face. 'You look like my mother – when she was a young woman, I mean.'

I'd never met his mother. She'd died before I was born, and his father had never had any interest in me. Mum's parents were the ones who'd remembered my birthdays and sent me Christmas presents, the ones we'd visited in the holidays. They were 'Gran and Grandad'; the other side of the family was just 'Brian's horrible old father'.

'Well,' he said, after another awkward pause. 'The car's outside. Can I take your suitcase?'

I let him take the suitcase, and we crossed the arrivals hall with a space between us, him a little in front, me behind and to the side, with my elbows stupidly tucked in so that they wouldn't knock against the invisible line between us.

We emerged from air-conditioning into a blaze of heat. The evening sun was golden in a smog-tinged blue sky, and the air smelled of exhaust fumes and hot concrete. Brian (easier to think of him that way than as 'my father') led me along the front of the building and on into a carpark. There were flowerbeds flanking it, filled with some pale fleshy-leaved plant with delicate pink blossoms. To my English eyes some of the cars looked equally exotic: enormous saloon cars and the notorious SUVs. Brian crossed a row of them to a dark glossy monster – not an SUV, but a shiny estate car of some type I didn't recognize. He unlocked it with a touch of the keyfob, stowed the suitcase in the boot, and waited while I shrugged out of the backpack.

Brian took the pack with a reminiscent smile. 'I back-packed right across Europe when I was your age,' he told me, placing it carefully in the car's huge boot.

'I know,' I replied, and he gave me a startled look. 'You did a lot of it with Mum,' I reminded him. 'She has pictures of it.'

'Oh,' he said, embarrassed now. 'Oh. Yes. I'd forgotten that.'

He shut the boot and went round to the driver's place, picking up a pair of sunglasses from the leather uphol-stery. He put them on; they were some kind of designer reflective shades, and looked much too cool for a man of his age and girth. I suppressed the grimace and climbed into the front passenger seat next to him. There was proper carpet underfoot, not cracked rubber mats like the ones in Mum's Metro. Brian started the car; the air-conditioning came on with the engine, blasting into the sun-baked inte-rior. We drove sedately out of the lot, pausing to pay five dollars to a tired Hispanic man at the barrier.

Brian said nothing for a time, preoccupied with getting on to the right road. The car cooled quickly. The sealed windows and the hum of the air-conditioning cut us off from the world around us, making the view of California seem like something from a silent film. I had never been to the United States before – never been further from Britain than France, in fact – and I looked at the country hungrily. There were hills to the east, covered with scrubby greenery, and as we drove towards them, the rise of the land gave me a view of the ocean behind and to the north of us. The late afternoon sun covered the blue of it with an overlay of gold, dazzling; maybe Brian had an excuse for his shades, after all. The big car glided smoothly on to a wide motorway where cars roared along multiple lanes.

'You can see the Hollywood sign from here,' Brian told me after a few minutes. I looked, and, sure enough, there it was: the big white letters spelling out 'Hollywood'. I felt more than ever that I was in a film.

'We'll take 101 north,' said Brian. 'It'll take about two hours. Hour and three-quarters, maybe, depending on the traffic.'

I nodded. I knew where he lived, though I'd had to look for it on the map.

'I hope you'll have a good visit,' he went on, nervously

now. 'It's, ah, very pretty country. Mountains. And the sea is only thirty minutes away.'

He said 'thirdy minuds' like an American. His accent wasn't really English any more, though it wasn't completely American. He'd been here a long time now – almost my entire life. I didn't know what to say. I didn't know what I'd expected, but this pudgy nervous foreigner wasn't it. Maybe I shouldn't have come.

I was here, though. I'd decided that I wanted to know more about the man beside me, this stranger who'd provided me with half my DNA. There was no point in quarrelling with him before we'd even got back to his house.

'There's . . .' Brian began again, hesitantly, just as I said, 'Sorry, I'm not taking much in.' He glanced over at me, and I added, 'I'm pretty jet-lagged.'

'Oh, right!' he exclaimed, relieved. 'Yeah, it must be what – two a.m.? – by your clock.'

He drove on for a few minutes in silence. The motorway raced past suburbs full of large houses, with green lawns and swimming pools, and past surface roads lined with ugly malls and fast-food joints. Exits were signposted 'Beverley Hills' and 'Sunset Boulevard'. There were palm trees, eucalyptus, the occasional bougainvillea drowning a wall or fence in an exotic burst of bright mauve. Occasionally the Californian countryside would break into the human landscape: dry hills covered in scrubby gray-green bushes and twisted gray-barked trees. The junction with highway 101 came up, and we turned northwest.

'I'm glad you agreed to come,' Brian said at last. 'I'm sorry I . . . I'm sorry we don't know each other. I'm hoping we can correct that, at least a little.'

I leaned my head back into the leather headrest. 'Look, I'm sorry. I really am too tired to talk now.'

'No,' he agreed quickly. 'I just wanted to make sure I said it.'

The motorway climbed into the arid hills. There was a sign to Malibu, but we'd lost sight of the sea.

'There's something I should warn you about,' Brian said at last. He took a deep breath. 'Um. There was an incident at my lab a couple of nights ago. I'm hoping it won't impinge too much, but, um, it may. The fall-out's been a bit of a nightmare. I'm sorry.'

I looked over at him warily. His profile was soft and plump; the mirror lenses masked his eyes completely. 'An "incident"?' I asked suspiciously.

He made a face. 'Some pro-life group posted our address on their website, and two nights ago we had a break-in. A lot of equipment was smashed, and we're still not sure what's been stolen and what's simply been wrecked. We've had the police round about it, and all the staff are very upset. We're trying to replace our equipment, and the insurance is a nightmare. I'm sorry; I really wish this had happened some other time.'

'Oh.' I didn't know what to make of this. I'd known that Brian was director of his own medical research company, but I couldn't see why he would have trouble with pro-lifers. So far as I knew, none of his research had anything to do with abortion. It sounded fishy to me. Brian had enticed me across the Atlantic with, among other things, the promise of a tour of California, and I wondered if this was just an excuse to back out of it. I almost said as much, then reminded myself that I didn't want to quarrel with him.

'A pro-life group?' I managed to ask at last. 'Why'd they pick on you?'

'We use stem cells in our research,' said Brian resignedly. 'The pro-lifers think that this is . . . I don't know, inciting and exploiting abortion.' He gave me another glance and added, 'The US government forbids the use of federal funds for stem cell research, so there aren't that many companies involved in it. Just small privately-funded ones like us. If you've only got a few targets, it's easier to shoot at them.'

'Oh.'

There was another long silence. I expected him to say more about the break-in, or explain what he used stem cells for, but in the end all he did was ask, 'You graduated OK? From Oxford?'

'Yeah.' I remembered the whole shebang: the stately Latin ceremony and the fake bunny-fur hood; the way it rained during the college garden party to commemorate the event. The dinner with Mum and Matt, made awkward and miserable by the fact that I'd just broken up with my live-in boyfriend, who'd been expected to join us. His empty chair sat at the table like the one reserved for the prophet Elijah at a Jewish Seder, and we all talked around his absence. I didn't feel comfortable telling any of it to Brian.

'In philosophy,' said Brian.

'Yeah. A two one.'

'Not bad,' Brian remarked appreciatively. He'd got a first, I knew. And a PhD and a string of post-doc positions in top institutions, and finally his own company. His brains obviously got watered down a bit in me.

There was a silence. 'How's your mother?' he asked.

I told him a bit about how Mum was – not that he seemed interested. The highway crested the hills and descended again to run along the sea coast. I yawned and slumped against the window.

I drowsed with my eyes open as we ran along the coast of south California, wondering afterward if I'd dreamed it: the surfers and the seagulls, the palm trees and pelicans, the vineyards and the orchards of avocado and lemon trees, the endless beating of the waves in the sunset. I woke up a bit when the highway turned inland, and we began to climb into the mountains. Looking at the map I'd imagined snow-capped peaks, but these were just big hills, rocky and dry, cloaked in gray-green scrub and scarred by gullies. The highway rounded a slope and descended again into an intermediate valley. Brian soon turned off the motorway on to a narrow road which climbed back up the hillside we'd just descended.

We came to some houses: big places, set well back from the road so that when you drove past all you saw was one of the stereotypical American mailboxes and maybe a glimpse of roof or wall through trees. The car slowed, and at last turned into one of the narrow drives. We went up steeply – the drive a mere slot flanked on either side by a rock wall and shrubs – then emerged on to a paved terrace in front of the house. There was a red sports car already parked there, with a dusty blue Honda next to it. Brian frowned at them, but squeezed his monster in over at the side and stopped the engine.

'Here we are!' he exclaimed, with false heartiness.

We got out of the car. The house was long and low, a designer creation of stained wood and non-reflective glass, surrounded by trees and tall yucca plants. The air smelled of eucalyptus, sage, and dry dust. It was just beginning to get dark. I was awake again, but with that middle-of-the-night hyper-lucidity where the whole world seems to vibrate on the edge of some enormous revelation.

Brian opened the boot and got the luggage, then paused a moment, looking at the two other cars again. 'Sharon's back,' he said, indicating the sports car. He frowned at the Honda.

Sharon was, I knew, his second wife. I knew nothing more about her than the fact of her existence. She had never been an 'other woman' hate figure – Brian hadn't met her until some time after he moved to California. According to Brian, Sharon had been eager for me to come, so I assumed she was at least *resigned* to my visit.

We went into the house, me carrying the backpack, Brian, the suitcase. The entrance hall was dim, floored with terra-cotta tiles and surrounded by open doors. Brian set the case down and called, 'Sharon?' There was an indistinct reply from our right, and we followed it.

The door led to a split-level lounge, carpeted in cream; one wall held a fireplace of natural stone. Opposite it, a picture window opened on to a wooden deck with a view over the shadow-streaked hillside; a swimming pool, darkly blue, was just visible below it. A beautiful woman was sitting on the earth-coloured sofa, looking like something from a fashion plate. Her long legs were draped in loose white trousers, a sleeveless black top showed off her tanned arms and shoulders, and her thick brown hair was pinned up with an artless elegance that probably took hours to achieve.

Sitting opposite her was a young man. Bespectacled and slim, with the kind of dark good looks that in Britain I would've identified as Mediterranean or Arab, but here were probably Hispanic, he wore a smart suit and perched nervously on the edge of his chair. When we came in he jumped to his feet, blinking owlishly at Brian from behind the rimless spectacles.

The woman also rose, and came over, smiling warmly at me. 'You must be Alison,' she said, extending a tanned and be-ringed hand. 'I'm so glad to meet you!'

She looked older close up: her skin was parched by too much tanning, and there were lines around her mouth and eyes. Her smile, however, seemed perfectly genuine. So, this was Sharon. I shook her hand with a fatuous smile.

'Dr Greenall,' said the young man urgently, 'I'm Roberto Hernandez, from the Los Angeles office of the FDA . . .'

'Please!' exclaimed Brian irritably. 'This is a very bad time for you to come. My daughter has only just arrived for a visit. I haven't seen her for twenty years.'

Hernandez glanced at me and away again, frowning. 'I'm sorry. I can see that it's a bad time. It's just that something's come up about that break-in you had. Did you . . . lose anything important?'

'Important?' Brian asked in bewilderment. 'What do you mean? We lost a lot of valuable equipment.'

Hernandez set his teeth. 'Look, what happened is this. The *LA Times* contacted us to ask what your company was working on and whether we'd licensed you. It turns out somebody phoned them with a story that you were working on a top-secret experimental genetic modification serum, which has now gone missing.'

'A *genetic modification serum*?' Brian exclaimed indignantly. 'What the fuck is that?'

'Your experimental skin therapy?' suggested Hernandez, with a faint smile.

'Oh,' replied Brian, disgusted. He grimaced. 'God, you made it sound like some kind of toxic gunge that turns people into mutants! Surely you know the difference between genetic modification and gene therapy? You gave us our licence: you know perfectly well we weren't working on anything hazardous.'

'*We* know that,' said Hernandez appeasingly, 'but the whole point of the phone call was to start a scare story, wasn't it? This guy who contacted the *Times* must've been one of the people who broke into your lab: he was trying to discredit stem cell research. Anyway, we told the *Times* that your work was properly licensed by the FDA, that you've never been guilty of any breaches of the biologicals code, and that you weren't working on anything hazardous to begin with. They probably won't just take our word for it, though, not with these other people telling them monster stories. They'll probably send somebody up here to check it out.'

Brian swore.

'I, uh –' Hernandez nervously licked his lips – 'that is, we're aware that you've been working on a very ambitious project, and we thought . . . we thought that this might make things difficult for you, in all sorts of ways. I thought that if you'd really lost your experimental therapy, after all that work . . . We tried to get hold of you by phone, and when we couldn't, my boss sent me up here.'

'Oh, you guys are *classic*!' Sharon intervened, with sudden anger. 'Brian always followed all the rules about safety and accountability. A gang of stupid fanatics break into his lab and cause tens of thousands of dollars worth of damage – and all you can do is come up here and harrass *us*!'

Hernandez looked shocked. 'I . . . look, you've got it all wrong! I'm not trying to harrass anybody. I thought Dr Greenall would appreciate a warning – and maybe some help.'

'Help!' replied Sharon contemptuously. 'And what, exactly, would you want in return?'

Brian frowned at her, and she subsided. 'I don't know exactly what's missing,' he told Hernandez. 'You've got to understand, the lab was a mess. Nobody's sure what was smashed, what was stolen, and what was just mislaid. If you come by tomorrow during the day, we might be able to work it out for you. For now, you're just going to have to take my word for it that there was never anything in the lab which could represent a danger to public health.'

'Yes, certainly. And your, uh . . . you had several patents . . .'

Brian gave him a sour smile. 'Our records are encrypted. They weren't compromised. As for biological material – if somebody *has* stolen some, they're unlikely to gain by it.'

'I'm glad to hear it,' said Hernandez. He sighed. 'I'm sorry to hit you with all this at such a time. I'll come by your lab tomorrow then, if I may.'

Brian nodded curtly. Hernandez made for the door; reaching it, he paused and looked back. Our eyes met, and he gave me a sweet smile – a movie-star flash of even white teeth that took my breath away. 'I'm sorry I gate-crashed your homecoming, Ms Greenall,' he said, and left.

The door closed behind the intruder. 'Shit,' said Brian wearily. He ran a hand through his hair.

'Lemme get you a drink,' said Sharon. She gave him a quick clasp of the shoulder on her way past him to the kitchen.

Brian shot me a look of helpless anxiety. 'I'm sorry,' he said wretchedly. 'This has been . . . if it had to happen, I wish it could've managed not to happen *now*.'

I let out a breath slowly. 'That's OK.' In fact, it was fascinating. Nothing this interesting had ever happened at the school in Slough where my mother taught, unless you counted the time the police raided it for drugs. 'The FDA's the American Food and Drug Administration, isn't it?'

'That's right.' Brian ran a hand through his hair again. 'One of their branches is responsible for regulating medical research.'

I wondered why the FDA was so worried about what Brian had been doing. They must be, otherwise why send Hernandez pelting up 101 ahead of the news media?

Sharon returned with a tumbler of something-or-other which she put into Brian's hand. 'Something for you, Alison?' she asked. 'And maybe something to eat?'

'I ate on the plane,' I told her, 'and I'm much too jet-lagged to drink.'

'Of *course*!' exclaimed Sharon with a wide smile. 'It's the middle of the night for you, isn't it? Brian said you'd probably just want to go straight to bed. We've got the guestroom all ready for you, if you'd like. Brian, OK if I show your daughter her room?'

It was a beautiful room, twice the size of my bedroom at home. It held an enormous double bed with a bedspread patterned in cream-and-terracotta blocks, with a matching armchair positioned next to a stripped pine dresser. The single large window looked out over the darkening hillside. There was an en-suite washroom, with big fluffy towels laid ready for me. I had a quick shower, then crawled into the bed. The sheets were clean and smooth and smelled faintly of flowers.

I rolled on to my back and lay looking up at the ceiling, listening. I could just make out the murmur of voices from the lounge, unless it was the television. Some insect made a chirring noise outside; there was no other sound. The dusk deepened outside the window.

I closed my eyes, remembering the previous night in my mother's house in Slough, then thinking about my room in the house I'd shared in Oxford. That brought an uncomfortable recollection of Steve, my recently-ex boyfriend, and I opened my eyes again hurriedly. I reminded myself that I'd finished university, that my lease on the house had expired; ditto my lease on Steve. He wanted more peaceful company, and I . . . Well, to be honest, I still wanted Steve. Lean, dark-haired, bright-eyed Steve, with his braying laugh, his historian's enthusiasm for detail, and his passionate desire to change the world. But I supposed I would find somebody else eventually.

I'd been so stupid with Steve: arguing, picking holes in his ideas just because I could, taking his beliefs apart because it's what philosophers *do*, and never mind that I'd known it bothered him. Steve said I confused him, that he never knew what I wanted, that he always seemed to be in the wrong. Maybe I didn't know what I wanted, either.

They say that women take their model of male behaviour from the way their fathers treat their mothers; where did that leave me?

The voices still murmured in the other room, where my father sat with his second wife. I got up, moving silently on my bare feet, preparing the excuse that I felt hungry after all and was just looking to see what was in the kitchen. Eavesdropping is a vile habit, they say, and they say one never hears anything good of oneself – but then, I didn't claim to be a model of probity.

I stole into the hallway. The door to the lounge was still ajar, and I could hear Brian and Sharon clearly.

'. . . bloody awkward time for it!' said Brian despairingly.

'She's come to see *you*,' Sharon consoled him. 'California's just a bonus.'

She had that right, I supposed – though if Brian was a wash-out, I relied on California to make the trip worthwhile.

'She wasn't eager to come at all,' he replied doubtfully.

'She did, though,' said Sharon. 'Look, I honestly think we can play around a bit with the touring; the emotional stuff's the priority, and if that goes right, the rest doesn't matter.'

'What if it goes wrong?' he asked gloomily.

'Don't be so pessimistic! She's *here*, isn't she, your long-lost daughter? And she's *cute*! I didn't expect that.'

'She looks like my mother,' said Brian. 'Apart from the shorts. Mum never wore shorts.'

Sharon giggled. 'I bet she didn't wear a "Wear Your Own Damned Fur" T-shirt, either.'

'She didn't!' agreed Brian, now relaxing. 'And if she'd worn shorts, they wouldn't have been such *short* shorts! When she came out of the Arrivals gate, I didn't know where to look.'

'It's nothing out of the ordinary,' Sharon remarked,

amused. 'Half the girls at SBCTV are dressed like that – well, not the animal rights T-shirt.'

'I suppose so,' he said ruefully. 'It's just that the last time I saw her, she was in a pink Babygro, with teddies on it. That's what I was remembering while I was waiting for her in Arrivals. Then out walks this . . . this red-haired vegetarian *punk* in a T-shirt, *radiating* disapproval.'

Sharon laughed.

'It was a considerable shock,' Brian finished with a sigh.

'There's obviously quite a lot of you in her as well, though,' Sharon said encouragingly. 'I mean, top-ranked university, challenging subject . . .'

'Philosophy!' he pointed out. 'I wish I knew something about it.'

'She's *here*,' said Sharon. 'She *did* agree to come, and I doubt that it's really the tour of the state that brought her. She wants to get to know *you*, Brian. Just relax and be yourself, and it'll be OK.'

'I hope so!' he said, and sighed again.

I waited in the hallway for a couple of minutes more, but there was no more discussion, only the murmur of the television. Weariness began to weigh on me again, and I crept noiselessly back to the guestroom and my bed.

Radiating disapproval? Maybe I had. I had reason, though.

It was – what? Gratifying? Satisfying? *Fair*? – that he really wanted the relationship now, and that he needed *my* attention and approval. *I'*d wanted his in the past, often enough, and never had it.

Too late, now, to form a model of male behaviour beyond whatever muddled one I already possessed. Too late, perhaps, to form any connection with the man at all – but part of me hoped. I told myself that I could at least learn the shape of the thing which had been missing all my life. That was a worthwhile goal.

I fell asleep still wondering about it. I woke – inevitably – in the small hours of the morning, when in England the day wore past noon. I'd reset my watch on the plane, and for a while I tried to believe what it said. My body, though, knew better than any stupid chronometer, and at last I got up and crept out to see if I could find a newspaper and a cup of coffee to keep me occupied until dawn.

I groped my way along the hall in the dark, feeling like an intruder. There was a big kitchen/diner the other side of the entrance hall – I could tell what it was by the blue glow of an illuminated clock on the microwave. I turned the light on. My reflection jumped into the black window facing me: a wiry redhead in shorts and an old Amnesty T-shirt, dishevelled from sleep. *Cute*? Not particularly. My father's blue eyes looked out at me from above my father's slightly snubbed nose. I imagined myself fiftyish and plump, smirking in a suit, then turned my back on the appalling vision and searched for coffee.

There was a fancy machine on the kitchen counter which appeared to make everything from Americano to Zanzibari, but I didn't know how it worked and wimped out of trying to teach myself. I rummaged in the cupboards instead, trying not to make any noise. Eventually I found a jar of instant coffee and a mug, but I couldn't locate a kettle. I used a small saucepan to boil some water.

I took my hard-won coffee across into the lounge, and found a copy of the previous day's *LA Times* there, on a redwood occasional table. I'd curled up with it and the coffee when Sharon breezed in, fully dressed in a light cotton trouser-suit, every glossy hair in place. It was still only four in the morning, and I gaped at her in guilty amazement.

'Good morning!' she said brightly.

'Morning,' I mumbled. 'I'm sorry. I didn't mean to wake anybody up.'

'Oh, I always get up about this time when I do mornings,' she said, amused. 'I have to be at the studio by five.'

'Oh. Uh . . . Brian never actually said what it is you do.'

That startled her. 'I'm a television news presenter. For SBCTV in Santa Barbara.'

'Oh!' Well, she certainly looked the part.

'We're on at seven, if you want to watch. I need to get myself some coffee and go.' She swished through into the kitchen; I followed out of a mixture of politeness and curiosity. She put some coffee in the fancy machine and tipped in water, then gave me a smile. 'Do have some breakfast,' she urged. 'There's bread there – it's sourdough, from a bakery in Santa Barbara, really good – or there's cereal here.' She opened a cupboard to display a selection of mueslis.

I helped myself to a couple slices of sourdough bread and bunged them in the toaster.

Sharon gave me a bright smile. 'You're a vegetarian, aren't you,' she remarked. 'I'll have to get something suitable for supper.'

'I can—'

'Oh, I like vegetarian food!' she exclaimed, cutting me off. 'It'll be a pleasure.'

'I can always make do with a couple bits of cheese instead of a meat course,' I finished.

'We'll get something nice,' she told me. She hesitated, then went on, 'I'm sorry your visit got off to such a bad start. Arriving in the house to find the FDA here and everything! Brian's been very anxious for everything to go well, and now we've got this mess!' She paused, then added softly, 'We don't have any kids of our own.'

I knew that. I tried to think how to respond to it, and Sharon laughed.

'You looked just like your father for a minute,' she told

me. 'That "I don't like what you just said, but I won't say anything about it because it would be impolite" freeze of the face.'

I scowled.

'What did I say wrong?'

I was irritated enough to tell her. 'You just made it clear that if you *had* had kids, Brian would've been perfectly happy to carry on ignoring my existence.'

'Ouch.' The coffee machine gurgled and spat out a stream of latte. 'Put like that it sounds pretty bad.' Sharon poured her coffee into an insulated mug and capped it with a plastic lid, then looked up and met my eyes. 'Look, he felt guilty. He didn't know how to approach your mother again, and the longer he put off contacting her, the harder it became. Now he's sorry for neglecting you for so long, he wants to make up. He's discovered that he wants a posterity, and you're all the posterity he's got.

'He's a good man. I can say that, because I've known some bad ones – married one once, the worst mistake I ever made. Brian is *civilized* and decent and fun and absolutely brilliant, and he's a been a wonderful husband to me. He wasn't so wonderful for your mother, or for you, and he knows it. He really wants to have another try at being a father, though, and I really hope you'll give him the opportunity to try. I'm sorry, I have to run. I hope . . . I hope today goes really well. You really are important to him.'

She sallied out of the house, insulated mug in hand; a moment later I heard her car door shut. The engine started. Then the early morning silence flowed back.

I wondered how important Brian was to *me*. I'd managed without a father for as long as I could remember. He had a nerve, abandoning a child for twenty years, and then, when all the hard work of parenting was done, wanting her to deliver him from his mortality!

Yet here I was, and my heart was beating hard – I had to admit it – stirred by that probably meaningless assertion: *You really are important to him.*

I fantasized for a moment about wowing him with my intelligence and my wonderful personality – and then walking out of his life the way he'd walked out of mine, telling him I never wanted to hear from him again. It gave me a jolt of vengeful pleasure, but I knew it would be cutting off my nose to spite my face. The fantasy itself was evidence that what I really wanted was for him to admire me and love me and be really *sorry* that he'd neglected someone so wonderful.

Childish. *Stupid!* The most likely outcome of this visit would be an annual exchange of Christmas cards, maybe a lunch together if he was ever in London or I returned to California. Those years of abandonment could never be cancelled out – not even if we *both* decided we wanted them to be. My mother had raised me, and she was, now and forever, my family. Brian was a stranger.

He hadn't wanted kids: that was always my mother's explanation for the demise of her first marriage. I wondered when he'd changed his mind. I wondered how Sharon felt about the absence of kids – whether she'd agreed with Brian, or gone along with him, or whether it was the fault of some bitter medical failure. Couldn't ask her, not yet. I hoped I could ask sometime, though, which surprised me. I'd somehow expected her to be a vapid Californian airhead, but she seemed to be something more substantial and interesting. Probably that shouldn't surprise me; after all, Brian had married Mum, and she certainly wasn't a vapid airhead.

I took my toast over to the breakfast bar and settled down with it, the coffee, and the newspaper.

Two

Brian got up about quarter to seven and came into the lounge in a dressing gown. For a moment he seemed startled to find me there; then he smiled eagerly and said good morning.

'Everybody gets up early round here,' I observed.

He grinned. 'There speaks a student. No, Sharon gets up early; I get up at a normal time. Lotta people round here start work at eight. My lab starts at nine, but I get up now so I can watch Sharon do her show.'

He fetched himself a coffee, put the television on, and together we watched Sharon present the local news. I was impressed. She was poised and cheerful, as she was in the flesh; she spoke smoothly and clearly, without any exaggerated emphases or other annoying verbal tics. Her announcements concerned such events as the decision by the local water board to refuse a licence for a new development, and an accident on a tourist fishing boat: in the water board story she conveyed a wealth of information without confusion; in the accident story she struck a good balance between neutrality and sympathetic concern. Brian watched her with a slight smile. When she'd finished, he stretched and switched the TV off.

'What would you like to do today?' he asked brightly. 'Just take it easy round the house? If that sounds boring I could drive you over to Santa Barbara, or to one of the beaches, or—'

'Don't you have to be in your lab to meet that guy from the FDA?' I interrupted.

'Well, yes,' he conceded. 'But I thought you could still do some touring. I could drop you off somewhere. If you decide to go in to Santa Barbara, Sharon could give you a ride home. She usually sets off from there about two.' He hesitated, then added, 'Look, about the tour of the state I offered. I'm still hoping to do it, but I always thought you'd want a couple of days around here first anyway, to recover from the jet lag.'

In the end I accepted the lift to Santa Barbara. Brian phoned Sharon and arranged for her to meet me after her day at work, and equipped me with a map and a mobile phone.

It was further to the city than I'd realized, a half-hour's drive. I asked Brian where his lab was, and he replied that it was only a few miles from the house; having dropped me off he would have to drive straight back again. I tried not to be impressed by his eagerness to do an hour's drive before what was undoubtedly going to be a very stressful and unpleasant day at work – but I was.

Santa Barbara was delightful. Of course, it helped that it had been such a cold wet summer at home: the sunshine alone would've made me fall in love with the place. The town, though, had even more going for it than its climate: it had wide, tree-lined avenues crowded with pedestrians; it had graceful white-washed Spanish-colonial buildings (mostly modern); it had a marvellous array of shops and outdoor cafes and restaurants where you could eat in little gardens shaded by orange trees; it had the blue Pacific lapping its shores, a marina full of pleasure boats, and a big wharf the size of Brighton Pier; it had a long sandy beach flanked by palm trees and public gardens. Most of my holidays had been to places like Cornwall or Wales – when I was small we never had the money for anywhere more exotic – and I was entranced.

I wandered happily all morning, touring the old court-house and the art gallery, and buying a few postcards to send to people at home. I hesitated before buying one for Steve, then decided that just because we'd broken up, there was no reason not to be friends. I chose a picture of the old Spanish mission church for him, even though I hadn't actually been to look at it; he'd prefer something histor-ical. I wrote:

Dear Steve,
　I'm visiting my father in California – it's really, really strange. The place is gorgeous, though. Thought of you last night, and wondered if you got that research job.
　Best wishes, Alison

Then I read it over, and cringed. There was so much I really wanted to say to him, and all I could manage was that banal drivel.

I found a post office, and bought some stamps. I put some on the other cards and sent them on their way, then re-read what I'd written to Steve. No, I couldn't send it. We weren't just friends: I was in love with him, and he'd dumped me. Maybe in twenty years we might meet and talk companionably about old times – but now, no, there was too much pain. I tore the card in half and binned it, then went back out into the sunny streets. I was on holiday. I would forget about Steve, and enjoy myself!

I bought myself some lunch from a little hole-in-the-wall that proudly claimed to sell 'The Best Tacos in Southern California!' I was nervous that it wouldn't cater for vegetarians, but I should have realized that Californians were into all kind of exotic diets: I could've asked for macrobiotic or gluten-free Vegan instead of just beans and cheese. I took the little cardboard box down to the beach and sat on a bench to eat, relishing the bite of the chillis.

All around me tanned Californians were flying kites and playing beach volleyball and frisbee and splashing in the sea.

When I'd finished the tacos I took my sandals off and crossed the beach to paddle in the actual Pacific Ocean. The sun tingled on my pallid shoulders, and I dug my toes into the wet sand. I felt gut-deep happy, and was after all glad I'd come.

I had strolled back into the town and was standing outside a Häagen-Dazs outlet, wrestling with temptation, when someone called my name. I turned and found the FDA man, Roberto Hernandez, just behind me.

'Ms Greenall!' he repeated, smiling and blinking at me from behind his specs.

'Mr Hernandez,' I replied, non-plussed.

'I, uh, just noticed you, and I thought I would apologize again for interrupting your homecoming last night.'

I grimaced. 'It's not a homecoming, just a visit. Weren't you supposed to be seeing Brian's lab today?'

'I already have,' he informed me. 'I just stopped off for lunch on my way back. Um, even if it isn't a homecoming, I'm sorry I interrupted it.' He glanced at the Häagen-Dazs. 'Can I buy you an ice cream, to make up for it?'

I frowned at him, wondering what he wanted. Maybe he was just trying to pick me up, but it didn't feel like that. Well, the way to find out was to let him buy me the ice cream: that would satisfy both my curiosity and my greed. 'OK,' I said equably, and smiled.

American Häagen-Dazs outlets are much better than English ones. They have more flavours and they give you bigger helpings and they charge less. I chose something called Burgundy Cherry Chocolate and pretended that requesting it in a little cardboard tub instead of a cone made it less fattening. Hernandez opted for mocha. We sat down inside the shop to eat it, because of the air-conditioning.

'Ms Greenall,' Hernandez began, 'I'm sorry, what was your first name again? Alice?'

'Alison.'

'Alison. That's pretty! I'm Roberto. It can't have been much fun, to come to visit your father and arrive in the middle of a circus.'

'Has it been a circus?' I asked innocently, licking a chunk of cherry off the little wooden spoon, and deciding that I wasn't going to call him Roberto until I knew what his motives were.

He frowned. 'He didn't . . . you didn't follow the news?'

'Was it on the news?'

'Well, not really – local paper, I suppose is all, but I thought . . . I mean, he *is* your father. I thought he must've kept you posted.'

'Look, last night was the first time I've seen him since I was a year old. He's had no contact with my mother and me since the divorce.'

'None? But . . .'

'Not one Christmas letter.'

'Oh. But . . .' He gestured helplessly with a spoonful of ice cream, indicating that here I was.

'He got into contact with me a year ago,' I conceded. 'Through my university email. We've exchanged a few emails and he invited me to visit. But it's been a pretty cautious, cagey contact –' I grimaced, admitting it – 'particularly on my side. No confidences, OK? Whatever it is you want me to tell you, I don't know it.'

He hesitated, then gave a sputter of guilty laughter. 'Was I that obvious?'

'Yep,' I assured him, and ate some more ice cream. Burgundy Cherry Chocolate! Why can't you get it in England?

Hernandez grinned at me. 'I thought you might know something about the anti-aging serum,' he confessed.

I set down my spoon and gaped at him, trying to decipher this. 'Is this the "experimental skin therapy" you were talking about last night? An *anti-aging* serum?'

'You didn't know?'

'My God, no! What . . . what is it? Does it work?'

'Nobody knows,' said Hernandez. 'Dr Greenall has published almost nothing the last three years. He's been conducting trials on cultured skin cells, though, so he must have something worth testing.' He studied me earnestly. 'Are you a biologist?'

'Nope.'

'Medic?'

'I'm a *philosopher*.'

'Oh.' He was taken aback. 'Oh, *that's* different. Uh . . . you know what gene therapy *is*, do you?'

'Yeah,' I said impatiently. 'It's when somebody has a defective copy of a particular gene – like in muscular dystrophy, or something – and they try to give them a good copy of the gene instead. I know it's very hard to get the new gene to take. Mostly the body just rejects it.'

'That's right,' said Hernandez, pleased to discover even this degree of scientific literacy in a non-scientist. 'There are hundreds of illnesses caused by genetic defects, and in theory all of them ought to be curable. In practice none of them are, because nobody's been able to insert the correct genes into the defective cells.'

'They've had some success!' I objected. 'There was that little boy who didn't have an immune system, who'd had to spend his whole life in a disinfected room in a hospital. They managed to cure him.'

'All right, I should've said nobody's *reliably* been able to insert the correct genes into the defective cells! There must be a hundred failures for every success – no, if you count conditions they haven't dared even try yet, *a hundred thousand*! Our bodies have some pretty strong defenses against genetic insertions. I mean, they have to. You wouldn't want your genome scrambled by every passing virus.'

'And you're saying that Brian Greenall, *my father*, has discovered a way to get past those defenses – to make a gene therapy *work, reliably*?' I couldn't believe that: it was too big, too scary.

Hernandez hesitated. 'As I understand it . . . no. It's something close enough to be a major breakthrough, though, and it's going to be really controversial. See –,' he tapped the table, meeting my eyes eagerly – 'Dr Greenall's approach to gene therapy involves the use of stem cells. The religious right is utterly opposed to stem cell research; they got the government to ban state funding for it, and they've made it such a hassle to do that most researchers have dropped the whole area. Dr Greenall, though, just changed his focus and went private. In the past he was working on genetic treatments for melanoma, but he changed to research on aging – specifically, to using stem cells to repair age-related damage to the skin. That allowed him to get funding from a collection of elderly billionaires and movie stars who want him to produce an elixir of youth. Now, he's . . . that is, he's *supposed to be* on the point of success.'

'Oh my God!'

'He's sort of a hero to most of the people in my office,' Hernandez admitted. 'Stem cell research is one of the hottest things in biotech; it was *stupid* to ban it, just to satisfy a lot of ignorant religious bigots. We don't know, though, exactly what it is he's got, and we're all *acutely* curious. Like I said, he hasn't published anything in the last few years.'

'And you thought I might know?'

'Well, you might've,' admitted Hernandez, with a smile. 'And it isn't exactly a hardship to eat ice cream with you anyway.'

'Ha!' I exclaimed, and frowned. 'An elixir of youth? *Really*?'

'It won't be *that*,' Hernandez assured me. 'He was only working on skin.'

'So it's more like skin cream with stem cells in it?'

'I think it's a serum, not a cream.'

'Shouldn't you *know* what it is? If your office licenses him?'

'Oh, the licence isn't from *my* office!' explained Hernandez, with a grin. 'The FDA is a discombobulated monster, and *my* office is part of the ORA, the Office for Regulatory Affairs. Like the name says, we regulate: check documentation, do occasional inspections, write reports and letters, that sort of thing. The people who grant licences for new research or new products in biotech are the CBER – the Center for Biologics Evaluation and Research – in Washington. They don't spill the details of a new product to the likes of us. Biotech is very competitive, and ideas are its capital. You can't have the regulators giving away your hot new ideas to your rivals.'

I mulled over this tangle of information and picked one thread out of the pile, more-or-less at random. 'So when you came to the house last night, what you were really worried about was the whereabouts of this anti-aging serum? You suspect that the people who broke into the lab may have stolen it?'

Hernandez flushed slightly. 'Well, yes. If there really was a threat to public health, of course I would've been worried about that, but there isn't, it was just a miscon-ceived attempt to scaremonger. But this serum . . . I mean, your father had original ideas and worked hard and dodged a lot of obstacles to get his work done. If those fanatics stole it, they could sell his work off to the highest bidder – and it must be worth a *lot* of money, even untested. There are probably foreign pharmaceutical companies that would pay *millions* for it.' He sighed and added, 'Luckily, it seems that even if some of the material *has* gone missing, it won't be much use to a thief – not unless he packed it in dry ice and had a freezer waiting for it. These pro-lifers don't sound like they knew enough about it to do that. From what your dad was telling me this morning, the serum breaks down pretty fast at room temperature – and it's hard to tell much about it just by looking at it even when it's kept frozen.'

'If the pro-lifers are trying to start a scare story about it,' I said slowly, 'that should mean that they haven't really even grasped what it is.'

'Right!' agreed Hernandez, nodding. 'Their main line on stem cells has been: "murdered babies used to make medicines!", and for sure they'd go for the "murdered babies used as skin cream!", if they realized they could. Instead they're trying this "toxic gunge" story. They're scientific illiterates.' He made a face and added bitterly, 'Like the police. *They* don't seem to have any idea what they're dealing with, either. Because all that happened was damage to property, they're not taking it seriously. To them it's just a question of vandalism, like a . . . a public toilet!'

'While to you,' I said, smiling a little, 'some vile unbeliever has nicked the Holy Grail?'

He started, then gave me a rueful smile back. He had nice eyes behind the specs: dark brown, with long lashes. I wondered if his enthusiasm for Brian's work was really as pure as it seemed, or whether it was principally a result of the 'millions' this experimental serum would be worth on the open market. From what I'd heard, the pro-life phone-caller had said the serum was *missing,* not that he had it. That might mean that it was out there somewhere – and somebody with the right clues might be able to find it. I hoped Hernandez was genuine. I *liked* him.

We finished our ice cream and went out into the sunny afternoon. Hernandez hesitantly offered to show me more of the town, but it was about time for me to meet Sharon.

When I said as much, he offered to escort me to the place appointed for the meeting. This wasn't her office, which apparently was away from the center of town, but a small park where I could sit or she could park the car, depending on which of us arrived first.

As we walked, Hernandez asked me about myself: was I at university? Oh, just graduated! From *Oxford*! He'd been to UCLA. What was Oxford like? He'd never been to England. He seemed interested in my replies, which was pleasing.

The red sports car was parked under the trees at the side of the road when we got there. The windows were open and I could hear the radio playing as we approached: talk, not music. Hernandez accompanied me over to the car. Sharon scowled at him through the window and put the radio off.

'Mr Hernandez,' she said sharply, 'what are you doing here?'

'I stopped off in Santa Barbara for lunch,' he explained, taken aback, 'and I ran into Alison. I was sorry for the way I barged in on her arrival, so I took the opportunity to apologize.'

'Thank you for the ice cream,' I told him, sketching the position for Sharon.

'My pleasure!' he replied at once. 'Could I, uh, see you again sometime?'

I was tempted: he was interesting and I liked him. I'd never really seen the point of holiday romances before, but now the idea of going out in the certain knowledge that we'd part in three weeks was attractive. Nothing very serious or terrible could happen in such a short time, and it might help me to get over the loss of Steve.

What was the point, though? Roberto Hernandez was really only interested in Brian. Besides, what if we started arguing? I probably disagreed with him about animal testing – strongly enough that the subject would quickly turn hot and angry. Argument is my Achilles heel: I can't resist pointing out the flaws in other people's logic, and I'm no good at dropping issues until I've beaten them to death. No, it would be better to end this sweetly.

I smiled and told Hernandez I was afraid I'd probably be busy touring until I went home. He sighed with what seemed flatteringly close to disappointment, and we shook hands. I climbed into the car and Sharon started the engine. We drove off, leaving him standing under the trees looking disconsolately after us.

'What did *he* want?' Sharon asked me as we headed back toward the motorway.

I reflected for a moment, then replied honestly, 'He wanted to know about Brian's anti-aging serum.'

Sharon's lip curled. 'Vultures. The smell of money brings them flocking from miles.'

I frowned. 'I *think* he sees Brian as a hero. A fearless scientist, battling the forces of oppressive superstition. He wants to rally to his side. He's wildly curious about the serum, too.'

She gave me a cynical glance. 'That wasn't how I read him.'

I was silent for a minute. Santa Barbara glided past in gardens and shopping malls; beyond them rose the mountains, their edges vivid in the dry air. Hernandez's motives were, I decided, beside the point: the thing I really wanted to know more about was the serum. 'This serum's missing, then?' I asked at last.

Sharon made a face. 'Brian thinks so. Some of it, anyway. He says it doesn't matter, since all the data's secure.'

'I didn't know anything about it,' I told Sharon carefully. 'I had no idea he was working on something so . . . so *science fiction-y.*'

Sharon gave a ladylike *huh* of acknowledgement. 'I

suppose you wouldn't've. Brian tries to keep it quiet, apart from what he says to the investors – and he would've been worried about talking about it to *you*, in case you thought he was trying to dazzle you or bribe you. What did the FDA man tell you?'

'That it wasn't exactly a genetic therapy, but was close enough to be a major breakthrough. That it uses stem cells to repair the effects of aging on the skin.'

She made the ladylike noise again. 'Well. He got that right.'

We reached the motorway and turned north. 'Your father's a genius,' Sharon said urgently. 'I hope you realize that.'

For some reason the statement annoyed me, and I slipped into philosopher mode – something I'd been trying hard not to do in social situations, since, as Socrates discovered, it makes people want to kill you. 'What do you mean by that?' I asked.

'I mean he's a *genius*!' repeated Sharon, more emphatically. 'He's done what nobody else could've!'

'Defining "genius" as "somebody who does what nobody else could" isn't very helpful,' I pointed out. 'By that definition, people who eat record amounts of pizza for the *Guiness Book of Records* are geniuses. Do you really mean that Brian is a very gifted molecular biologist who has made important discoveries in his field? Or do you mean that he displays exceptional intelligence and insight in every field he turns his mind to?'

Sharon gave me a startled sideways glance. 'I guess I meant that he's a very gifted molecular biologist.' She gave another type of small snort, this one amused. 'He can be pretty stupid about things like car maintenance and doctors' appointments.'

'So you'd say that Brian is a genius at molecular biology, but that in other ways he's just an ordinary man, and that in some ways he's actually stupid?'

'What *is* this?' demanded Sharon, taken aback.

'You told me that he's a genius as though you believed it ought to be an important factor in my view of him. Since his genius-hood is confined to biology, and I'm not a biologist, I don't see how it has much relevance to me.'

Sharon's brows drew down. 'I don't see what you're getting at,' she said levelly. 'Don't you *want* to be proud of your father?'

That shut me up. I did, but I wasn't.

Sharon gave me another sideways glance, this one full of misgiving. 'You're not some kind of pro-lifer who *disapproves* of using stem cells, are you?'

'I don't think it's a straightforward issue, if that's what you mean.'

'Jesus!' Sharon exclaimed in disgust. 'It seems straightforward enough to me. Stem cells are by-products of other treatments, medical waste: they'll be created whether they're used or not, and if they're not used, they'll be incinerated. They represent the greatest hope of finding a treatment for a number of particularly foul diseases. I don't see any good reason for banning research on them.'

'So do you want to recycle *all* medical waste?' I asked. 'You'd make it compulsory for everybody to donate his or her body to science? Turn all morgues into reprocessing centers? You'd have no qualms about buying soap made from human body fat, *à la Fight Club?*'

'That's . . . it's not the same thing!' She drew in a sharp, irritated breath. 'We don't *need* to make soap of human fat; there are plenty of other sorts of oil around. There's no replacement for human stem cells – or, if there is, we won't find it unless we can learn more about how they work.'

'So you're saying that there is indeed something repugnant about exploiting human body tissue, but that the importance of what it's being used for, and the impossibility of replacing it, justifies its use in this case?'

Sharon gave me a wary look. 'Philosophy,' she said, as though she'd just remembered it. 'If I agree that that's what I meant, you'll spring something else on me, won't you?'

I made a face: she was right. 'I just don't think it's "straightforward",' I said defensively. 'I think it's a complicated, murky, moral issue. I suppose I'm not in favour of banning all research on stem cells, but beyond that I don't even *know* where I stand on it – and I certainly wouldn't feel happy about dismissing somebody else's position as stupid, out of hand.'

'You haven't had your partner's lab address posted on the internet by a bunch of people who are known to have bombed clinics. You haven't had to watch Brian find out his lab has been broken into and smashed up.'

'That's a reason to *ignore* their rationale, is it?'

'Ouch!' Sharon shook her head, then suddenly grinned. 'Should've realized that I wasn't going to win an argument with you. I never can with Brian.' She gave me another sideways glance, this one friendly. 'You'll have to take it up with him yourself. I'll look forward to listening in.'

She drove on, leaving me with the familiar frustration of having a mind churning with arguments and nothing to do with them.

We arrived back at the house at about quarter to three. Brian wasn't there. Sharon suggested that I relax by the swimming pool while she went to do some shopping. 'But you'd better put some sunblock on,' she added, studying me critically. 'It looks like you're starting to get a sunburn.'

She was right: I could already feel the heat in the skin of my face and shoulders. I never tan; I just burn and freckle.

I went to my guestroom and changed into my swimming costume. It was at the bottom of my suitcase, which

I hadn't unpacked the night before, so I shoved a few things in the wardrobe while I was about it. I'd brought some high-factor sun-block with me – Mum had picked it out when we were shopping for the trip, and thrust it firmly into my hands with the injunction to 'use it!' The memory made me smile when I slathered it on.

By the time I came out, Sharon was gone. I found my way out on to the decking and down to the swimming pool, then slid into the water with a shiver of pleasure. The swimming pool was small and kidney-shaped. It wasn't very deep – in the middle it only came up to the middle of my chest, and the ends were shallower – but the water was marvellously clean, with only the faintest scent of chlorine. The decking enclosed about two thirds of it, and the rest was flanked by a rockery. I swam round it a couple of times, then rolled over and floated on my back, looking up at the blue sky. It was eleven p.m., English time, and I was starting to feel . . . not so much *tired* as disoriented, adrift in time and space. It seemed unbelievable that forty-eight hours ago I'd been in bed in my mother's two-bedroom terrace house, and now I was here.

I would have to phone Mum . . . no, not phone, not at this time of night. Email her. Brian must have a computer I could use. A computer full of encrypted data, probably. That thought led me to stem cells.

You got them from human embryos in the very early stages of development, when they were simply a lump of undifferentiated cells, long before the embryo has a nervous system or a heart. That was the source of their value: the cells had in them the potential to become any sort of tissue, poised as they were at the very top of the long cascade of development that would eventually lead to a human being. Once collected, the cells could be cultured in a laboratory, creating a 'line' of stem cells for use by many different researchers.

You could get stem cells from umbilical cords, too, and there were even supposed to be a few in the blood and bone marrow of adults, but presumably Brian was using embryonic stem cells, or he wouldn't have a problem. Embryonic stem cells were supposed to be the most potent and versatile sort, the most interesting to the researchers. They were generally obtained from surplus embryos created for fertility treatments. When infertile couples undergo *in vitro* treatments, doctors normally harvest and fertilize half a dozen or more of the woman's eggs at a time, but only one or two are selected for implantation in the mother's womb during a given cycle of treatment; the remainder are frozen for the next try. If the treatment's successful, though, the fertilized eggs are spare. They're normally saved for a few years, in case the parents want to try for another baby, but once it's definitely decided that they're never going to be implanted in a womb, the doctors sometimes ask permission to use them in stem cell research.

I supposed that some parents might view it as equivalent to donating a dead child's organs to help another child live. Sharon, or Hernandez, undoubtedly saw it as a generous humanitarian act. To a religious fundamentalist, however, the same grant of permission was incitement to murder: to a fundamentalist, an embryo possesses an immortal soul from the instant of its conception. I wondered where *I* stood on the matter. In my second year at university I'd taken a class called 'Ethical Dilemmas in Modern Medicine'. It had been fascinating, but quite scary, and I'd been glad I didn't have to deal with the dilemmas personally. Now it seemed that my long-lost father was a hero to one side of just such a debate, and a villain to the other. I needed to do some thinking.

If there is such a thing as a soul, I didn't see how it could adhere to a speck of undifferentiated tissue. Even naturally fertilized ova at that stage don't always succeed in implanting themselves in the womb; many of them get flushed out of the mother's body at menstruation without her ever becoming aware that they exist. To believe that they all have immortal souls commits you to a very peculiar concept of a soul's value in the scheme of things, as well as a funny idea of its nature.

On the other hand, I didn't think it was just a straightforward matter of using up medical waste, either. To turn a person into a thing – literal dehumanization – is the ultimate expression of contempt; it's why those Auschwitz lampshades made of human skin are so shocking. A sixteen-cell embryo isn't a person, but it has the potential to *become* one, given the right conditions. I could see ways to justify dehumanizing it to treat a deadly illness – but to provide a cosmetic treatment for elderly billionaires? I had a problem with that.

I climbed out of the pool and sat on the deck, dangling my feet in the water. OK, so I had a problem with Brian's work. What should I do? Have a furious row with him and march out of his house in righteousness anger? Stay, and make the most of his hospitality while secretly despising him? Allow myself to be corrupted by swimming pools and the admiration of people like Hernandez, and end up agreeing that there was no moral problem after all?

I sighed: none of the above. I didn't need a new reason to despise my father; I had plenty of old ones. I'd come on this visit largely because I wanted reasons *not* to despise him. This was a setback, but not a fatal one. Brian was probably acting morally, according to his own beliefs; I could accept that even if I disagreed with him. He was a medical researcher, used to dealing with donated human tissue and not questioning where it had come from; to him, stem cells were probably nothing more than samples in tubes. He would have had no contact with the parents of those embryos, and probably none with the clinic which had collected and cultured the cells; all the real moral choices involved had been made before the cells reached his hands. Anyway, Hernandez had said that Brian had wanted to work on melanoma, and had switched to anti-aging serums because that was the way to get funding after his grants were cut off. Probably his work still had a lot of relevance to skin cancer. I shouldn't jump to conclusions, particularly in an area I knew so little about. I should ask him about it in a civilized fashion, as soon as I had a good opportunity to do so.

I went back into the house to have a shower and get changed.

Three

B rian got home at about six. By then Sharon and I were sitting on the deck, drinking white Zinfandel; Sharon was telling me about dry-country gardening. Brian wandered out into the golden evening, looking sombre, and Sharon sloshed the wine bottle at him.

'I think I want something stronger,' he told her. He went back into the house and returned with a gin and tonic.

'Cheers,' he told us, and took a deep gulp of it.

Sharon set down her wine and got up to rub his shoulders. 'Horrible day?' she asked sympathetically.

'God!' he agreed, with feeling. 'It was a contest between the police, the FDA, the *LA Times*, and the insurance people as to who could be the worst pain in the ass.' He had another swig of gin and tonic. 'The insurance people won, of course. When it comes to greed and dishonesty, you can *count* on 'em.'

'What did you say to the *LA Times*?'

'The usual. Cutting-edge biotech research, wide range of applications in human health, blah, blah, blah. Oh, yes, and that the scare story is an illustration of the ignorance of the people behind the break-in. I think I finally convinced the reporter that I'm not in the business of making toxic gunge. He seemed disappointed.'

'I could set you up to do a slot on TV or radio,' Sharon offered.

He shook his head morosely. 'I'd prefer to lie low.'

'These people are trying to start a story,' Sharon warned him. 'It might be better to get your side out first.'

'Yeah, but they might not succeed in starting the story,' Brian pointed out. 'With any luck, the *Times* will decide that a vandalized biotech lab isn't very interesting. After all, there weren't any explosions and nobody was hurt. Any sensible newspaper would conclude that what happened isn't worth more than a paragraph in the crime report. In that case, there'd only *be* a story if I were stupid enough to start it myself.'

Sharon thought about that. 'You might be right,' she conceded. 'It's worth a try anyway.' She went back to her seat. 'I got us some fresh pasta for supper. I figured you wouldn't want to go out.'

We ate pasta and salad sitting on the deck while the sun slid down behind the house and the mountainside turned to ochre and blue shadow. It was extraordinarily pleasant. Brian asked me about my day in Santa Barbara, commented on my sunburn. I tried to hang on to my wariness, my disapproval – but it was difficult.

I'd sort of hoped to have a chance to ask Brian questions about stem cells, but by the time we finished the wine I was too tired and too comfortable. Sharon was yawning, too: it was seventeen hours since she'd got up. We went to bed, leaving Brian alone in the lounge with the television.

I slept a bit longer that night, waking at the soft chunks that were Sharon getting ready for another morning's broadcast. I wanted, somehow, to avoid human communication in the dangerous early hours, so I waited until the car door had slammed shut and the house was quiet again. Then I got up, put on some more after-sun, and made myself some coffee.

The previous day's *LA Times* was again in the lounge, and I wondered when it had appeared there and who had picked it up. I looked through it for a story about Brian, but there was nothing. Presumably it was still too early for that. If they ran the story, it would be in today's paper.

The paper itself was peculiar: thicker than an English one, but with less news. Some of the extra wood pulp had been devoted to feature stories of one sort or another, but most of it was advertising. There was very little foreign news, and none of it was European; the political slant seemed to me very right-wing. The whole thing was a reminder that I was in a foreign country which just coincidentally spoke the same language as my own.

It was still before five when I finished the paper. I looked around the lounge for something else to read, but there were no books, only a couple of fashion magazines. I didn't quite dare search the rest of the house for reading material while Brian was still asleep, so I let myself out on to the deck and looked up at the arid mountain. Where I stood was shadow, but the hillside above me was bathed in salmon-pink light, like the special effects in a surreal Western movie. An unfamiliar bird was singing an intermittant *chrrrrr-chik*, loud in the still air.

There was a faint track climbing the hillside just beyond the dry-country garden. I went back into the house, put on socks and boots, and set out to see where it led. My track quickly petered out into prickly bushes. I almost gave up, but then I spotted another trail a few yards over. I struggled over to it at the cost of a few scratches, and it rewarded me by leading to a proper hiking trail of beaten earth with the occasional yellow trailmark on a creosoted post. This led me steeply upward. After maybe half a mile I reached a tree-filled gully.

Sharon had mentioned live oaks and when I studied the trees I could see that they were indeed oaks, although the familiarly shaped leaves were tiny; they had dropped acorns on the path. I picked one up and turned it in my fingers, then slipped it into the pocket of my shorts.

'What was that?' a voice from among the trees shouted. I jumped, startled to the point of shock.

'What was that?' the voice called again, and a young man emerged from among the trees. He was a little older than me, good-looking in a blond, tanned, Californian way. His jeans were stained with oil, and his dirty T-shirt strained over a muscular chest and arms. His expression was suspicious, verging on hostile. 'What did you just pick up?'

'J-just an acorn!' I stammered. I fished it out of my pocket again and showed it to him. I was acutely aware that I was wearing the running shorts and Amnesty T-shirt I'd slept in, with nothing on underneath.

'Oh,' he said, and glanced down. 'Oh. I thought . . . see, we lost something around here the other day, and I thought maybe you'd found it.'

'No.'

'It was in a box about this big.' He held his palms out a couple of inches apart. 'A black plastic box.'

'I haven't seen anything like that.'

'Sorry.' He shook his head. 'Sorry I startled you.' He gave me an apologetic smile.

My heart began to slow down; it seemed this was not going to be a 'lost tourist raped in mountains' story after all. 'When did you lose it?' I asked helpfully, trying to atone for my suspicion.

There was a moment's hesitation. He frowned. 'You're not from around here.'

So, he'd noticed the accent. I'd already had several people in Santa Barbara tell me how 'cute' it was. 'I'm a tourist,' I confessed.

'What, from *England*?'

'Yeah.'

His frown deepened. 'What're you doing up here so early?'

'I'm still jet-lagged,' I explained. 'In England right now it's about two o'clock in the afternoon.' Belatedly, it occurred to me to wonder what *he* was doing up here so early.

'Yeah? And you're staying round here somewhere?'

'Just down there.' I pointed negligently back along the trail and downslope. I was becoming nervous of him again. 'I'd better get back. This was just a walk before breakfast.' I took a few hesitant steps backward. 'If I see your box, I'll bring it up here.'

'OK. Thanks.'

I turned and started back the way I'd come, trying not to hurry, listening fiercely for the first sound of him following me. There was nothing; when I reached a bend in the path I glanced back and saw him standing where I'd left him, staring after me. I broke into a run as soon as I was out of sight. I knew it was stupid and paranoid, but I ran anyway.

I missed the track from the house in my hurry. I jogged on along the hiking trail in the brightening daylight, then slowed to a puffed-out walk, looking carefully for any turn that would take me down the slope to my left and back to the road.

After what might have been a mile, and felt like several, the trail itself arrived at the road. There was a small carpark and a sign saying 'LOS PADRES NATIONAL FOREST', with an incomprehensible map etched into the wood. I followed the road back to my left, and eventually – to my intense relief – arrived at the familiar slot-like drive of Brian's house.

The front door was locked, so I made my way around the back. Brian was awake and watching the news when I stumbled back through the picture window. He glanced at me, then stared. 'I thought you were asleep,' he told me. On the box, Sharon earnestly discussed the effects of the latest El Niño with a climatologist.

'I went for a walk,' I informed him. 'I found a hiking trail just up the slope from here.'

'Oh yes!' he exclaimed, smiling. 'The new trail from Nojoqui Falls to the Los Padres Forest. It goes right by my lab. You like hiking?'

'Yeah.'

'There are a lot of trails in the region. I have some maps somewhere, if you're interested. You have to make sure you take plenty of water, though – and watch out for rattlesnakes.'

Rattlesnakes. Such an outré hazard had never crossed my mind. I grimaced and went to shower off the dust and sweat.

Putting on a clean shirt in my room, I wondered about the man on the mountain. He'd been looking for a box he'd lost *the other day* on a trail that went *right by Brian's lab*. It could be complete coincidence, but he'd become uneasy after he identified my accent. Had he wondered about a connection between me and Brian? Would a pro-life activist even be aware that Brian lived in the neighbourhood? No, I was just being paranoid . . . I wondered, though, if I should tell Brian about the meeting.

When I came back to the lounge, however, Brian at once began organizing my day. He would be obliged to go into the lab again, he told me, to deal with the insurance, but he could once again drop me off somewhere. Did I want to see Lake Cachuma? One of the beaches? More of Santa Barbara?

I opted for Santa Barbara again; Sharon had told me I ought to see the Botanic Gardens, and I wanted to view the Mission whose photo I'd purchased for Steve. Once again, Brian drove me back along the coastal highway and deposited me in the town, this time further uphill, by the old Spanish colonial mission church. He thrust some money at me as I got out of the car, stretching to reach across the seat. 'For a taxi,' he explained, 'to take you up to the gardens.'

After a moment's hesitation, I took the money with an embarrassed mutter of thanks, and he drove off. The money turned out to be sixty dollars, which seemed a lot for a taxi which only needed to take me about a mile, according to the map. I remembered, with a sudden churning of the stomach, a time when I was fourteen and my school organized an end-of-term trip to Paris. I'd desperately wanted to go, but my mother had said we couldn't afford it. Where was my father then?

I shoved the money angrily into my pocket, deciding not to spend it. I could return it that evening, explaining that I'd walked to the Botanic Gardens. That might be silly – I was compromised anyway, since I'd let Brian pay my air fare and I was a guest in his house – but accepting cash handouts would take me over some boundary I wasn't prepared to cross.

The Santa Barbara Mission – 'Queen of the Missions', according to the blurb in the tourist handout – was an imposing white building with twin bell towers. I found an unpleasant reminder of recent concerns even there, however. Outside the church and over to one side of it stood one of those folding tables favoured by pressure groups; it was hung with lurid pictures of fetuses, and its signboard identified it as being run by 'The Coalition for Human Dignity'. A couple of earnest young women were foisting pamphlets on to anyone who came near. I gave it a wide berth.

I wondered about the group a little, though. Of course, the Catholic church is opposed to both abortion and stem cell research, but the pressure group's position, outside and away from the main entrance, seemed to indicate tolerance rather than active support from the Santa Barbara Mission. Presumably someone on the staff of the church was sympathetic to the cause, and had granted the group permission to set up their table, but they were obviously not supposed to annoy the tourists.

The history of the church – its mission to convert the native Indians, and its uneasy relationship with the Spanish authorities – proved to be quite interesting. My tour took a while. When I eventually emerged, I'd almost forgotten about the pro-life group. It was almost by chance that I glanced over at them, and saw that the man I'd met on the mountain was there, talking to one of the girls.

He noticed me and smiled, so the option of sneaking off wasn't open. I could still have walked past pretending not to recognize him, but there seemed no reason to; even if he had been one of the people responsible for vandalizing Brian's lab, he had no real reason to connect me with Brian. I smiled back and walked over. 'Hi,' I said, 'did you find your box?'

He began to speak, then stopped. The girl beside him, a dark Mexican type in a green dress, looked a question at him. The other young woman seemed to have left.

'No,' he said at last. He turned to the girl. 'I met this lady on a hiking trail when I was looking for something I dropped there.' He turned back to me. 'You didn't see it?'

'Sorry, no.' I picked up one of the leaflets on the table. 'SLAUGHTER OF THE INNOCENT', it read, above a gruesome picture of an aborted fetus. 'Ugh!' I set it down again.

'It is "ugh",' said the girl earnestly. 'Little babies *murdered*: you can't get any worse than that! But it won't stop just because you stop looking at it.'

Abortion is a subject where arguing only makes differences more irreconcilable: I'd learned that listening to student debates. I gave her an embarrassed smile and looked away.

'Are you staying up around where I met you?' asked the man. 'Round Nojoqui Falls?'

'Yeah,' I agreed. I noticed another leaflet, this one headed 'STEM CELL RESEARCH: PROFITING FROM MURDER'. I picked it up.

'With some friends?'

'With a relative.' The stem cell leaflet had lots of assertions in bold capitals, but not much text; what there was had poor grammar and spelling and a low information content. '**FACT!**', it screamed, '**MEDICINES MADE FROM STEM CELLS DON'T WORK! FACT! THE MURDER OF EMBRYOS ARE CONDENMED BY ALL MAJOR RELIGIONS!**'

I put it back on the table. 'I'm on holiday here for a few weeks.'

The man hesitated. 'You're not related to Brian Greenall, are you?' he blurted out.

I widened my eyes. 'Who?'

'Brian Greenall. He's a professor who does stem cell research. English, lives near Nojoqui Falls.'

'There's no way I'd know every English person in California!' I protested.

'No,' agreed the man, relieved. 'Sorry.'

'Stem cell research is *evil,*' said the girl feelingly, looking at me with large doe-like eyes. 'They kill babies and use their poor little bodies to make medicines! And the medicines don't even work!'

I hesitated, the philosophical questions already ranging themselves in my mind: *In what sense is a lump of undifferentiated tissue, conceived in a dish, already condemned never to be implanted in a womb, a 'baby'? You think it has a soul? What do you mean by 'soul'? Would you still be saying this if you had a child dying of muscular dystrophy?*

It was useless to argue, and I didn't want to alarm the

man. He might be worried that his search for that black box was suspicious – which, actually, it was. I wasn't really afraid of physical attack – we were in front of a major tourist attraction, after all, there were busloads of tourists around, and, anyway, it would be stupid. Why incriminate yourself with assault and battery, when at worst you might be charged with criminal damage – a less serious offence? It was perfectly possible, though, that he and the girl would make a scene, and I hate scenes. 'It's not something I know a lot about,' I said at last. I nodded to the man. 'I hope you find your box.'

'Thanks.'

I pulled out my map and tried to determine the best way to the Botanic Gardens.

'Where are you trying to get to?' the man asked helpfully.

'The Botanic Gardens,' I told him. 'I've been told they're really good.'

'Yeah, they are. You need to go up Mission,' he waved at the street that climbed past the church, 'and then fork left on Tunnel Road.'

It was further than I'd realized: I'd misread the scale of the map. I looked at Mission Road without enthusiasm; as far as I could tell the pavement for pedestrians gave out a bit past the church, and there was quite a bit of traffic. It was hot, too. 'Is there a route for pedestrians?' I asked. 'Or a bus?'

The two Californians boggled. 'You mean you don't have a *car*?' asked the girl, horrified at European deprivation.

'I'll give you a ride,' offered the man. 'I'm going back that way anyway.'

'Aren't you busy here?' I asked doubtfully.

'I just came down to drop off some more leaflets,' he told me.

'Yeah, that's right,' agreed the girl, nodding. 'We just got that one –' the stem cell effort – 'printed up this morning.'

They seemed perfectly straightforward and above board, and I didn't fancy walking up that road in the traffic fumes and the hot sun. 'Well, if it's no trouble . . .' I said.

'No trouble!' The man waved cheerfully to the girl and escorted me over to a battered yellow van which was parked in a drop-off zone by the church. He unlocked it and removed a toolbox from the passenger seat before going round to climb up behind the wheel.

'Thanks,' I said, as he pulled out on to the road.

'What do you think of it, then?' he asked. 'What we're doing?'

'I think it's good the issues are raised,' I responded carefully.

'No, what do you think of abortion? Should it be legal?' He asked it with a kind of triumphant challenge. I cursed myself: I should have known better than to get into a car with a known proselytizer.

'Oh, come on!' I pleaded. 'Everybody other than the complete nutcases think there are *some* circumstances when abortion should be legal – when it would kill the mother *and* unborn child both if the pregnancy continued, for example. The debate isn't really about whether it should be legal, but about *under what circumstances* it should be legal.'

'You think human beings have the right to end other human lives when it's just inconvenient to the mother, though?' he demanded belligerently. The left fork into Tunnel Road came up, and he swerved into it with a cavalier disregard for traffic that had me grabbing the armrest.

'If you really want the truth,' I said, hoping to head him off, 'I think the whole debate is howling stupidity. Both sides are conceptually confused to the point of incoherence. In many ways, given their ideologies, they ought to be taking the opposite positions to the ones they do.'

This surprised him so much he took his foot off the accelerator and looked at me. The car wavered and slowed and I clutched the armrest harder. He returned his attention to the road with a jerk. 'How do you figure that?' he demanded.

'Look,' I told him, 'I'm sorry, but we must be almost at the Botanic Gardens.' I flourished my map. 'There isn't time for a philosophical discussion!'

'Yeah, but that was an outrageous thing to say! You can't just say something like that, and then leave it.'

A brown wooden roadsign painted with SANTA BARBARA BOTANIC GARDENS appeared on our left, and I made an urgent noise and pointed to it.

He hesitated, then flicked the indicator. 'I'm not in a hurry.' We pulled off the road into a large carpark, and he parked in an empty space, switched off the engine, and turned toward me with a look of challenge.

I refused to debate with him in the hot car. The Botanic Gardens had a proper reception building, complete with cafe and shop, and I led us there, hoping for a cold drink that wasn't too expensive. The cafe obligingly provided water for free, so I got myself a glass. My companion bought himself a coffee. We took them out on to a terrace overlooking a lawn punctuated by beds of bright annuals and exotic trees.

'So,' said the pro-lifer, stirring in sugar and frowning at me like a school head faced with a girl caught smoking in the washroom, 'how do you figure the pro-life movement is . . . what did you say? "Conceptually confused"?'

'I said *both* sides are,' I pointed out. 'Look, most pro-lifers are religious, right? Evangelical Christians, Catholics, devout Muslims, yeah? They share a belief that human beings have an immortal part, a soul, and that the goal of human life is for that immortal part to be united with God in an afterlife.'

'Yeah,' he agreed, suspiciously rather than enthusiastically. He was looking for the catch.

'They believe that this life, here and now on Earth, is only a prelude to eternal life, or Heaven, or whatever you want to call it. In contrast, most pro-choicers are secular humanists, and believe that the here and now on Earth is all there is, that if you lose your chance at this life, you have nothing.'

His frown deepened. 'I think I get what you're saying. If you think this life is all you're gonna get, it ought to be more precious to you than it is to someone who believes that death is only the beginning. Yeah, I can see your point. What you haven't got, though, is that Christians believe that human life is precious to *God*. Every human life is equally precious, no matter how small the human. Your so-called humanists never really have any respect for anybody's life except their own! If somebody else's life is inconvenient to them, they want to end it. An unborn baby's, a sick old man – abortion or euthanasia – they're for it. They're not into looking after anybody but number one.' He gave me a steely look and added, 'And don't give me any of that crap about how we don't protest about the death penalty, or wars. Societies have to have justice, and countries and individuals have a right to defend themselves. Without those rights, you couldn't have any sort of society, everything would fall to bits. There's no way there's any justice, though, in killing innocent unborn babies.'

I made a face. 'Where's the justice in the four million Third World babies who die of preventable causes every year, because of poverty and poor medical care? Vaccination programs, water treatment plants and improved access to health care in the Third World would save a *lot* more innocent babies than banning abortion would, but I never hear about pro-life groups agitating for those things.'

My companion looked annoyed and uneasy. 'Just because you can't right *every* wrong in the world, doesn't mean you shouldn't work on the ones you come across! I'm not against charity to people in other countries . . .'

'Scuse me,' I interrupted, 'but I'm not talking about charity, I'm talking about justice. A lot of those deaths are down to unfair trade rules and debts to Western banks.' Steve was passionate about trade justice.

He waved this aside. 'OK, but the thing I've run up against in my own life is abortion!'

I held up a hand; I was tired of this, and I wanted to go look at the garden. 'I already said I thought the whole abortion debate was howling stupidity, OK? So can we not get bogged down in it? You asked why I said I thought it was conceptually confused. I told you. You want me to make it plainer? If you accept the premises of either side in the debate, you get absurd conclusions. Are you an evangelical Christian, or some other sort of pro-lifer?'

He looked uneasy. 'I'm . . . sort of a Christian. I don't go to church much any more, but, yeah, I believe in God.'

'You believe that each individual has a human soul from the moment of conception?'

'Uh, right.'

'OK. Tell me what you mean by "soul".'

By now the headmaster look had given way to the expression of a rather stupid witness being cross-examined by a very sharp lawyer. 'I, uh . . . it's what you said. The immortal part of a person.'

'Yes, but how do you conceive of it? For example, a Buddhist would think of the soul as a kind of bullet of life-force which can be reincarnated as completely different individuals. Do you think of it like that? Or do you think it's individual, unique to the person?'

'Ah. Now I got you. It's individual.' He became a bit more confident. 'It's more than that: it's what *makes* you an individual, what *makes* you a person.' He pressed a big hand against his T-shirt. 'It's the you inside.'

'So what happens with identical twins? They start off as a single fertilized egg, and don't split into two separate individuals until a couple of weeks after conception. Does their unique individual soul split, too? Or did they have two souls from the start, in which case, is it possible that there are failed twins walking around with more than one soul in the same body?'

He looked annoyed. 'I don't know! That's God's business. It's human business to look after them.'

'That's a pretty sneaky way out of a paradox,' I complained. 'And you know, it leaves you with another problem. If something like that is God's business and we can't know it – how is it you *do* know, with absolute certainty, that an embryo has a soul from the instant of conception? I mean, there *are* other possibilities, even given the assumptions of your religion. In the Middle Ages the Catholic church used to think "ensoulment" occurred at around five months' gestation.'

He scowled, lost for a response.

'Try it another way,' I suggested. 'Is the soul mutable?'

'Uh . . . what?'

'Does it change? Does it grow and develop as you grow and develop? Or is everything it's going to be completely fixed from the moment of conception?'

He frowned, trying in his fumble-brained way to come to grips with the idea. 'It has to be able to change,' he decided. 'Otherwise you wouldn't have any freedom of choice. You couldn't be saved or damned.'

'OK. It's mutable. So if you died tomorrow, your soul would reflect the way you are now, not the way you were ten years ago?'

He looked confused, but nodded. 'Yeah, that sounds right.'

I looked at him pityingly. 'OK, can you explain to me how the soul of an unborn baby is different from that of, say, a calf?'

'Animals have no souls!' objected Mountain Man indignantly.

I made a face: I hate that attitude. 'Well, this is your definition of the soul, so you can say what you like – but do you see my problem? If you conceive of your soul as something that grows and changes with your body, then the soul of a newly conceived embryo ought to be as tiny and simple as its body – no brain, no mind, no personality, no moral capacity whatsoever. In that case, just what is it about it that's distinctly human?'

Mountain Man opened his mouth, shut it. 'It could *become* more!' he exclaimed triumphantly.

I cast my eyes heavenward. 'Do you really mean that? Because if something has to *become* human, then it is, in fact, not human at that moment.'

He glowered. 'What if I said the other thing?'

'Oh, well, if you say that the soul is fixed and immutable, then you need to explain why it needs to have a life at all – particularly if you believe in Hell and damnation. Do you?'

'Yes,' he said flatly. His tanned face was grim. 'I believe people can damn themselves.'

He looked like he suspected I was one of those people. 'What do you believe happens to the soul of an aborted baby?' I asked, disregarding the look. 'Does it get another chance at being born? Does it return to God? Or do you believe that, because it couldn't make an adult choice to be saved, it's stuck in limbo or damned to Hell?'

He was shocked. '*Shit*, no, I don't believe *that*! I know my baby's soul is in Heaven!'

My baby's soul, I noticed, with a quiver of unease; this was personal. I was well into the game now, though, so I sailed on anyway. 'OK, then. Say there are ten women who are able to have abortions under the current legislation; according to what you believe, the souls of their ten babies will go to Heaven, right?'

'Wait a minute . . .'

'However, if abortion is banned, and those women are obliged to bear the babies, things are different. Those kids are not going to grow up as good Christian children – good Christian mothers wouldn't have wanted to abort them in the first place, would they? Even if you stack the odds and say that *most* of them end up OK, even so, some of them are going to grow up poor, unwanted, neglected, possibly abused. They'll become damaged, nasty adults. So the result of your intervention to protect them will be that their souls, which *could* have gone to Heaven, end up in Hell. You are keeping them alive here and now in order to condemn them for all eternity.'

He stared at me, slightly panicked, as he tried to find the flaw in the reasoning. 'The women . . . the mothers would still be committing murder,' he said, a bit desperately.

'Yeah, but they could repent and be saved, couldn't they? And if they didn't, well, they probably had other sins that would've damned them anyway.'

'God intended those babies to be born, to take their chances in the world!' he snarled. He was going red in the face. 'One of them might have become a great man, a doctor who discovers a cure for cancer, or something. For human beings to thwart God's will is wrong!'

'Oh, come on!' I exclaimed in disgust. 'Go on, explain to me why abortion is thwarting God's will, but a Caesarean section that saves two lives is a miracle of modern medicine.'

'One kills, the other gives life!'

'So? They're both human interventions that change the natural outcome. If you're entitled to say that the aborted baby could've become a life-saving doctor, I'm entitled to say that the Caesarean baby will become a mass murderer, and God *intended* him to die.'

'God never intends babies to die!'

'Then he's bloody incompetent! Until modern medicine came along, *half* of all children died before they reached the age of five. That's still true in many parts of the world. You'd think God could manage a hit rate of better than fifty-fifty!'

'We live in a fallen, corrupt world, full of human sin!'

'So it's *just* the place for innocent little babies, is it?'

'We don't know, we can't know everything that's going to result from what we do! We have to obey the moral law we know, and it says "Thou shalt not kill!".'

'So, you're abandoning the claim that human interven-tion – "playing God" – is wrong in and of itself? And you're claiming that we should not consider the conse-quences of our actions when we make a moral choice?'

He gave me a look of fury. 'You're real good at arguing, aren't you, you . . . snotty smart-ass bitch! This is all a game to you, isn't it? Just tricks with words! But you should thank God you're here, that you *can* argue – that your mother didn't want to abort *you*.'

I shrugged, trying to play it cool, though the sudden descent to name-calling was unsettling. Besides, it reminded me that my father *had* wanted my mother to abort me. 'Look,' I said, 'You wanted to talk about this; I didn't.'

'I thought maybe you'd be willing to listen to the *truth*!'

'I'm not the one who's stopped listening and started shouting.'

He hit me. It caught me completely by surprise: a

swinging slap to the face that knocked me off my chair and sent me sprawling on the terrace, elbow cracking against the paving slabs. Shocked and stunned, I looked up to see him looming over me, his face crimson. 'Bitch!' he spat. Then he turned on his heel and strode off.

A woman from one of the other tables hurried over and tried to help me up. 'Are you OK?' she asked anxiously.

I sat up and cradled my stinging face in my hands; to my shame, I was starting to cry. 'I'm OK,' I muttered.

'You shouldn't have anything to do with a man like that!' the woman exclaimed indignantly.

'I don't even know him!' I protested, sniffing and wiping my face.

'He wasn't your boyfriend?'

'I don't even know his *name*! He just gave me a lift up here, then said he wanted to talk!'

My helper shot a look of awed horror in the direction he'd gone. 'You ought to go to the police!' she exclaimed. 'He's *dangerous*!'

Four

I didn't go to the police. Instead, I spent the next couple of hours in the Botanic Gardens, trying to calm down. There was a stream in a wooded gully, a little beyond the flower-garden part of the establishment, and it was very quiet and peaceful. I sat on a bench for a while, listening to the water purling over the rocks and watching the dance of the insects above it, doing some thinking.

I decided that I wouldn't say anything about what had happened. The whole incident now made me feel embarrassed and ashamed. I should've known better than to have accepted a lift, let alone one from a man I suspected of being the next thing to a terrorist. I'd been very stupid, and lucky to have escaped with nothing worse than a scraped elbow. Besides, I had only a few weeks in California, and I didn't want to waste them in court proceedings. I was unlikely ever to see the Monster of the Mountain again, and the best thing I could do was forget him.

I was also guiltily aware that the guy had been right: I *had* been a smart-ass, more interested in scoring points than in illumining the issues. I'd noticed, too, that the pro-lifer was a rubbish debater *and* had personal baggage – I should've backed off. No, I wasn't proud of myself, and I wanted to forget the whole business.

I could've demolished all the arguments I'd used. That question about the soul had been a false dichotomy: if it's not x it must be y, when, in fact, there's no reason it couldn't be *a,b*, or *c* instead. Arguments about metaphysics always end up being totally governed by the definitions you use.

I thought, though, that singling out the definition of the human soul as central to any argument about abortion made some sense. You could even recast the argument in purely secular terms as 'how do you define a human being?', and get exactly the same division into camps. Pro-lifers think humanity begins *ab ovo*; pro-choicers think it's something that develops gradually. I supposed that I ought to decide what *I* thought about it, if I wanted to have anything more than a knee-jerk response to what my long-lost father was doing.

When I first got interested in philosophy I'd believed that you could use it to find the Truth. I don't think like that any more. Partly it's because once you get into the subject you learn to argue both sides of any case, but mostly it's because you discover that you can't prove anything, not even – *pace* Descartes – your own existence. The trouble is that logic itself dissolves if you look at it hard enough, and without logic, where's proof? I still think the truth is out there – that there really *is* a universe, for example – but I no longer believe it's wholly knowable. The most you can do is rig up a system that satisfies *you*, avoid all definitions that lead to absurdity or self-contradiction, and be ready to adapt to new ideas.

I'd hit the question of consciousness and the soul before, in my own pet cause of animal rights, so it was something I'd thought about. The traditional view is that human beings possess consciousness – or souls, or minds, or whatever you want to call it – and that animals don't, and that therefore human beings are entitled to do whatever they please to animals. I hate that view. Animals clearly possess minds of some sort. There may be some sort of phase change between humans and other animals; some critical point where the mind becomes so complex that it shifts to a different form of organization; I wasn't sure about that. What I don't believe, though, is that human beings have some sort of ghostly doppelgänger inside them, made of an immaterial quintessence that's totally lacking in the rest of creation. There are all sorts of problems associated with that view of things.

If I threw out the Monster's ghost, what *did* I think the soul was? Did I even think it existed, in any meaningful sense? Is there anything that makes us an individual – the *same* individual from birth to death! – when everything else about us changes over time?

Yes, I decided. I would define the soul as being a particular package of abilities and weaknesses, inclinations and aversions, that characterize a conscious, self-aware human individual. In a sense, too, I believe it existed from the moment of conception, since individuality is inherent in our genes. The double helix strand ties 'the subtle knot that makes us man'.

Genetics, though, isn't everything. One of the speakers who'd lectured my Ethical Dimensions class had been scathing about genetic determinism: the idea that our fate is written in our genes, and that you can look at the gene set and predict the individual. Human beings, he'd pointed out, have fewer than thirty thousand genes – less than the number possessed by roundworms. Genes switch on and off; they trigger one another; they form fountains and cascades. We're designed to interact with our environment, and from conception to death, we do. Our DNA is not so much a blueprint as a musical score – and one written for a jazz piece, where the instruments respond to one another ad lib. In other words, that subtle knot is only the seed: the soul is the plant that grows from it. So when does it come into being? When is an acorn an oak? When it germinates? When it's a seedling, three inches high? How can you pinpoint the moment of change, when change is something that happens over time?

I had no trouble with viewing 'ensoulment' as a process, one that begins at conception and ends . . . well, with death, I supposed. Or maybe there's a 'desoulment' process that happens with senility or foul degenerative diseases or the horrific kind of brutalization you see in war criminals. Anyway, by this definition, destroying or exploiting an embryo was wrong, but it was less wrong very early in development and more wrong the later it happened. In the early stages it might be justified by the benefit it could bring to others, just as a lie can be justified if it saves a life.

I felt quite pleased with this definition. To be sure, there were people in Oxford who'd have it in pieces in ten minutes, but it would give me something to keep hold of when I talked to Brian about his work.

Sharon, when she arrived to collect me from the Botanics carpark, asked about the bruise on my face and the scrape on my elbow, but accepted the explanation that I'd slipped climbing down the gully to the stream. She drove me back along the coast chattering happily about how beautiful the gardens were.

Back at the house, we both had a dip in the pool, and then Sharon went to have a nap while I checked my email. I used Sharon's computer, not Brian's: she'd offered it the day before when I asked about emailing my mother. It was in a room she called 'my office', which was next to my bedroom, and contained a second television and a couple of filing cabinets as well as the computer.

Mum had sent a reply to my 'I arrived safely' note. She said she hoped I was having a good time in the Californian sunshine, because in Slough it was raining. I smiled, and sent her a reply about my sunburn.

I'd received a few other emails: from some of the societies I'd joined at university; from a couple of my friends;

one rather disheartening one from an NGO where I'd applied for a job. (Nothing from Steve. I hadn't expected there to be – but it still hurt.) Everything else in my inbox was spam, and I deleted it and quit. As Outlook Express folded itself away, I was left staring at Sharon's desktop. She was evidently a tidy person: everything was neatly put away in folders, with no stray files or junk applications left out to litter her desktop photo of a beach. A folder called 'Litigation' caught my eye, and out of idle curiosity I clicked on it, then wondered if I was invading her privacy.

It didn't seem to be personal litigation, though; she'd downloaded several articles about employment legislation, as well as a collection of court cases. Still curious, though now slightly furtive, I glanced through the latter. They all concerned women who claimed that their employers had unfairly dismissed them when they grew too old; the employers usually seemed to get away with it. Several of the cases concerned television presenters, sacked and replaced with younger models.

I closed the folder, feeling guilty. Did Sharon have some reason to fear that she would lose her job? It's perfectly clear to anybody watching that television prefers its female presenters young and pretty, though it has no objection to statesman-like white hair in the males.

I wondered if she hoped to be one of Brian's first customers, and if that was why she was so enthusiastic about his research. A serum to restore the fresh face of youth could, for her, be about more than just vanity. It could mean the difference between having a respected career, with all the satisfaction of doing a job and supporting herself, or trundling into underemployed cipherhood in middle age.

I shivered. I felt that if mature women *were* able to pander to the media's preference for youth, it would only encourage disdain for female experience, but I was twenty-two, and I didn't expect my career ever to depend on my looks. I still didn't like the idea of using human embryos to make cosmetics, but I could see why Sharon might.

I switched off the computer and went to see if the household had any general books on stem cell research. I eventually located the household's books, in a largish room off the kitchen which might have been designed as a dining room but now seemed to be principally Brian's study – at least, I assumed that the computer was his. There were several bookshelves along the wall, but none of them held what I was looking for. Most of the books were serious molecular biology texts, far too technical for my limited knowledge. For the general reader there were only novels, divided about equally between thrillers and historical romances: clearly a his-and-hers affair, with nothing of much interest to me. I was distracted into browsing anyway, and eventually picked up a historical whodunnit and took it out on to the deck to relax with until supper.

When Brian got back, it seemed to have been decided that we would all go into the nearest village to eat. This proved to be a place called Solvang, which had been settled largely by Danes. The center of the town had been done up in a twee Olde Worlde Danish style, complete with windmill, and the restaurant provided a rather surreal Danish smorgasbord with south Californian trimmings. Brian was in a much better mood than he'd been the night before: apparently the insurance company had agreed in principle to pay up, and the *LA Times* had decided not to run the toxic gunge story. He ordered a bottle of champagne to celebrate.

I returned the sixty dollars quietly, explaining that I hadn't bothered with a taxi. He took it with a startled, slightly hurt look. 'It can't have been a very nice walk,' he remarked. 'Right along . . . it's Tunnel Road., isn't it?'

I shrugged. 'It wasn't all that far.'

Brian stuffed the sixty dollars back into his wallet with a dissatisfied air, but said nothing more about it. He was full of suggestions of places for us to go on the following day, which was a Saturday. It seemed, though, that his presence would be required in the lab on the Monday at least, to negotiate with the insurers, so the tour of California had to be postponed again. He didn't want to go too far afield, either: he wanted to be available to his staff if anything came up. LA was in; a weekend trip to San Francisco was out. 'Next week,' he told me, 'we can go north. For now I really am stuck. I'm sorry.'

I tried to feel indignant at the way my tour of California was receding. The champagne, however, had gone to my head, and I was feeling happy and relaxed. I agreed that later in the week would be fine, and that we could go to LA in the morning.

It was a strained and pretty stupid day, really. We went to Universal Studios, because Sharon said nobody should visit LA without doing so; after all, wasn't Hollywood the city's most famous contribution to world culture?

It was fun, though probably only about half as much as we pretended. I think we were all acting a little, to encourage and reassure each other about how much fun we were having together. I wished afterward that I'd insisted on the Getty Museum, one of the other proposals. You don't have to pretend anything with great art.

On the way back there was heavy traffic. We were all hot and tired, and Brian began to lose his temper. He did so quietly, making *sotto voce* catty remarks about other drivers and driving just that bit too aggressively; it was disconcerting, because that's exactly what I do myself. Sharon soothingly suggested we stop in Santa Barbara for supper. When we finally reached the city and parked, Brian and Sharon made straight for their favourite restaurant.

It was a fish place. 'I'm a vegetarian,' I reminded them, when I saw where we were going.

'But you eat *fish*, don't you?' asked Sharon impatiently.

I don't know why there's this expectation that a vegetarian will eat fish. Why should fish be honorary vegetables?

'No, I don't eat fish,' I said. 'Uh . . . I'd be happy just to eat the vegetables, if this place is good.'

There was a brief, rather disgruntled discussion about where else we might go. I could see that it was felt that I was being awkward. I reiterated my willingness to eat at the fish place, so we did.

It wasn't a hardship: they had a huge and fabulous salad bar. Brian, however, was still displeased with me for turning my nose up at the fish.

'Why are you a vegetarian?' he demanded suddenly, while I was eating salad and he and Sharon were waiting for their fish. 'You think eating meat is unhealthy?'

'No,' I said, trying to keep my tone mild. I don't like to preach – not now, anyway. (When I first became a vegetarian, in my early teens, I was unbelievably obnoxious about it; I still cringe at the memory.) 'For me it's a private moral choice. It isn't like it's *hard* to be a vegetarian; I actually like the taste of vegetarian food more than I like meat. This salad is fantastic, by the way.'

'A *moral* choice?' asked Brian. 'You think it's immoral to kill animals?'

I hate it when carnivores see vegetarianism as an implicit insult. 'Not *per se*,' I said, trying to stay mild and friendly. 'I don't think animals are "furry people" or anything like that. I just think that where you have a choice whether to kill or not to kill a sentient creature, you should choose not to kill it. Animals are certainly sentient: nobody disputes that they feel pain and fear, at least.'

'Other animals kill to eat,' Brian objected. 'Does that make them immoral?'

I put my fork down. 'Please! I never said I think people who eat meat are immoral. In our society eating meat is a default. You only make a conscious choice about it if you decide *not* to do it, and I don't think it makes sense to talk about morality unless somebody's making a conscious choice. I don't think meat-eating's such a pressing issue, either, that everybody needs to make up their minds about it right away.'

Brian didn't give up. 'Yeah, but what do you think of it when an animal kills to eat?'

'I think it's natural behaviour,' I said resignedly. 'I don't think animals make moral choices.'

'Meat-eating is part of natural human behaviour,' Brian pointed out triumphantly, as I'd expected him to. 'In fact, it's probably one of the things that allowed our species to evolve the way it has. The brain's a hungry organ: it needs richer food than fruit and roots.'

'I've heard this theory,' I said politely. 'I think it may even be true. I don't feel it's particularly relevant, though. Ape-men on the savannah didn't have much else in the way of high-calorie, high-protein food available to them; modern humans do.'

Brian rested his elbows on the table. 'You think we're more highly evolved, more *moral* creatures now?'

I wasn't going to fall for that one. 'No, I think we have more choices. You don't think technology gives us more choices?'

The fish arrived then, a single large one for Brian and Sharon to share between them. It was some Pacific species, grilled whole and garnished with parsley. I turned my attention back to my salad, trying not to catch its dead white eye.

'Alison thinks stem cell research is immoral, too,' said

Sharon teasingly, when the meal had been dished out. Brian looked up at me sharply.

'I never said that,' I said wearily. 'I only said I think it's a murky, complicated issue.'

'Why?' asked Brian quickly.

I grimaced, wary of confrontation while Brian was in this snidely belligerent mood.

'No, it's important,' Brian insisted. 'I'd like to know what my daughter thinks of my work.'

'All right.' I put down my fork again. 'First, whatever else stem cell research is, it's commercial exploitation of human body tissue. That raises all sorts of questions about human dignity and about the ethics of consumption. Second, it involves the destruction of a potential human life, and that has its own ethical dilemmas.'

'Huh!' Brian sat back in his seat. After a moment he added, 'Most people would put those two the other way round, if they mentioned the first one at all.'

'I put them that way round because the second one is the same problem as early-stage abortion,' I told him. 'If early abortions aren't a problem for you, stem cell research won't be either. The first issue is a problem no matter what.'

'Huh,' he repeated. After another silence he said, 'OK, those are the moral problems you see. You going to enlighten me with your opinion about them?'

I gritted my teeth. 'I don't have much in the way of an opinion. I've never had to wrestle with the issue personally, and I'm not required to legislate on it. My point was simply that it's a very complicated moral issue, not a straightforward one.'

'I never said it *wasn't* morally complicated!' Brian protested irritably.

'I did,' admitted Sharon. 'I was pissed off about those morons invading your lab. Your daughter practised logical judo on me, and was disappointed when I declined to continue the bout.'

Brian smiled at her, then turned his attention back to me, quizzically now. 'You really don't have an opinion on it? I thought *everybody* had an opinion on it.'

'Look, if you want me to be honest, then, yes, I have doubts about the morality of using stem cells for a *cosmetic* treatment, but I haven't jumped to any conclusions. I've been wanting to talk to you about it, but I'd prefer to leave it to another time if it's just going to be a confrontation.'

Brian frowned. 'Why should it be a confrontation?'

'Because you seem to be looking for one,' I said shortly. He blinked.

'You were,' said Sharon, amused. 'You were trying to pick a fight with her over the fish. I thought it was pretty neat, actually, because she wouldn't fight and she still won.'

He laughed suddenly, his face relaxing. 'You're right.' He gave Sharon an affectionate glance, then turned a smile on me. 'I *was* working on skin cancer,' he told me. 'Melanoma, in particular – that's the most virulent kind, kills seven or eight thousand people a year in the United States alone. But I lost my funding when the neo-cons banned federal funding for stem cell research.'

'I heard that.'

'Those neo-cons who banned it,' murmured Sharon. 'I'd like to introduce them to a few people who're dying of melanoma, and hear them explain why it was such a moral thing to do.'

Brian smiled at her again. 'Diverting to the study of aging wasn't as big a switch as it sounds,' he continued. 'Skin aging and skin cancers have a lot in common. Skin is an organ, you know, the largest in the body. It's a complicated, sensitive organ that does a lot of vital jobs: it protects the body from infection and dehydration, cools it and keeps it warm . . . it even manufactures essential vitamin D, just from sunlight. Because we wear it between us and our environment, however, it's subject to constant assault. Bacteria, viruses, fungi, chemicals, radiation – skin has to handle everything. It suffers a lot of wear and tear, and some of the damage it takes is genetic. Luckily, normal skin has its own genetic repair kit. Abnormal skin . . . I don't know whether you've ever heard of a disease called *xeroderma pigmentosa*, or XP?'

I shook my head, very interested now.

'It's rare, luckily.' Brian was speaking eagerly now, barely pausing to gulp down the odd mouthful of fish. 'People with XP lack the normal genetic repair mechanisms in their skin. Any damage to the cells can cause cancer. They don't dare expose themselves to sunlight – have to stay indoors or come out at night. UV radiation is the worst offender when it comes to genetic damage, see. Anyway, XP provides a sort of a window into the workings of the skin's genetic repair kit. It's inherited, see, so you can use it to work out exactly what genes are involved and what's missing. It turns out that the mechanisms involved in genetic repair which are missing in XP, and which cause cancer when they fail in normal people, are also implicated in the effects of normal aging.'

'I thought aging was . . .' I began, then rephrased it. 'I heard there's a particular kind of genetic material stuck on the end of every chromosome, and every time a cell divides, it gets worn down a bit more. A sort of biological counter in every cell of our body.' It had been a sobering piece of information.

'Teleomers,' supplied Brian. 'Yes. They're not the whole story of aging, though. For example, there *is* a type of cell which is immortal, and can go on dividing indefinitely: it's called cancer. The point of teleomers, like the point of the genetic repair mechanisms which are missing in XP, is that they *protect* the working parts of the DNA. Skin cells need all the protection they can get. They get degraded with all the wear and tear they suffer, and cease to function well. The skin becomes thinner, the collagen that supports it becomes weaker. There are lots of other changes, too, but they all boil down to degradation of the cells' ability to repair damage. Find a way to splice a fresh DNA repair kit into the failing genes, and you can restore the skin to its flush of youth – *or* you can treat XP *or* cure a deadly cancer like melanoma. Oh, it won't be the identical same serum for all three, but if you've got *one* serum that works, the rest is just fine tuning. So – to get back to the point you raised – as far as *I'm* concerned, I'm *not* using stem cells for a cosmetic treatment. I'm using them to save lives, and the cosmetic application is just a way to get funding.'

'*I* don't see what's so bad about using stem cells to stop aging, anyway,' put in Sharon. 'The world we live in is obsessed with youth. If you're old, you're on the scrapheap. Anything that can help change that has got to be good.'

'And you've actually got your one serum that works?' I asked Brian.

He grimaced. 'I'm close. Maybe a year till we can go to clinical trials. The latest version of the serum is very promising indeed; the take-up by the skin cells in culture is *excellent*. I need more time and more funding.'

'It doesn't help when a bunch of bigots trash your lab,' said Sharon.

'Well, at least the insurance has agreed to pay up,' said Brian. 'Though I still need to satisfy the investors.' He caught my eyes again and added, 'See, my funding now comes from a couple of foundations set up by old men, and from a few wealthy private individuals. They'll only keep the money coming if they can see results, and they find raw data too hard to understand. You have to show them pictures before they'll sign the cheques, and all the photos we'd got ready for them got trashed. I just have to hope they'll accept that as an excuse.'

'Remind them how much money they'll make,' suggested Sharon, 'when the drug hits the market.'

Brian continued to speak enthusiastically about his work throughout the rest of the meal, backed occasionally by supportive comments from Sharon. I said very little; I wanted to think about what I'd heard. They were both in a jovial mood when we returned to the car and drove back to the house.

We were eating breakfast outside on the deck next morning when the phone rang. Sharon put down her coffee with a look of disgust and went off to answer it, then came back and fetched Brian. He was away for several minutes, and came back looking anxious.

'I have to go in to the lab,' he told us. 'The police say they need to check something, and they need somebody to let them into the building.'

We'd just been finalizing plans for a day at the beach. 'Will it take long?' Sharon asked. ''Cause you could run down there now, and I could get the stuff together. Then we can head off as soon as you get back.'

Brian thought it wouldn't take too long, so I offered to accompany him; I was curious to see his lab. He was surprised, but pleased, and we climbed into his monstrous great car together. The lab was, as he'd said, only a couple of miles down the road, not very far from the carpark where the hiking trail crossed it. The site was enclosed by a chain-link fence, the building invisible up the drive from the single unmarked gate. Two cars were pulled over at the entrance: a marked police car and a blue Honda.

Brian pulled over, switched the engine off and got out. The doors of the other cars also swung open, disgorging a pair of policemen from the one and Roberto Hernandez of the FDA from the other.

'Alison!' Hernandez exclaimed, smiling at me in pleasure, then: 'Dr Greenall!' with respect.

Brian frowned at him.

'Dr Greenall?' said the larger of the two policemen. He was a stout, red-faced man; his companion was dark and wiry. 'I'm Detective Ronald Kermode; I've just been assigned to your case. This is my assistant, Lt Stevens.'

Brian shook hands. 'And you want me to let you into the lab, right?'

'If you please.'

The other policeman, Stevens, put in, 'We've been told that this treatment of yours is worth a lot of money.'

Brian glanced at Hernandez, who looked embarrassed. 'Yes,' agreed Brian quietly. 'Millions, if it's as successful as I think it will be.'

Kermode and Stevens exchanged a look of apprehensive commiseration.

Brian glanced uneasily at Hernandez again. 'What are you doing here, Mr Hernandez?' he demanded bluntly. 'What's this got to do with the FDA?'

Hernandez blinked. 'I, uh . . . that is, your insurance people have approached us, um, about what sort of security is normal at a research establishment like yours. Basically, they wanted us to say that you'd been negligent. They were worried that the missing serum might've been stolen rather than just destroyed, and they're afraid you're going to try to claim compensation for it. I offered to investigate it personally.' He paused and added hopefully, 'When I spoke to the police about it, they upgraded your case.'

'I've already told you,' said Brian irritably, 'the real secrets are in the computers. The processes are patented and the data's encrypted. Even if the serum was stolen, if it wasn't kept under controlled conditions, it would soon be no use at all.'

'Yes, but,' replied Hernandez unhappily, 'I came across some evidence that somebody's trying to buy it.'

Brian stared.

'I checked out some websites belonging to the more militant pro-life groups,' Hernandez elaborated. 'There was a . . . message left on several of them which . . . well . . .' He fumbled in his jacket pocket, brought out a very nifty little personal organizer, and began pressing keys to bring up the message.

Kermode forestalled him by pulling out a little note-book. '"To the brave night owls who perched in the green tree",' he read, his voice heavy with distaste for the theatrical words, '"the bluebird would pay well for the elixir". It was posted on Tuesday, the day after your break-in was discovered. There was a contact email – blue-bird12@safemail – but it seems to have been set up at the time, and we haven't been able to trace it.'

'And the day after this was posted,' Hernandez continued, 'the *LA Times* got that phone call about the genetic modification serum. The caller said that the serum had "gone missing". If they'd just destroyed it, that would be an odd thing to say. I . . . I just wondered whether one of the people who broke into your lab might have been more scientifically literate than the others – whether he could've understood what he'd found, and taken it to sell.'

'Oh.' Brian looked slightly sick.

'Can we see the lab, Dr Greenall?' asked Detective Kermode.

Brian obediently dug out his wallet, selected a keycard, and ran it through the box next to the gate. The chain-link doors rolled aside with a buzzing groan. The others climbed back into their cars, but Brian waited while they drove through, and I realized that he intended to lock the gate behind us. I offered to close it for him.

I didn't need the keycard; it closed with a button. I rested my fingers on the gate as it groaned back along its runners, and felt the metal vibrate with a deep resonance. The fence was heavy.

Brian had the car waiting just inside the gate. I climbed back in. 'Must have been an expensive fence.'

Brian snorted in agreement. 'Yeah. The insurance company insisted. They were really only worried about theft, though, when they had us set it up.' He made a face. 'I think if they'd worried about pro-life terrorists, they would've asked for something like the Berlin Wall.'

We drove on up the drive to a small carpark, one that could hold perhaps fifteen cars. It was empty, apart from Hernandez and the police – as one would expect, at half past nine on a Sunday morning. The building beyond it was a very ordinary block of glass and concrete; it could've been a tax office. I hadn't known what to expect of a cutting-edge biotechnology laboratory, and I was slightly disappointed.

The others had parked and were waiting by the building's main entrance, and Brian and I came and joined them. It was very quiet, and you could smell the sage on the hillside above us. Sharon had told me that the dry scrub was called 'chaparral'. It sounded improbably wild west for a biotech research establishment.

Brian took out another keycard and began to unlock the door. 'Do I understand that you want to check the deep freeze?' he asked the policemen.

Kermode nodded. 'We've found an item which we think may have come from there.'

'Oh.' Brian opened the door and led the way into the building. 'May I ask what?'

'Let us look first,' said Kermode forbiddingly.

The interior of the lab was no more dramatic than the exterior. There were a couple of large rooms filled with work benches and light industrial equipment; locked doors probably led to offices. There were a couple of shiny patches on the wall where someone had tried to wash away felt-tipped pro-life slogans which were now faded but still clearly visible: BABY-KILLERS! and HUMAN LIFE IS SACRED! PROTECT THE INNOCENT! Apart from that there wasn't really much evidence of the 'tens of thousands of dollars worth of damage' which had supposedly been done. I supposed the broken glass and so on had all been cleared away.

Brian led us through one of the big rooms and into a second, then pressed a panel on what looked like a big safe. He picked up some insulated gloves and face masks from a box beside it. 'Safety regulations,' he explained, offering them to the policemen. 'The freezer's kept at minus 70 C., much colder than a domestic device, and the cell cultures are immersed in liquid nitrogen. If you touch anything that cold with your bare skin it will burn you.' The policemen grunted and accepted the equipment.

Brian opened the safe, and a cloud of chilled air flowed out. The policemen, masks hastily wedged on, took it in turns to look inside. Kermode grunted, drew on a glove, and pulled out a simple plastic freezer basket. It was white, stamped with 'Sunset Scientifics Inc.' in square red lettering, and empty.

'You keep all your frozen samples in crates like this?' he asked Brian.

Brian nodded. 'That's what you found?'

Kermode gave a grunt that was probably affirmative. 'I can't see anything else in your freezer. Am I just being blind?'

'No.' Brian told him. 'When we came in here the morning after the break-in, there were a few things still in there, but the power was cut off during the break-in. The guys who did it cut the power to the alarms, and so the power to the freezer went, too. It might've been OK, but the pro-lifers had thrown a lot of stuff from the fridge on to the floor. Eventually we decided that since we didn't know how long the freezer'd been open, we had to conclude that everything left in it had been damaged or contami-nated. We had to throw it out, and we haven't yet been able to replace anything.'

Kermode grunted again, and peered into the steam. 'The freezer was open when you arrived?'

Brian hesitated. 'We're not sure. I was about the fourth person to get here the morning after the break-in. The freezer was closed when I got here, but somebody could have closed it before I arrived. Nobody actually *remembers* closing it, but it's an automatic action. You know, like switching off the coffee maker: you can forget you've done it.'

Kermode grunted in a more human fashion. 'Yeah. Whenever we go on holiday, my wife's always worrying about whether she remembered to switch off the dryer. You keep the freezer locked normally?'

'No.' Brian was resigned. 'We have a small staff, and we don't have many visitors. We'd never had any need to lock up our research supplies.'

'What was it you kept in there?'

'I told your colleague that before. We kept biological material: tissue samples, skin cultures, the stem cells that caused all this trouble.' Brian hesitated, then added, 'The serum I was working on.'

'The valuable one. That was kept in a box like this?'

'It was stored in test tubes, each containing five mils of serum. We put them in sealed cases: little black boxes which each contained four test tubes. We stored six boxes in a freezer tray. We had two trays prepared, and we think we recovered the contents of one of them.'

'So one's missing?'

Brian sighed. 'You've got to understand, everything was just jumbled together and dumped on the floor. We're sure that some of the trays are missing. We think that these people were after the stem cells when they opened the freezer, and that they took them off to . . . I don't know, give them Christian burial. It looks like they took some of the serum as well, but they may have thought it was more stem cells, and just have dumped it somewhere else when they discovered their mistake. Where did you find the tray?'

'Couple of miles east of here, along the hiking trail,' answered Kermode.

Brian blinked, then let out his breath unhappily. 'That would explain why there's no sign of anybody forcing the gate and why nobody noticed them parked on the road.'

'Oh, they brought a ladder, and climbed the fence in back,' said the policeman confidently. 'We found the marks where they did it. They wouldn't have attracted any attention, even if they came while your people were still around.'

Hernandez stirred. 'There's a gully with some trees a couple of miles along the hiking trail,' he informed Brian. 'That's where the police found the freezer tray.'

I cleared my throat uncomfortably. 'These little black boxes . . . they wouldn't be about so big?' I held my hands a few inches apart, as the Monster of the Mountain had.

Everybody looked at me in surprise.

'I met a guy on the hiking trail who was looking for a box like that,' I told Brian. 'When I went for that walk before breakfast, day before yesterday.'

Brian's face reddened. 'Why didn't you tell me this before?'

I felt guilty now that I hadn't. 'I didn't know it was significant, did I?' I replied defensively. 'He was just a guy I met on a hiking trail. When I met him I didn't even know the trail went near your lab.'

'What did he look like, this guy you met?' Kermode asked eagerly.

I described the Monster of the Mountain as well as I could, and the policemen made notes.

'We'll look into this,' promised Kermode. He hefted his plastic freezer tray. 'Mind if we take this back with us?'

Brian waved them permission and closed the freezer. He started back toward the entrance to the building with the air of a man who'd had enough and wanted to get away. The policemen hurriedly stripped off their gloves and followed.

Hernandez fell into step with me. 'You were lucky that guy you met didn't know who you were,' he said seriously. 'Those people can be violent.'

I knew from experience that the Monster was violent, but I still hated that phrase 'those people'. I found myself saying, 'Most of them aren't. Most of them are honest, well-intentioned people who campaign peacefully.'

Hernandez made a noise of contempt. 'Most of them, yes. Some of them have blown up clinics and assassinated doctors.'

'Some animal rights activists use violence and intimidation,' I said irritably. 'I always hate it when I get lumped in with them because I share some of the same beliefs. The people we're talking about *didn't* blow up Brian's lab. They broke into it in the middle of the night when nobody was around, damaged some property, and carried off the stem cells. There's no reason to think they belong to a violent group.'

Hernandez looked at me in amazement. 'You're into *animal rights*?'

He sounded as though he'd never heard of such a ludicrous idea. It was probably just as well that we emerged into the carpark at this point, and the conversation came to an abrupt halt.

Five

Brian had recovered his manners enough to invite Hernandez and the two policemen back to the house for a cold drink. The policemen declined; Hernandez accepted eagerly.

Sharon was not pleased to see him, and was even less pleased by the news that somebody might be trying to sell the missing serum. She nevertheless played gracious hostess, and brought everyone iced orange juice.

'You seem to have gone to a lot of trouble on my behalf,' Brian commented, sitting down opposite Hernandez in the lounge.

Hernandez smiled eagerly. 'I really admire your achievements, Dr Greenall. I totally disagree with the government's attitude to stem cell research and I'd really love to see you succeed. I'll do anything I can to help.'

'I see!' Brian was taken aback a bit. 'Well, thank you.' He sloshed the orange juice around in his glass and added, 'I still don't really think I'm in much danger of having my work stolen, though. The key to it isn't the composition of the serum, it's the processes involved in making it. Most of them are patented, and none of them will be apparent just from looking at the serum. Even if you're right, and one of the people who broke in did decide to try to sell it, I still think they must've ruined it by the time they got it home. It'll be useless if they haven't kept it cold.'

'How cold do you actually have to keep it?' asked Sharon, perching on the arm of his chair. 'I mean, you have that industrial-grade freezer, but does it really *need* to be that cold?'

Brian shrugged. 'I suppose it would be all right in an ordinary deep freeze, for a few months, anyway. But it must've thawed out when they stole it, particularly if they had to hike a couple miles along a trail with it. If it was allowed to thaw out, and then refrozen, it wouldn't be safe to use.'

'Yeah, but they weren't planning to *use* it,' objected Hernandez. 'They were planning to sell it to someone who would *analyze* it. The sort of thing I was thinking of was maybe the thief slipped it into a cool box or something until he got home, and then stuck it in his freezer.'

Brian frowned.

'Why would they have a cool box available?' asked Sharon.

'Cold drinks,' Hernandez said at once. 'They must've wanted to check the lab out before they broke in. Probably they were sitting up on that hiking trail for a while, waiting for a good time to hit. They'd have had some drinks in a cooler.'

'You've really thought it out, haven't you?' asked Brian.

Hernandez flushed slightly. 'It's a lot more interesting than sending warnings to internet snake-oil peddlars, or writing reports on how some research trial breached the guidelines on informed consent.'

Brian was amused now. 'I suppose you do a lot of that.'

Hernandez rolled his eyes. 'Somebody has to.' After a moment, he added quickly, 'I like the FDA, but the thing I really *wanted* to do was get a PhD and go into research. I needed to pay off my student loan, though, and my family had other commitments, so it was too much time and money.'

Brian was now openly sympathetic. 'Where'd you get your degree?'

'UCLA. Biochemistry.'

'It's a good school. Maybe you could go back. Grad students can usually support themselves.'

'I've looked into it, a couple of times,' Hernandez told him eagerly. 'I was thinking of going back once my little sister's finished school. She's a junior at Cal State.'

'Brian,' interrupted Sharon pointedly, 'are we going to the beach, or not? All the things are packed up and in the hall.'

Hernandez looked disappointed, but got to his feet. 'I didn't realize you were planning to go out,' he said. 'Sorry.'

'Not at all,' said Brian politely. 'Thanks for your help. Please stop off and see me if you discover anything more, or just if you're in the area.'

Hernandez flushed again. 'Thank you, Dr Greenall. I will.'

When he'd gone, Sharon said disgustedly, 'What a boot-licking creep!'

'That's unfair,' said Brian.

'He's trying to get you to give him a reference for grad school,' Sharon informed him with distaste.

Brian shrugged. 'If he is, he's wasting his time. I'm not an academic, so any reference I could give him would be no use for academic work.'

Sharon gave a snort of contempt. '*He* doesn't realize that, though.' She leaned over to kiss her husband on the ear. 'Let's not talk about him, OK? Let's just go to the beach.'

The nearest beach was only a ten-minute drive away. It was a beautiful place, with a wide stretch of yellow-brown sand nestled under a steep headland. There were trees – eucalyptus, live oak, a few pines – and birds in abundance. We didn't have the place entirely to ourselves, as there were families barbecueing and a group of teenagers playing volleyball, but by European standards it was marvellously uncrowded. We went for a swim in the bitingly cold blue water, then sat down to eat the picnic Sharon had packed. Then we lay in the sun.

Sharon lounged in a white bikini like a true Californian beach babe, her skin glowing golden in the light. She had a wide-brimmed hat (white, like the bikini) and designer sunglasses. She'd brought one of her historical romances to keep herself entertained, and she leafed through it as she toasted. I sat beside her for a while feeling dowdy in my old blue one-piece, pallid skin heavily coated with sunblock. Then I got bored.

I get bored quickly on beaches. I can't sunbathe and the light's too bright to read comfortably. I got up, pulled on my shorts, T-shirt and sandals, and told the others I was going for a walk.

'I'll come with you,' said Brian quickly.

'Enjoy,' Sharon wished us, without looking up from her book.

Brian and I crunched along the sand toward the headland. 'Sharon loves the beach,' he told me. 'We don't go often enough.'

I eyed him sideways. 'You think it's boring too, huh?'

He grinned sheepishly. 'I thought that for you it would at least have some novelty value.'

'Yeah,' I agreed, amiably enough. 'I suppose I couldn't come back from southern California and admit I never sat on a Pacific beach. It'd be like going to Munich and not trying the beer.'

We crunched a bit further. 'What do you actually *like*?' Brian asked. 'Before you came, Sharon was telling me to take it easy on the culture. She thought you'd like to see Hollywood and Malibu and the malls. She was planning to take you shopping. She told me that you're twenty-two, you're a student, you were going to want to have fun. But I have a feeling that maybe your idea of fun is closer to mine than to Sharon's.'

I laughed – or, to be honest, sniggered. 'I like culture. I suppose what I'm really eager to see, though, is more of the countryside. The Sierra Nevada, the giant sequoias – the sort of thing you don't get in England. I really don't enjoy shopping very much, though it's nice of Sharon to worry.'

'She's very keen for this to work,' said Brian. 'She . . . I suppose the best way to describe it is that she's been hoping that you'll see her as an aunt, a young aunt. That you'll look forward to visiting.'

I wondered again whether Sharon was childless by choice, and what she'd said when Brian first suggested contacting me. It was possible she'd actually pushed him toward it.

I picked my words very carefully. 'I'm keen for this to work, too. I don't know, though, how much it's realistic to hope for.'

Brian stopped, turning to look at me squarely. 'I was a very immature, selfish young man when I walked out on you and your mother. I know that now, OK? And I'm very sorry for it.'

So. It seemed we were finally going to talk about it. 'Mum said you didn't want kids,' I replied, watching him. 'That you tried to persuade her to have an abortion.'

'It's true. I can't deny it. Alison, your mother and I got married when we were your age. When you were born we had a one-bedroom flat. I was working on my PhD and your mother was teaching on a short-term contract. Having a baby – it meant having no money and no space; it meant never going anywhere, because we couldn't get a babysitter; it meant living in squalor. I was used to freedom, to being able to cut loose and go on the spur of the moment.

I was crazy about films and theatre, I liked travel and books and parties. I didn't think I could cope – and, as it turned out, I couldn't. Your mother expected me to babysit while she was at work, and I was no good at it: she'd come back and find you screaming with hunger and the place a mess, and she'd lay into me. It was hell, and after a year of it I walked out. I was a *failure*, OK? I failed as a husband and father, and I was so ashamed that I couldn't bear even to think about it, and didn't dare go back and apologize. I'm not *defending* what I did, I'm just saying that's how it was: a mess, not a policy. But please believe me when I say that when I wanted your mother to have an abortion, it wasn't because I didn't want *you*. I didn't know anything about you: there *was* no such person. All I wanted was to preserve my marriage and my way of life. When you were born, I felt all the things new fathers are supposed to feel: amazement, awe, protectiveness. Love. It was just . . . you just wanted attention *all the time*, and if you didn't get it, you had this yell that was worse than a dentist's drill. Still, I *never* forgot you. Whenever I saw little girls playing, I'd think of you and wonder what I was missing. I don't accept, though, that I was a monster because I didn't want you to be born. If your mother had had the abortion, like I wanted, the marriage probably would've lasted, and we might well have had other children.'

'Oh, please!' I protested. 'I don't trust might-have-beens. Yeah, maybe the marriage would've lasted, but maybe it would've broken down over something else. Maybe *she* would've walked out on *you*, because she wanted kids and you didn't; maybe one or the other of you would've been knocked down by a bus! Might-have-beens can never justify an actual decision, because they aren't real. To tell the truth, it doesn't really bother me that you wanted to abort me. Maybe I'm just weird, or maybe it's because I can't conceive of never having existed, but it's never been an issue for me. The fact that you walked out wasn't really the issue for me, either; that was between you and Mum. I don't remember you ever being there, so I can't honestly say I missed you when you left. The things *I* minded about growing up without a father were different.

'*Other* people's divorced dads took *some* interest in them. They took them on holidays, they sent them birthday presents, they gave them money. Not you. God, when I arrived at the airport, the only way I even knew what you *looked* liked was Mum's old photos! And I always got dumped in after-school clubs and holidays clubs when Mum was working, and for years we never had the money for the kind of house or car or holiday that other people did. Maybe that sounds greedy and callous, but that's where it hit me. You say you never forgot about me, but you never paid any child maintenance, either. How real is an interest if you're not willing to spend any money on it? Would you believe somebody who said he was a big opera fan, but never actually went to any shows or bought any CDs?'

Brian flushed and just stared at me unhappily. He didn't offer to defend himself. I found, to my shame, that I could do it for him. He'd been living in another country, where nobody sent him any forms asking him to pay. He would have had to volunteer – and he'd been angry at Mum anyway, and probably resentful of the demand that he support a child he'd never wanted. Perhaps he hadn't even *decided* not to deal with the matter, but had only put it off, until so much time had passed that an intervention would be an embarrassment. Oh, I could see it.

'That's all water under the bridge,' I said, more quietly. 'It's twenty years later, and the question is what happens now. I would *like* to work something out between us, I really would, but I just don't think we should expect too much.' I wondered which of us I was warning.

Brian regarded me soberly. 'You're an alarming young woman.'

I'd heard that one before. Steve thought that, too. Probably it was true. 'Oh, thanks!' I turned away and looked up at the headland.

'You're not at all what I expected. I thought you'd be more like Claire – like your mother. Excitable and vivacious.'

'Mum always said I was a lot like you.'

'That's the really scary part,' he told me. 'How much that's true.'

That was the part that scared me, too. I glanced back at him, then started on along the beach.

'What made you pick philosophy?' he asked quietly.

'I was interested in the big questions,' I said honestly. 'What's real, how do we know what we know, what should we value and how should we live? And I'm good at arguing.' Too good. Oppressively good, as far as Steve was concerned.

'Doesn't seem to me that there are any answers to those questions – at least not ones that everyone can agree on.'

'Yeah, but with philosophy you can understand the questions better.'

He snorted in acknowledgement. 'I suppose I was interested in the big questions, too. I picked molecular biology because I wanted to understand what makes us what we are.'

'Molecular biology always seems to me a subject which has lots of answers, but nobody's sure what the questions are.'

Brian smiled hesitantly. 'There's some truth to that.'

We'd reached the end of the sand; before us the headland rose sheer out of the Pacific, cloaked in the dry scrub. 'There's no trail from here,' Brian told me. 'You have to go back to the carpark.'

'You've tried?'

He nodded, ruefully. 'I've been bored here before.'

We turned and crunched back along the beach the way we'd come. Even though the things I'd said had been perilously like a quarrel, we walked side by side companionably, as though we'd effected some kind of reconciliation.

The next day was a Monday. Sharon again left early – Brian told me that she generally had two weeks doing mornings, followed by two weeks on evenings, which included the weekends. Brian and I rose around seven, watched her present the morning news, and then Brian dropped me off to do some touring and went to his lab. I'd been in the country less than a week, but the pattern of the day already seemed routine.

My tourist activity for the day was a hike – not on the trail behind the house, which I now wanted to avoid, but further afield, along the Santa Ynez river.

I had another lovely day. The countryside was stunning, the sun shone, and there was swimming in the river. The birdlife was amazing: there were golden eagles, hummingbirds, and even some little burrowing owls which stuck their heads out of a mound of dirt and glared at me with disgusted yellow eyes. When Sharon picked me up, about three, I was hot, sweaty, tired, and immensely happy.

Sharon, however, seemed tense and short-tempered. She listened to my enthusings without interest, not even commenting on any of the plant life, which I'd gathered was something of a hobby of hers. I shut up quickly and sat silent in the passenger seat of the red sports car, wondering whether I should ask if she'd had a rough day at work. I feared that it would only irritate her, that what she was really annoyed about wasn't work, but me. I was not the friendly niece-figure she'd hoped to go shopping with, and she was having to do quite a lot of running about to collect me.

When we reached the house, however, she gave me a tired smile as she turned off the engine. 'Sorry,' she said. 'I've had a lousy day.'

'Oh!' I said, relieved but trying to look sympathetic. 'What happened?'

She shook her head, stretched, and climbed out of the car. 'Let's have a swim and a drink before we do anything else, OK?'

After a quick dip, we sat on the deck with a bottle of cold Chardonnay, and Sharon had a good moan about her place of work. It was pretty much what I would've predicted: an aggressive and critical boss, a supercilious male colleague and an ambitious female junior. The current complaint concerned the junior overstepping her job description, and the boss and colleague taking the view that Sharon was making a fuss about nothing when she objected. It was clear that this wasn't the first time this had happened, and that Sharon was worried and defensive. I made sympathetic noises.

When she ran out of things to say, Sharon fell silent, then stretched and rubbed the back of her neck. 'Thanks for listening,' she said.

I made that embarrassed sound you make to try to indicate that no, it wasn't a chore.

'I *hate* getting old!' she said bitterly.

'You're not!' I protested. 'You're . . . I don't know? Forty? That's not old. It's barely even middle-aged!'

'Forty-six,' she said sourly. 'No, I'm not really *old* yet. But I'm not young any more, either, and I'm getting older every day.' She leaned her head back into the deck chair. 'It won't hit you for years yet. Fresh out of university, you're rushing out to conquer the world with all your life ahead of you. One day, though, you'll suddenly find that the best bit of your life is already behind you, and you haven't achieved anything you hoped for, and everything ahead is just a long roll downhill. You don't have the energy or the resilience you did. Your tits sag and your ass spreads and your skin dries up like old newspaper. Nobody whistles at you when you walk down a street – and I know you think it's just a stupid pain in the ass when guys do that, but you'll find you miss it when they stop. Your enthusiasm fades and your cynicism grows. I know, you're thinking to yourself "I'm an intellectual, I won't mind". But you will. All around us, everything celebrates youth and beauty – and *we're* getting older.'

I said nothing. I was shocked.

'Sorry,' said Sharon, and sighed. 'I don't mean to be so gloomy. It's just I'm tired . . . God, I'm tired! And we've got nothing in the house for supper!'

'I could take the car and buy something,' I offered hesitantly. I was a bit nervous; I'd had a driving licence for four years, but never a car of my own, and Sharon's sports car was a far cry from my mother's old Metro. I'd noticed, however, that the local roads were quiet, and that Sharon's car had an automatic gear shift. If I kept reminding myself to drive on the right I should be OK, and I wanted to do something helpful. Sharon had been extremely kind to me, considering that I was her husband's child by another woman, and a prickly one at that.

'You can drive?' Sharon asked, gazing at me in surprise; then, recovering a little, 'Of *course* you can, you're twenty-two, aren't you? Would you really be willing to pick something up for us? I think the insurance would stretch.'

A few minutes later, and I was behind the wheel of the red sports car, steering it carefully down the drive.

I wondered if Sharon was right, that I'd mind getting older. Probably she was, though I doubted, still, that I'd mind it as much as she did. I wasn't beautiful; that had never been part of my image of myself, so I wouldn't feel that I was losing a part of myself when my looks began to fade. If my *mind* started to go it would be different.

Aging suddenly struck me forcibly as a fundamental horror: God, what a monstrosity, to be trapped in a body that is subject to a slow and remorseless degeneration, losing resilience, strength, beauty, senses, wits! What a world, what a terrible world! Sitting there, clutching the steering wheel, I looked at my hands – pale, smooth-skinned, freckled, young – and really believed, for perhaps the first time, that one day they would be old, wrinkled and frail. It lay ahead of me, as it lay ahead of everything that breathes.

I looked up, saw another car in the distance, and realized with a jolt that I was driving on the left. I swerved rapidly over to the right, and I decided that I'd better concentrate on driving. Aging may be a horror, but the alternative is worse.

Sharon had directed me to a supermarket in Solvang, and I found it without any trouble. It was quite fun: the fruit and vegetable section was selling six varieties of chilli pepper, and I gave up counting the flavours of ice cream after I found the Burgundy Cherry Chocolate. I returned with ice cream and an oven-ready Chinese, triumphant and pleased with my driving skills. The police car in front of the house rather punctured my bubble.

It was only Detective Kermode again, though. It seemed he had a folder of mugshots he wanted me to look at. He'd been sitting out on the deck with Sharon while he waited for me, sipping a glass of cold water, but we all came into the lounge and looked at the pictures.

The third face in the folder was the Monster of the Mountain. 'Him,' I said, with a quiver of misgiving. It was a prison mugshot, full face and profile with a number printed beneath.

'You're sure?' asked Kermode, watching me closely.

I nodded uncomfortably. 'Is he . . . has he blown up clinics?'

Kermode jutted his lower lip and examined the page beneath the pictures, which he'd covered with his notebook. 'Naw,' he said dismissively. 'Curtis Langford, resident of Carpinteria, automotive mechanic. Six months for domestic violence. Sent his girlfriend to hospital with a broken nose and a fractured rib.'

Because she'd aborted his baby? I suddenly found I could imagine the whole thing: he'd been jealous and short-tempered; she'd wanted out of the relationship and had opted for the abortion; he'd turned on her in horrified rage. He'd said he was 'sort of' a Christian. I suspected that he'd been brought up on some fundamentalist faith which he'd never actually rejected but had long ceased to observe. When his girlfriend committed what his faith saw as murder though, it had struck him like a visceral blow. Perhaps he'd attacked her out of a confused desire to revenge his own lapses. And perhaps I just had an over-active imagination. I thought about telling Detective Kermode about my second meeting with the Monster – and found myself reluctant. It would be embarrassing to admit I'd accepted a lift from the guy; it would be more embarrassing to explain why I hadn't said anything about the slap before. ('I thought it would be a lot of hassle, and I'm on holiday.') Besides, I felt, uneasily, that the bare description of what had happened would be somehow misleading – that it would make me look too good and the Monster too bad. It hadn't been a case of Innocent English Girl vs Thug; it had been a case of Intellectual Bully vs Half-Educated Brute. I'd deserved to get my comeuppance. Maybe I hadn't deserved a slap in the face – but if I added in all the other people I'd bullied over the years – if I added in all the things I'd said to *Steve* – maybe I did.

'What will you do?' I asked Detective Kermode uneasily.

'We'll pick him up for questioning,' said Kermode, closing his file. 'See what he says about this missing serum, search his place of residence. If we have enough evidence, we'll charge him with grand larceny. Thanks for your help, Miss Greenall.'

No, I'd already caused Curtis Langford enough trouble by siccing the police on him. I'd keep my mouth shut about the slap in the face.

Sharon had seemed flustered by the presence of the police, and she heaved a sigh of relief when Kermode left. 'I hate this whole business,' she told me. Then she gave me a singularly false smile and added, 'Have some more wine!'

The following day, Tuesday, found me once again playing tourist in the Santa Barbara area; Brian still couldn't tear himself away from his stricken lab.

It was pleasant enough, though by now I was mopping up the second- and third-division sights. If Brian didn't manage to fix the insurance problem by the next day, I would have to think about doing some travelling on my own. I'd enjoyed the last week, but I didn't want to spend the next week the same way. Brian and I had been making some progress toward an understanding, but there was a lot of tension between us, and if we didn't get something new to focus on, it was bound to flare up. I wondered how much it would cost me to rent a car for a few days.

I ran out of enthusiasm for sightseeing after lunch, and retired to the park where I was to meet Sharon. I'd found a really nice second-hand bookshop, so I had plenty to keep myself amused. I sat down with one of my purchases on a bench under a tree.

I was in the middle of the second chapter when somebody called my name. I looked up, and there was Roberto Hernandez.

'Oh,' I said. 'Hello.' I wasn't sure whether or not to be pleased.

'Hello,' he replied, smiling appeasingly. 'I was hoping you might be here.'

I raised my eyebrows, but took my new bag of books off the bench beside me and put it beside my feet. Hernandez sat down, well forward on the bench, hands locked together, and looked at me with a smile.

'You're saying you came here to meet me?' I asked, after a lengthy silence.

'Yes,' he agreed. 'That is, I was here in Santa Barbara for a meeting, but when it finished I, uh, came *here* just on the chance I might meet you. I didn't want to . . . that is, I get the impression your step-mother thinks I'm being a pest, so I didn't want to stop by your father's house again. I don't have anything to tell him, anyway.'

'So what did you want to talk to me about?'

He gave me a sweet smile. 'I was just hoping to see you again.'

'Oh!' My heart sped up and I stared at him. Maybe it was Sharon's influence, but I wasn't sure I believed him – and yet, I wanted to.

'I didn't think you'd be here,' he added. 'You'd said you were going on a tour of the state.'

'It's sort of been delayed by all the fuss,' I admitted. 'Look, I probably *am* going on it before long, and anyway, I go home in two weeks.'

'I know. I just . . . look, I . . . don't know any other philosophers. I've always thought of them as old guys with beards, not cute redheads with freckles. It just seemed to me that you'd be really interesting.' He drew a deep breath. 'Would you like to go on a boat cruise? They do cruises round the harbour here. I could drop you off at your dad's place afterwards.'

'Well,' I said, helplessly. I knew I was blushing, and

that he would probably notice as much; it's pretty obvious with my sort of skin. Agreeing would probably be a bad idea. I didn't trust him, *but* – that awful *but* that so easily overpowers good sense – I liked him.

Steve hadn't emailed me, either. Was it wrong to enjoy a little male admiration?

'Yeah,' I muttered. 'Thanks. Let me phone Sharon.'

Sharon was disgusted and suspicious when I informed her that I was going on a boat with Roberto Hernandez, but didn't try to talk me out of it. We went down to the harbour and wandered along the waterfront and the wharf. Eventually we found the company that did harbour cruises. The next one left in half an hour, so we sat down to wait.

'Are you really into animal rights? Roberto asked.

'Moderately,' I told him. 'I'm not a believer in Animal Liberation or anything; there are a lot of places I'd disagree with Singer, for example. But I think the issues he raises are valid ones.'

'Who's Singer?'

'Peter Singer? *Animal Liberation, Practical Ethics*? You haven't heard of him?'

'Uh . . . no.'

'Oh.' I realized that it would be much easier to talk about what Singer thought than about what *I* thought; it would be a good way to defuse the issue. 'Well, he's an ethical philosopher, one of the most original and contro-versial around. He says there's no moral reason to privi-lege the human species over any other kind of animal, that in considering the morality of an action, the relevant ques-tion isn't what sort of creature it affects, but how much suffering it causes. Mind you, he thinks that to kill or injure a human being is worse than killing or injuring another sort of animal, because we're more aware of what we're losing, so we suffer more. But he thinks it's as wrong to hurt an animal as it is to hurt a human being.'

'Oh!' He mulled that bold idea over, then observed, facetiously, 'I guess he must be a vegetarian.'

'Strictly so.'

'What does he think of using animals in research?'

'What do you think?'

'Even if you discover a medicine that saves human lives?'

'You've got no moral right to save human lives at the cost of inflicting pain and death on thousands of rats and mice.'

'Wow. I can see why he's controversial.'

'Oh, he upsets a *lot* of people! He got into terrible trouble with the religious right, too, because he doesn't think killing a baby is any worse than killing a calf, except inasmuch as the parents suffer more than the cow. In his view, neither the calf nor the baby is fully sentient – that is, fully aware of themselves and what they're losing – so their suffering would be about equal.'

Roberto gaped in amazement. 'That's *insane!*'

'It's *exactly* the same argument that's used to justify abortion,' I corrected him. 'I presume you don't think *that's* insane, since you have no trouble with the use of stem cells.' Then I bit my lip; I couldn't seem to get away from that subject these days.

'The pro-choice lobby doesn't believe in killing babies!' objected Roberto. 'An embryo *isn't* a baby until it's developed enough to survive on its own.'

'Hey, be fair to Peter Singer! He doesn't believe in killing babies, either; he doesn't believe in killing *anything*. Look, the commonest pro-choice argument is that because a foetus is not a fully sentient, self-aware, independent individual, it isn't really human. A woman who is such an individual has a right to end its life to protect the quality of her own – right? Well, by that definition a newborn baby isn't fully human, either. It isn't fully sentient, can't possibly survive on its own, and is certainly a terrible burden to its mother. What's more, the same can be said of a disabled person or a demented old one. Now, you don't have to tell me that the pro-choice lobby isn't in favour of euthanizing unwanted babies and disabled old people: I *know* that, OK? The point I'm making is that if the *argument* is accepted as valid in the case of abortion, then it is necessarily also valid for infanticide and involuntary euthanasia. You cannot logically agree with it in one case, and then call it "insane" in the other; that's just incoherent. If you can't agree with the conclusions of your own argument, then you need a better argument.'

Roberto sat frowning over this for a moment. Then he gave a little snort, and grinned. 'I thought this would be interesting.'

Well, as a response I liked that more than a slap in the face, even though it meant he wasn't taking the ideas terribly seriously.

'So, you disagree with this man Singer?' he went on.

'I think he's a very exciting and challenging thinker, but yes, I disagree with him. I think it *is* reasonable to privilege humans above other animals. The syllogism runs something like this: if there is nothing unique or special about being human, and if it's morally acceptable for other animals to kill and eat one another as part of their natural behaviour, then it must be morally acceptable for humans to do the same; if, on the other hand, it's fair to expect more of humans because of our greater awareness and greater freedom of choice, then there must be something unique and special about us.'

Roberto laughed.

'Singer's got a response to that argument, of course,' I admitted. 'I just don't find it particularly convincing.'

'And this . . . this is what you do? This is what modern philosophy's about?'

'Oh, well.' I looked down at my hands. 'This is ethics; it's comparatively practical. I mean, it's about problems people face living in the real world. A lot of modern philosophy is much more abstract. There are an awful lot of papers about the meaning of meaning and so on. Those can be interesting, too, in their way, but they really do your head in. I suppose the people who write them don't get hate mail the way Singer does, though.'

'So what do you do with a philosophy degree? Work for a government agency?'

I looked up at him again, surprised. 'Yeah, quite a lot of people *do* go into the civil service.'

'I can see it. That sort of skill at hair-splitting would come in handy. Is that what you plan to do?'

'I've applied. I'd really prefer to work for an NGO or an international agency.'

'Not go on and get a PhD?'

'I'd prefer to do something *real*, which is just as well, really, because I couldn't afford another three years at university.'

'I would've thought your father . . .'

'He hasn't offered, and I wouldn't accept it if he did,' I said sharply.

He blinked at me, surprised.

'From what you were saying, you'd go back to university like a shot,' I said, to change the subject.

'Yeah,' he agreed, brightening. 'I'd really like to do research.'

When the boat turned up, he was explaining why molecular biology research was so fascinating. Our tour of the harbour was fun; there were sealions and even a couple of dolphins, and we talked non-stop: about animals, about universities, about working for government agencies. We managed to keep off the subject of animal experiments, and everything stayed sweet. When the boat returned to the wharf, we wandered into the town, stopped for a coffee, and talked some more. Then it was evening. Roberto suggested dinner, and I regretfully informed him that I'd told Sharon I'd be back at the house for that.

Roberto drove me back up the coast and around the side of the mountain. As I climbed out of the car he asked, 'Could I see you again on Friday?'

'I don't know whether I'll still be around,' I told him, blushing again.

'If you are?'

'Yeah,' I said, blushing harder. 'If I am, I'd like that.'

He grinned, caught my hand, and pulled me closer so he could kiss me: a romantic kiss, not too pushy, warm and thrilling. I came away from it glowing, and we exchanged phone numbers.

Six

As I'd expected, that night Brian was full of apologies about how he still couldn't leave his lab – not for a couple more days, maybe not until the weekend.

I made my suggestion about renting a car. Brian and Sharon were embarrassed, but also, I thought, tempted. I'd arrived at an extremely difficult time, and it was a strain looking after me; of course they wanted some time to themselves. I pushed and – after some concerned hemming and hawing – they gave in. Wednesday morning found me heading off for the Sierra Nevada in a rented Honda, with a sleeping bag and some camping gear borrowed from one of Sharon's friends tucked into the boot.

Brian had paid for the car rental, which made me uncomfortable. I excused myself by deciding that it was less than he would've been paying for travel and hotels on the delayed tour.

It was a longish drive – by my standards, anyway – but an easy one: most of it on excellent motorways, with only the last twenty miles or so scenic and twisty. I arrived at the Sequoia National Forest by late afternoon, and was lucky enough to find a campsite almost at once.

It was idyllic. I saw the giant redwoods, did some walking, and was befriended by a group of English students I met at the campground. The peace and freedom made me realize how tense I'd been at Brian's: getting away

100

was like walking from a hot and noisy party into the stillness of a quiet night.

I was away two nights, or three days. I'd decided to come back on the Friday, partly because Brian and Sharon were making plans for the weekend, and partly, I admit, so that I could meet Roberto. I arranged to see him on my way back; the way the highways worked, it was as quick to return via the northern edge of Los Angeles as it was to hack across the mountains to Santa Barbara.

We'd agreed to meet at a restaurant in an LA suburb called Thousand Oaks. It was an Italian place, on the edge of a mall and next to the freeway. When I pulled in, Roberto's blue Honda was already parked. I started for the restaurant, but he unfolded himself from the car and came over before I reached the door. 'Hi,' he said, smiling, and greeted me with a kiss.

'Hi,' I said, savouring the taste of it on my lips and smiling back.

He cleared his throat. 'I don't know anything about this place. It's just somewhere I've noticed when I drive past. If you think it looks lousy, say, and we'll go somewhere else.'

It didn't look lousy; it looked nice, but not so posh that I felt out of place. I was wearing shorts; I'd put on a nice shirt with them, pink silk without slogans, but still, it wasn't appropriate dress for a good restaurant. I was a bad match for Roberto, too, who was wearing his FDA suit.

We sat down, looked at the menu, placed our orders. Roberto asked if I wanted wine; I declined on the grounds that I had to drive back to Santa Barbara when we finished.

'You look like you had a wonderful time,' Roberto told me. 'Funny. Somehow I never associated philosophers with camping trips.'

I laughed. 'Yeah, but you thought philosophers were all old men with beards. No, it was *fantastic*. Those *trees*!'

We talked for a while about giant sequoias and camping. I was so full of what I'd seen that it took me until the food arrived to realize that Roberto was uneasy, worried about something.

'So,' I said at last, sticking a fork into my pasta primavera, 'what's the matter?'

He flinched very slightly. 'Nothing.'

'Bad day at work, then?'

He made a face. 'I . . . oh, look, you know your father was conducting trials of his new serum? On cultured skin?'

'Yeah,' I said, frowning a bit.

'Well, the police arrested one of the guys they think was involved in the break-in. They . . .'

'What, the guy I met? Curtis Langford?'

'I think that's the name. They went to his place with a search warrant, and they found a stash of things that looked like they'd come from your father's lab – so they arrested him. They asked me to look at the things they'd found, to see if they included the serum; they weren't sure what anything was, and I'd been volunteering to help.'

'Oh!' I said, rather weakly. So, I'd got the Monster of the Mountain arrested. The responsibility made me wince. '*Did* they include the serum?'

'No,' said Roberto unhappily. 'The police told me afterwards that the guy's said he never had it, that he went back looking for it because he thought he might've dropped it on the trail, but he couldn't find it. But . . .'

'He admitted the break-in?'

'From the sound of things, he's *proud* of it. He's a martyr for the cause, though he isn't so enthusiastic about martyrdom that he wants company in it. He's refused to say who was with him that night. But that's not the point. What I meant to say was that . . . well . . . among the junk from the lab were some photos of the skin cultures. Not – not in any sort of sequence, you understand, just sort of jumbled together, like the guy had just snatched up a handful of stuff at random. And . . .' Roberto stopped, biting his lip.

There was a silence. 'There was something wrong with them?' I asked at last.

He nodded unhappily. 'Lesions. Small ones. Only in a couple of the pictures. I don't know, maybe they were the "before" pictures, and the ones without lesions were the "after" pictures. But he wasn't *supposed* to be researching cancers.'

My appetite vanished, even though I barely understood what Roberto was implying. 'What are you worried about?' I asked anxiously.

'Look, one of the things I do, in my office, is check that trials of drugs and biologicals are being properly conducted. I go over the paperwork, check it against the procedures. Inconsistencies between the results shown and the results claimed – mostly that's picked up at the peer-review stage on publication. We know what it looks like though, and occasionally we're the ones who pick it up. Then I write a letter asking the company to explain itself. If I'd been looking at your father's work officially, I would've sent him a letter.'

'Oh.'

'I think I'm probably worried about nothing,' Roberto insisted valiantly. 'I don't have all the paperwork, and the pictures aren't sequenced. I . . . I just don't know what to make of it. It worries me. I don't want . . . I don't want to offend Dr Greenall, but . . .'

I remembered Brian talking about how his investors operated: '*They'll only keep the money coming if they can see results, and they find raw data too hard to understand. You have to show them pictures before they'll sign the cheques, and all the photos we'd got ready for them got trashed. I just have to hope they'll accept that as an excuse.*'

If his magical serum wasn't as close to completion as he'd led his investors to believe – if the present batch had nasty side-effects – was it inconceivable that he could've trashed most of the photos himself, *after* the lab was broken into? After all, it would help secure his funding, and the serum wasn't actually going to be used in human trials yet. It would have seemed a perfectly safe thing to do. He wouldn't have expected some of the photos to turn up again.

'Do you think I'm worrying about nothing?' asked Roberto.

'I don't know,' I told him honestly. 'I don't know much about biochemical research, and I don't know my father very well.' I considered it a moment longer, then said resolutely, 'I'll try to sound him out. Very tactfully.'

Roberto slumped in relief. 'Thanks. I . . . really don't want to bring it up, and be wrong.'

I found driving difficult when I left the restaurant. I'd already done far more driving that day than I was accustomed to, it was dark, and I was tired. I kept the hired car steady in the right lane, paid attention to the road ahead, checked behind me regularly, and put the radio on to some public broadcast station. With all of that to concentrate on, I almost forgot to worry whether Brian was guilty of some kind of scientific fraud.

When I left the motorway, however, I was so distracted that I started off by driving on the left, and had to swerve over to the right abruptly when a car's headlights appeared in front of me, horn blaring. Shaken, I made my way along the quiet back roads, missed Brian's house, and had to reverse back past it. At last, though, I was able to pull up safely on the terrace and pry my fingers loose from the steering wheel. The door of the house opened while I was still collecting my frazzled wits, and Brian and Sharon came out together.

'We were wondering what had happened to you!' said Sharon warmly, helping me out of the car. 'Come in, have something to drink, tell us about it!'

A drink sounded very good. I came in, leaving the camping gear until the morning, and sat down in the lounge. Sharon bustled over with a whisky and ginger ale. The few days' break seemed to have done her good: she seemed fresher, more cheerful, more beautiful than ever. Brian looked relaxed as well.

'So, how were the sequoias?' Sharon asked, settling herself gracefully on the sofa.

'Fantastic,' I told her, remembering them again.

'I love those trees,' she told me warmly. 'Though "tree" hardly seems the right word for them. They seem like another kind of plant entirely. Every ordinary word seems too small for them.'

'They had me whispering poetry,' I agreed. '"Your vegetable love should grow Vaster than empires, and more slow".'

Sharon smiled. '"Vaster than empires". I like that.'

Brian was looking thoughtful. 'That's Andrew Marvell, right?'

'Brian!' exclaimed Sharon in surprised amusement. 'I never thought I'd hear *you* identifying a poem.'

'I looked that one up a couple of years ago,' he said sheepishly. 'There was a line from it that got stuck in my head, so I looked it up on the internet. I think I must've read it in school, though I didn't remember anything but the one line.'

'What was the line?' asked Sharon, still amused.

I knew, somehow, what it was going to be, and I tensed, knowing that the feeling which had driven it into his mind also lay behind my own presence.

'"But at my back I always hear,"' Brian duly quoted, in a low voice, '"Time's wingéd chariot hurrying near."' He paused, then continued, with a touch of horror,

> 'And yonder all before us lie
> Deserts of vast eternity.
> Thy beauty shall no more be found
>   nor, in thy marble vault, shall sound
> my echoing song.'

There was a silence. 'How gloomy,' said Sharon at last. There was a trace of real bitterness in her voice at the reminder: *'thy beauty shall no more be found'*.

I cleared my throat uncomfortably. 'Yeah. I don't see how he expected it to persuade her go to bed with him.'

She gave me a surprised look which quickly cleared. 'Of course! It's "To His Coy Mistress", isn't it? "Come on, baby, let's go to bed, 'cause we're a long time dead." I'd forgotten that that was what it's about.' She grinned. 'No, I wouldn't have gone to bed with the gloomy bastard, either.'

'He wasn't *all* gloomy!' protested Brian.

> 'Now therefore, while the youthful hue
> Sits on thy skin like morning dew,
> And while thy willing soul transpires
> At every pore with instant fires,
> Now let us sport us while we may;
> And now, like amorous birds of prey,
> Rather at once our time devour,
>   Than languish in his slow-chapp'd power.'

Sharon got up and went over to kiss him. 'Well, I agree, that's a lot more cheerful.'

I decided that I wasn't going to ask any awkward questions that night.

I did no better over the weekend. Brian had finally roused himself to supply some of the long-promised tour – not the whole thing, it's true, but he had got as far as arranging a weekend in San Francisco. He'd booked flights from Santa Barbara's small airport, and we flew out Saturday morning after returning my hire car. We stayed in a plush hotel, ate at good restaurants and generally conducted ourselves in the touring style Brian and Sharon were accustomed to. This was a style that involved spending more in a day than I'd normally spend in a week, and I was, frankly, dazzled. I couldn't bring myself to do anything to rock the boat. This glamorous dream-life would end soon enough; there seemed no reason to spoil it prematurely. I could always have a confrontation with Brian once we got back to Santa Barbara.

We returned on the Monday afternoon. Sharon was supposed to be working that evening, so Brian dropped her off at her studio straight from the airport. She'd left her car parked there on Saturday morning, so that she could drive herself home after her work's late finish. Brian was silent as we drove on up highway 101.

'You mind if I go check in at the lab?' he asked abruptly as we turned inland. 'I just want to see how Dave's getting on with the purchasing.'

Dave was, I knew, the senior-most member of his staff, who had been left with a list of supplies to buy from the insurance money. From the frequency with which Brian had referred to this task during the weekend, I had the feeling that 'checking in' at the lab was likely to take some time. 'Maybe you could drop me off at the house first?' I suggested. I'd been longing for the swimming pool ever since the plane left San Francisco.

'Sure,' agreed Brian with relief.

He dropped me at the bottom of the drive, stopping the car only long enough to detach his house key from the ring. I trudged slowly up the drive to the big fancy house, feeling dissatisfied and a bit flat. I was more than halfway through my visit, and I didn't feel that I understood my father significantly better than I had when I arrived. True, I'd expected all along that it would be too late for us to establish much of a relationship, but I discovered again that I still had hopes.

As I let myself into the house, it occurred to me that my swimming costume was with the luggage in the back of Brian's car, still damp from the pool of the hotel in San Francisco. The house was quiet and close. I went to my room and contemplated the shower without enthusiasm. It was odd, I decided, how quickly one could get to prefer a swimming pool.

I wondered if I dared swim without a costume. There seemed no reason not to: the neighbouring houses didn't overlook us. I didn't think the hiking trail did – after all, I hadn't noticed the house when I was on it – but even if it did, from a distance my panties and bra would look like a bikini.

I stripped off to my underthings, then wrapped myself in a towel and went out on to the deck. I arranged the towel at the side of the pool and slid into the water.

I'd swum two lengths when I looked up and saw Curtis Langford, the Monster of the Mountain, standing on the decking staring down at me. He had a gun in his hand.

I shrieked and recoiled like some stupid girl in a fifties horror flick, then darted to the middle of the pool where it was deepest. I stared up at him fearfully.

'I thought it was you,' he said angrily. 'I looked down at Brian Greenall's house, and who do I see but the smart-mouthed English girl who says she doesn't know him.'

I felt utterly feeble and stupid and vulnerable, standing there in my underclothes, crouching a bit to keep my body under water. 'What are you doing here?' I wailed.

He gave me a nasty smile. 'This house is Dr Brian

Greenall's. You're in his swimming pool. Seems a pretty funny place for you to be, when you don't know him.'

'I wasn't trying to trick you,' I told him. 'I just wanted to avoid some kind of scene.'

'You got me *arrested*!' he told me furiously. 'I may end up in *prison* because of you!'

Yeah, that was what I'd thought. I had no idea what he was doing free, hanging around my father's house. Nothing good, of that at least I could be sure. 'I wasn't *trying* to,' I said inanely. 'Just the police came round, and they were asking about a black plastic box like the one you were looking for.'

He crouched down beside the pool and struck the surface with his left, gun-free hand, sending a sheet of water over me. The rage in the gesture scared me; I had no doubt that in his mind the blow was aimed at my flesh. 'Don't play dumb, bitch!' he snarled.

I wiped water out of my eyes. 'It's true. I didn't know what the black plastic box was, until the police came round.'

'And then you pointed them straight at me! You must've laughed yourself sick when I gave you a ride and tried to convince you of the truth!'

'No,' I told him. 'I wasn't laughing.'

'Not after I hit you,' he said, with satisfaction. 'You know, I was really sorry that I did that. I thought, oh God, my stupid temper again, why the hell can't I keep it under control? I was looking out for you in tourist places, 'cause I wanted to *apologize*!' He hit the water again, hard. 'You bitch, you've fucked up my *life*! The police were talking about grand larceny and it'll be my second conviction! You know what that means? Come out of there!'

I shook my head. 'I wasn't laughing,' I insisted. 'Look, Brian – my father – wanted my mother to abort *me:* would I laugh about that?'

I'd said it in a vague hope that it would defuse some of that rage and let me escape in one piece. It certainly got his attention. He crouched motionless, frowning, his eyes fixed on me. Blue eyes, they were, pale and cold.

'You're lying,' he said at last.

I shook my head again. 'No, I'm not! When my mother was pregnant with me, Brian wanted her to have an abortion. She wouldn't, and about a year after I was born, he walked out on us. This summer is the first time I've seen him since. That's *true,* I promise you! I was never laughing at you. I don't think abortion is the least bit funny.'

He took his hand out of the water and put it on his knee, frowning at me. 'You're lying,' he said again, after another silence, but he sounded less sure of himself. 'When I talked to you before, you were pro-abortion.'

'*Nobody's* pro-abortion!' I objected. 'Some people just think it can be a lesser evil. I don't even *know* where I stand on it. Yeah, sure, I think your side is conceptually confused, but I think the other side is, too. I *said* that, you know I did!'

He scowled and abandoned the argument. 'Come out of there,' he ordered again.

I once more shook my head.

'I won't hurt you!' he told me impatiently. 'Just don't make me come in there after you.'

I'd known that the water was no real protection, of course, but the words still chilled me. I could imagine him jumping in, splashing over and grabbing me. I didn't think I could get away, not half-naked and barefoot. He was bigger and stronger than me, and much, much more ruthless. If he thought I was getting away, he might even use that gun.

'I don't have any clothes on!' I protested wretchedly.

He eyed me sharply, probably registering that what I was wearing *wasn't* a bikini, then rolled his eyes in disgust. 'What the fuck was wrong with a bathing suit?'

'It's in Brian's car,' I admitted tearfully.

'Just get out of there!' he ordered impatiently. 'I don't care about the swimming things. I'm not some pervert. I won't touch you.' He picked up my towel and stood.

'You can have this. Now, come out. I want to go inside and have a look around, and no way am I going to leave you here while I do.'

He *could* go inside, I realized. He wouldn't even need to break and enter: I'd left the picture window on to the decking ajar. I wondered how long he'd been hanging around the house, what he'd been planning. I wondered how his plans had changed, now that I'd given him this opportunity.

'I'll count to ten,' he said, surveying me with a cold glower. 'If you're not out of the water by then, I'll come in after you – and I'll be pissed off, because I wasn't planning to get wet. One. Two . . .'

I edged over to the end of the pool, at right-angles to him. He tossed the towel down in front of me, and I draped it over my shoulders before climbing out. I held it wrapped close. I was shivering. It was pure fear: the day was hot.

'That's better,' said Curtis Langford. 'Now, where's Dr Greenall?'

'He went to check in at his lab,' I whispered.

'When will he be back?'

'I don't know.' The Monster glowered and raised his hand, and I added quickly, 'I really don't! We went away for the weekend, but he had a lot of business at his lab because of the break-in. He was so worried about it that he didn't even want to stop here; he just dropped me off and drove over there. He might be back soon, or he might not be back for hours.'

'Huh.' Langford scowled. 'Anybody else in the house?'

'No. Sharon – Brian's wife – is working an evening shift. She won't be back until late.'

He chewed on this for a moment, then gestured along the decking. 'You go in, then. I'm gonna be right behind you. Don't try for a telephone or do anything stupid. I don't want to hurt you, but I will if I have to.'

I edged slowly across the decking to the picture window, pulled it open, and went in; as he'd promised, he was right behind me, the gun held loosely in his hand.

We paused in the lounge; Langford glanced around it assessingly. 'Nice place,' he remarked bitterly. 'Murder obviously pays.'

I don't know why I felt I had to defend Brian. 'He isn't a murderer,' I said. 'Not even by your standards. He's never performed an abortion, and even the stem cells he uses are things he only got after somebody else harvested and cultured them.'

Langford turned a pale glare on me. 'He's making money out of it; he's a *fucking* murderer at heart! Where's his office?'

'Please can I get some clothes on first?' I asked. I desperately wanted to dress, and get some shoes on my feet, so that I could at least run for it if I saw a chance.

'I'm not letting you out of my sight,' he told me, with grim satisfaction. 'Where's your dad keep his computer?'

I showed him to Brian's office. He glanced around it incuriously, then switched on the computer. The system came up and asked him for a password. Langford turned toward me, gun level, face cold. 'What's the password?' he demanded.

I took a step back. '*I don't know!*' I protested desperately. 'For God's sake, how could I? I told you; I hadn't even *met* Brian until week before last. I've never even seen this computer turned on before!'

He stared at me with narrowed eyes. 'Where's your room?' he demanded at last.

I swallowed. 'I don't . . .'

'I told you, I won't hurt you unless you make me! I just wanna see whether you really live here or not.'

It made sense: if I was really a visitor, then he couldn't reasonably expect me to know Brian's password. I showed him my room, which still looked like a guestroom, though now it was messy, the bed still unmade from the last time I'd slept in it. My backpack was propped against the chest of drawers, full of dirty things still left over from my camping trip as I'd taken the suitcase to San Francisco. The shirt and skirt I'd discarded for my swim were lying on the bed, and I grabbed the T-shirt at once. I glanced at Curtis Langford, who was looking around thoughtfully. I pulled the T-shirt hurriedly over my head, letting the towel drop. When I stuck my head out the neck, Langford had the gun on me again.

'I just want to have some clothes on!' I told him, with strained dignity. Defiantly, I picked up my skirt. 'You want to check my air ticket? It's on the dresser.'

He scowled, but went over to the dresser and picked up the flimsy sheaf of papers. I pulled my skirt on. He set down the ticket with a grunt.

'I told you,' I said. 'I'm just a visitor. Anyway, why would I've been doing all those tourist things if I came here all the time?'

He gave another grunt, conceding the point. Feeling a bit more confident, I slipped my feet into my sandals. My wet underthings were already soaking through my outfit, but I felt enormously better for being clothed.

'I'm going to have a look around,' said Langford slowly. 'You're coming with me.'

We looked around the house. Langford went first to the kitchen, opened the freezer, and examined the contents: two cartons of ice cream, some frozen vegetables, and a couple of TV dinners. He grunted and lifted one of the dinners, then set it down in frustration and closed the freezer again. I knew then what he was looking for.

He didn't give up: he searched Brian and Sharon's bedroom, then their bathroom, then Sharon's study. He examined the bookshelves in the bedroom, checked the knick-knacks in the study. In the bathroom he opened the medicine cabinet and examined the jars of aspirin and the bottles of antacid, the array of expensive face creams and scrubs.

He seemed increasingly frustrated, and at last he turned to me and demanded, 'Where is it?'

'Where is what?' I replied, though I'd guessed.

'The thing he was working on, the elixir!' Langford's face was starting to flush red, and his voice rose. 'The thing he's accused *me* of stealing!'

'It's *missing,* isn't it?' I replied. 'Why would he say it was stolen, if he had it?'

'*We* didn't touch it!' protested Langford. 'We just took the stem cells. When I . . . that is, I thought for a while we might've taken it as well, by accident, and I checked, but the only things we buried were the stem cells. I went back and checked whether we could've lost it along the way – you met me! – but it wasn't there. We didn't steal it; we never even *saw* it!'

'Well, maybe it got smashed up when you trashed the lab!' I said. 'Brian *said* he wasn't sure what was smashed and what was missing.'

Langford made a gesture of impatient anger. 'You don't understand! We didn't trash that lab; we didn't do much damage at all! Sure, we had to cut the power cables and break a couple of windows to get in, and we wrote some slogans on the walls and grabbed a few documents to see if they had any information we could use, but we weren't . . .' He trailed off, then resumed, meeting my eyes, 'We're not *criminals*, OK? We were trying to make a point about respect for human life! We have that sort of respect; we weren't going to just go in and smash and burn! The object of our mission was to take the stem cells and give them a decent burial. They were human remains; they deserved to be laid to rest like human beings! We didn't steal, and what we destroyed, we destroyed to make that sort of evil research harder to do. What your precious father said to the police, it's *lies*.'

I believed him. Maybe I wouldn't have, if Roberto hadn't already raised a question in my mind, but a fraud to get money out of insurers wasn't too different from a fraud to get money from investors, and I already suspected Brian of that. I bit my lip, feeling sick.

'He must've hidden it somewhere,' said Langford, in a low voice. 'To get money off the insurance or something.'

My numbed mind stirred back into action. Why was *Curtis Langford* so bothered about what had become of the serum?

Answer: because he'd realized he could get money for it. He was suspected of having stolen it anyway, and he was probably going to end up in prison for the break-in: he must feel that he might as well get some benefit for his pains. He'd referred to it as 'the elixir' which was the word used by whoever it was that had asked about it on the website. For all his pose as a champion of human dignity, his reasons for being here with a gun were as venal and dishonest as Brian's for accusing him.

'Maybe the serum never existed,' I said, aloud.

Langford gave me a wild look. 'What d'you mean?'

'Look,' I said, 'do you know how the money works? Brian has a set of investors who fund his company because they believe he's developing an anti-aging serum. He doesn't actually have a *product*, only the hope that there will be one, sometime in the future. He . . . he must be doing real work, because he's got that licence from the

FDA, and I think he said he's patented some of his processes, but what sort of serum he's got, and how well it works . . . nobody seems to *know*. Apparently he hasn't actually published anything for *years*. Maybe he has less in the way of results than he says he does. Maybe there *wasn't* a serum.'

Langford stared at me, stricken.

'Whatever happens,' I told him, 'I don't think you're going to be able to get your hands on anything you can sell. Even if the serum does exist, the physical stuff isn't all that important. Brian says that what matters is the processes he used to make it, and that all that information is encrypted so nobody can get at it.'

'They're going to charge me with *grand larceny* for stealing it!' said Langford shrilly. 'That means *years*. I don't think I could take it!'

'They *can't*!' I said impatiently. 'There's no evidence you ever had it, let alone that you demanded money for it. I can testify to the fact that you were looking for it along the path. For that matter, Brian's never actually claimed it was stolen: he's just said that it seemed to be missing. The police really can't charge you with anything worse than breaking and entering, unless they hit you for what you're doing now.'

He glared at me.

I pressed on in the teeth of that glare. 'I mean, what you're doing now is much worse than what you did at the lab. Holding people at gunpoint, threatening them – that's false imprisonment or assault or something. I'd be surprised if you got much of a sentence just for vandalizing a lab, but for something like this you could get *years*!'

'I haven't touched you!' he exclaimed indignantly.

'You've threatened me, and you've put me in justifiable fear for my life!' I said, and swallowed, because my voice had come out shrill. 'You don't think that's serious? The best thing you could do for yourself is just go away now. Then it's nothing worse than trespass.'

Langford shook his head vigorously. 'No!' he said grimly. 'I'm gonna wait for your precious father.'

'Are you out of your *mind?*' I demanded. 'You do that, and then what?'

'Then I can find out what happened to the elixir,' he said with satisfaction.

'Yeah, and what're you going to do with it? You really think you can just carry on, sell the data to some anonymous guy you met on the *internet?* You don't think the police would catch on? You think your buyer will stick around and pay you, when you're this hot? And what do you plan to do about Brian? Kill him, so he can't tell anyone how you forced him to hand over the key to his priceless encrypted data? You'd have to kill me, too, wouldn't you, to eliminate the witness. Don't you think the police would come after you for a *double murder?* Your own pro-life friends would turn you in for something like that!'

'I'm not planning to kill anybody!' he protested angrily. 'I'm not a murderer!'

'Then just how *do* you intend to get away with this?'

He looked sick and angry. 'I just want to find out what *happened* to the stuff!' he protested. 'I don't even want to sell it anymore; I just don't want to get nailed for having stolen it!'

'If you just go away now,' I said urgently, 'it'll mean that the only thing you can be convicted of is the old business of breaking into Brian's lab. Even if I start screaming to the police as soon as you're out the door, what could I say? If you choose to say that there wasn't a gun, and that you never threatened me, just asked nicely if you could have a look around, it'd only be your word against mine.

I'd have to admit in court that you didn't break in, that you haven't done any damage, and that you left, quietly, when asked. That's scarcely a crime at all!'

'You bitch!' he said angrily.

'Well, what else are you going to do?' I demanded. 'Lock me in the bathroom while you *torture* Brian for his password? March us both away from here at gunpoint and keep us hostage? Do you have any sort of plan *at all*?'

He didn't, clearly. He'd been watching the house because he wanted the serum, and he'd lost his temper when he saw me – the girl who'd fingered him – in the swimming pool. He'd wanted to confront me, but he hadn't been planning murder. In his own eyes he was a hero.

'You're not going to find the serum here or prove anything,' I told him. 'You must've seen that by now. Just go, OK? It's the best thing you could do for yourself. Just go!'

He stared at me for several interminable seconds, his nostrils flared. 'Swear you won't tell anyone I was here,' he said at last.

My heart gave a frantic double thud of relief. 'If I say you came here and talked to me,' I said slowly, 'but don't mention that you had a gun or that you came inside, then you'd be OK.'

He gave me a bitter look. 'Except the police will be on my case about it.'

That was the idea; I certainly didn't want him coming back. 'Yeah, well,' I said. 'If you insist, I'll swear not to say a word.'

He opened his mouth, then closed it. 'You'd lie, wouldn't you? You'd swear it and lie.'

I snarled at him. 'No, of course not! You're pointing a gun at me: I'll swear whatever you like!'

He shoved the gun into the waistband of his jeans. 'It isn't loaded,' he told me bitterly. He walked quickly through the lounge, out the glass doors, and off up the arid mountainside.

Seven

Iphoned the police immediately. It took a while to get hold of Detective Kermode, but I reached him in the end.

'Ms Greenall,' he said warily. In the background I could hear voices, as though he were in an office or, to judge by the tinkle of crockery, a cafe.

'Is that guy Curtis Langford out on bail?' I demanded. ''Cause he just came over here.'

There was a startled silence on the other end of the line. 'Over where?' asked the policeman cautiously.

'Brian's house. My father's. Brian dropped me off here when we got back from San Francisco, and Curtis Langford came up while I was in the pool. He scared me.' I swallowed; saying it made me realize just how much he'd scared me.

'Shit!' said Kermode. 'Yes, he is out on bail. Is he still there?'

'No. We talked, and then he left.' I drew a deep breath. 'He said that he and his friends didn't do much damage to Brian's lab, and that he never had the serum.'

There was another silence, punctuated only by indistinct laughter from people who had nothing to do with us. 'We are aware of his claims,' said Kermode guardedly. 'Ms Greenall, what is it you want?'

I opened my mouth, then closed it. 'I just don't want him to come back here!' I said, too shrilly. 'He didn't do anything this time, but he might. He doesn't strike me as the most sensible or self-controlled person I've ever met, and if he lost his temper he might do something horrible.'

A pause, and then Kermode said – with amusement, damn him – 'That's a perfectly legitimate worry, Ms Greenall. I'll send somebody to talk to Langford at once. We'll warn him off. To tell the truth, I didn't realize he knew the address. I'm relieved to hear that all he did was *talk*.'

'Yeah,' I agreed.

When I'd cut off, I wondered why I'd kept quiet about the gun, and about the way Langford had searched the house. Because I'd semi-promised to say nothing about the whole matter?

The law wouldn't consider an oath sworn at gunpoint to be binding; I didn't either. I acknowledged, bitterly, that I'd glossed over Langford's crimes because I had doubts about my father's. Probably the police did, too: that silence before Kermode's terse '*We are aware of his claims*' had spoken volumes. Yeah, the police, too, suspected that Brian had exaggerated the losses he'd suffered in the hope of increasing his compensation from the insurance company.

I was the one who'd fingered Langford for the police: I felt responsible for what happened to him. I didn't want to see him punished for things he hadn't done. Keeping quiet about something he *had* done . . . seemed to redress the balance.

I suppose partly it was just that when it came to attacks on laboratories, in the past I'd always been on the same side as the perpetrators. Not that I've ever done anything illegal on behalf of animal rights – I don't think it can be justified in a democratic society – but I can't help sympathizing with the balaclava'd students who break into research establishments in the middle of the night in order to rescue beagles. Intimidation and violence are different

– but Langford's group hadn't engaged in those. Pro-life activists and animal rights people have a lot in common. Both groups see themselves as knights in shining armour, riding to the rescue of abused victims too weak to defend themselves. I respected, too, the fact that Langford had kept his mouth shut about who'd been with him that night. He almost certainly hadn't acted alone, and the police had probably promised him more lenient treatment if he named his accomplices – but he hadn't. I simply couldn't leap in with more condemnation and make things worse for him.

On the other hand, insurance companies rarely pay their customers the full amount they're due. Perhaps Brian's only way to recover his losses was to exaggerate them. There certainly had been *some* damage done to his lab: Langford hadn't disputed that. Langford was obviously going to paint his own conduct in the best possible light.

I wondered if I were making excuses for a corrupt schemer, or if I were being a self-righteous prig. I roamed around the house, restless and angry. I thought about going for a walk, but I was afraid of running into Langford again. I put the television on: it played an imbecilic ad for Pepsi, and then another one, even worse, for some shampoo. When it started to try to sell me a dancing tampon, I switched it off again.

I checked my email. Mum had emailed to say that she and Matt had booked a week's holiday on the Dordogne on lastminute.com, she hoped everything was going well, she looked forward to hearing about it when I got back. There was a forbidding response from a firm where I'd applied to work, and a pile of spam. (Nothing from Steve: nothing.) I switched the computer off, then switched it on and googled stem cells. There were a few hundred thousand hits, but none of them seemed to make sense.

Brian didn't get back until half past five. I hurried into the entranceway the moment I heard the door open, and he paused in the tiled hall, looking at me quizzically.

'Something the matter?' he asked in concern.

'Yeah.' I swallowed. 'Curtis Langford, the guy who broke into your lab, the one I met on the mountain – he came round here. I was in the pool, and I looked up, and there he was.'

'God!' exclaimed Brian, shocked and alarmed. 'Are you OK?'

'Yeah.' I swallowed again. 'We talked, and then he left. He scared me, but he didn't actually do anything. I called the police after he left, and they said they'll warn him not to come back.'

'Good.' Brian ran a hand wearily through his hair. 'I had no idea he knew where I lived.' He grimaced and added, 'He must've found something at the lab with the address. I never post it.'

'Maybe.' My mouth was dry; I'd been so desperate to question him and now I couldn't seem to get started.

'You're all right?' Brian asked again.

'Yeah,' I said, then burst out, 'He said that he never had the serum, and that he and his friends didn't do much damage to the lab.'

Brian frowned uneasily. 'I think we need a drink.'

We went through to the lounge and he poured himself a gin and tonic, then, after a questioning look, poured another for me.

'I never really thought he and his friends had stolen the serum,' he told me. He sipped the gin and tonic and set it down, meeting my eyes honestly. 'They're scientific illiterates; they thought a genetic therapy was toxic gunge. Some of the serum does seem to be missing, but it always seemed to me far more likely that it got lost or destroyed somewhere between the freezer and wherever it is the pro-lifers disposed of the stem cells. It was your friend from the FDA who was worried that they'd stolen it and were going to sell it.'

'My friend from the FDA,' I said slowly, 'says that when the police searched Langford's place, they found some strange photos from your lab. He wanted me to ask you about them.'

Brian went very still, his eyes nervous. 'Photos?' he repeated at last.

'Photos of skin cultures,' I agreed. 'He says they were out of sequence, but he was worried about them because some of them show lesions. See, the police asked him for advice on the stuff that'd been taken from your lab, because they didn't know what any of it was and he'd been helpful.'

'Shit.' Brian had a gulp of the gin and tonic.

I felt his reaction go through me like ice. 'You were cheating, weren't you?' I asked accusingly. 'Your serum has side-effects. You took advantage of the break-in to destroy the evidence of the problem, to keep your investors happy. *And* you claimed that the damage to the lab was worse than it really was, to get the insurance money!'

He grimaced. 'Alison, I'm *close*! It's not my fault that my investors don't understand how research works.'

'You *lied*!'

'Not in any way that matters!' he protested. 'Yes, this batch of serum had some undesirable side-effects – but that isn't because it doesn't work, it's because it works too well. The stem cells are potent; they get into the DNA and start coding for proteins, vigorously. Don't you see? It means the gene therapy is *working*; the only problem now is to turn off the genes we don't actually want! My investors won't understand that, though. I know them; they'd look at the lesions, and if they heard that word "cancer" they wouldn't hear anything else. But if they just keep faith, they'll have a working serum! Only a year or two, and then they'll make a lot of money, and get exactly the kind of results they want! Suppressing a few pictures

. . . it's not really a *lie;* it's just making the truth easier for them to grasp.'

'And the insurance fraud?' I demanded in disgust.

'It's not *fraud*!' he replied angrily. 'Those idiots did real damage! Windows smashed, wires cut, the entire contents of the freezer wrecked. Adding a couple of items to the bill . . . the insurance *ought* to cover equipment damage anyway. Alison, it really isn't a big deal!'

I put my drink down, got up, walked around the room. 'How the hell do you expect me to believe you?' I asked angrily.

'I haven't done anything wrong!' he protested impatiently.

'No, and neither has Curtis Langford!' I replied bitterly. 'In fact, he's a *hero*, fighting to preserve human dignity and the lives of unborn children! Just like you're a hero, fighting for scientific truth and the lives of cancer sufferers! Only both of you are willing to compromise on the heroics, as soon as it comes to money.'

'And you're so pure,' said Brian sarcastically, 'that you didn't mind missing a father's love, but bitterly resented losing out on his cash.'

I whirled on him, glaring. 'Maybe I would've minded missing the love more, if I'd ever had any experience of it.'

We stared at one another, furious and hurt. Brian moved first, brushing the whole conversation aside with a restless gesture of the hand. 'I'm sorry,' he said. 'What do you expect, though? I never said I was a hero. I know I let you and your mother down. I've already admitted it and apologized for it, for God's sake! This business, these things you've got so worked up about, they're nothing. If you're going to hate me because of them, then I might as well give up, because you'd hate any father who was less than . . . than Mahatma Gandhi!'

'Shut up!' I cried desperately.

'The thing that matters,' he continued, as though I hadn't spoken, 'the thing that's important is that you're my daughter, my only child.' His eyes met mine, blue and fierce and desperate. 'Blood *counts*. I didn't think so when I was your age, but at your age I thought I was immortal. Now I look back into the past, I see my parents and my grandparents and my great-grandparents, their blood flowing through me to make me what I am, and I know that something of them endures in me. When I look into the future, though, there's only you. If anything of me and the people who shaped me is going to carry on into years to come, it'll be through you. And that *matters*, Alison! It'll matter to you, too, one day. One day you will *want* to feel that you are part of a life that endures. You will *want* your past, your heritage, I promise you!'

'I have Mum,' I told him bluntly. 'I'm part of *her* family. I don't think I *want* to be part of yours.'

I saw it hit and hurt, and part of me wanted to unsay it. I didn't. 'I'm . . . I'm going for a walk,' I said instead. 'I need to think!' I strode past him, out through the entrance-way and into the warm dry evening.

I didn't go up on to the hiking trail, but instead headed off along the road. It was quiet: only one or two cars went past before I reached the carpark which provided the official access to the trail. I strode on past it, taking long, angry steps, breathing hard.

I wanted to love my father, and he was a cheat. If the going got tough, he opted for a short-cut. Fatherhood had made him work, so he'd kited off to America, leaving his wife holding the baby. His chosen line of research lost funding, so he'd adapted it to please a collection of vain and ignorant old men, and when it didn't produce the results they wanted, he suppressed those results to keep the money flowing. He complained about the insurance people even as he lied to defraud them. He was a cheat, a cheat, a lying cheat.

I wanted to go home. Mum, however, was headed off to the Dordogne with her darling new hubby, and anyway, my return flight wasn't for another nine days.

I reached the gates of Brian's lab and paused a minute. I wondered if I could exchange my air ticket and fly home early. Even if Mum wasn't there, I could sleep in my own bed, phone up some of my old school friends, settle back into my old life. . . . Maybe contact Steve . . .? No. Steve said it was over. I could see friends, though, and do some job-hunting.

I'd still need my luggage. I would still have to go back to the house, inform Brian, argue with him, pack up, ask for a lift to the airport. I couldn't face it. I walked on along the road, blindly now, with no idea where I was going or what I intended to do if I got there.

The road carried on along the hillside, going nowhere, like me. I followed it for another mile or so, and then simply sat down on a rock. The light was beginning to fade, and in the dusk everything was silent, a vast sweep of rock and fragrant scrub, empty under a darkening sky. A few lights twinkled mysteriously halfway up the opposite hill; everything else was dim. I felt all at once immensely weary. I was lost, a stranger in a foreign land.

I took out the phone I'd been loaned and stared at it. The only person I knew to phone was Roberto Hernandez, and somehow I didn't want to phone him. If I phoned him, I would have to tell him that his fears were well-founded, that my father was a cheat. I couldn't bring myself to do it. Roberto's job required him to take steps to prevent scientific fraud. He might or might not obey its demands; either way it would be painful and embarrassing, to him and to Brian both.

Anyway, the person I really *wanted* to phone was Steve.

Steve would never cheat. I supposed that was the thing I loved most about him – that idealism, that passionate goodness. He could be silly, he could be naive, he could be cringingly embarrassing, but he never cared about his own advantage, and he never said or did anything just because it would impress somebody else. I remembered the moment when I'd fallen in love with him. We'd gone in to London, him and me and some other mad student activists. There'd been a rally for trade justice, his favourite cause, but after it ended we'd slipped away from the crowds. We'd walked along the Embankment, and he'd talked about the history of trade, the romance of it, and the frequent horrors and injustices. His face was vivid and alive, full of the desire to save the world. Oh, flip the old song on end; he *did* want to set the world on fire, and that's what lit the flame in my heart. I'd put my arm around his shoulder and leaned against him, and he'd suddenly flung his round me, then paused, grinning. 'That was London's life-blood once!' he'd said, waving at the Thames. 'All the wealth of the world flowed up it! You want to go in?' And he'd threatened to jump in with me, and I'd shrieked and clung to him until he kissed me.

The coded signal from my American phone would never reach so far – and if it could, he wouldn't answer me. I put the phone away again and began to cry.

Crying never solves anything, of course. Eventually you stop crying, and then whatever it is you were crying about is still there, and you still have to deal with it. When I ran out of tears it was full night, and the only thing I could do was turn around and walk back along the road the way I had come.

I had reached the carpark for the hiking trail when a car loomed out of the night, a huge black shape with glaring headlights. It braked sharply, the door flew open, and Brian leapt out. 'Oh, thank God!' he exclaimed, rushing toward me into the glare of the headlights.

'What, you came to look for me?' I asked bitterly.

He stopped abruptly. 'It's dark,' he replied seriously. 'You hadn't come back.'

'I told you I was going for a walk.'

'But it's *dark*,' he repeated.

There was a silence, and then he said nervously, 'Here, let me drive you back.'

I thought about saying that I'd walk, but the fact was, I was tired. I climbed into the passenger seat. Brian did a three-point turn, and the big car rolled quietly back in the direction it had come.

In the house there was light and safety and the smell of toasted cheese. 'Would you like some supper?' asked Brian, escorting me inside. 'I had some, before I started getting worried. I could make you a cheese sandwich.'

I became aware that I hadn't eaten since breakfast that morning at the hotel in San Francisco. 'Yeah, OK,' I agreed gruffly.

He gave me Monterey Jack cheese toasted on sourdough bread, with salsa, and watched as I wolfed it down.

'Look,' he said at last. 'I'm sorry.'

I shrugged. I knew perfectly well that he wasn't at all sorry for cheating his investors and insurers; he thought that was just good business. What he meant was that he was sorry I'd taken it so badly. I was too tired and depressed, though, to argue with him about it.

'This isn't going to work,' I said instead. 'I think I should go home early, if I can exchange my ticket.'

'Because of this stupid business?' he asked, appalled at my pettiness.

'Because I can't trust a word you say,' I told him.

He was silent a moment, taking that in. 'I haven't lied to you,' he said at last.

'Oh, come on!' I protested. 'You told me that you hoped your investors would understand that you couldn't show them pretty pictures of how well the serum works. You complained to me about the insurers. That was all unadorned truth?'

He grimaced. 'It wasn't anything to do with *you*.'

'The trouble with lying,' I told him, 'is that once people know you do it, they can never be sure that you're telling the truth.'

He winced. 'What I think is, you should sleep on it,' he told me. 'Right now you're tired. You were understandably upset when that thug turned up here. He told you a lot of poisonous half-truths and got you all worked up about it. You're overwrought and everything looks impossible. In the morning everything will seem much more manageable.'

I sighed. He was probably right to an extent. 'In the morning, then,' I told him.

I went to bed early, then lay awake. The house was silent, the television switched off. It struck me that I had never heard either Brian or Sharon playing music. Come to think of it, I hadn't even found any music CDs in the house.

> The man that hath no music in himself
> Nor is not moved with concord of sweet sounds,
> Is fit for treasons, stratagems and spoils;
> [. . .] Let no such man be trusted.

But that was excessive, unfair. I knew at least one cloth-eared philosopher who was perfectly sweet. Besides, Brian wasn't particularly 'fit' for treason; it'd require far too much passion and commitment from him.

Was I being unreasonable? Was I, in fact, being a self-righteous prig? I'd known from the start that my father was no hero. I hadn't expected him to be. I'd just wanted him to be a father. I wasn't perfect myself, but I still wanted people to love me. Was Brian any different? What should he have been like, to make things work?

I didn't know. Maybe I'd had no expectations. Lying there, though, thinking about it, I saw that I was less shocked by what he'd done than by his complacency about it. I could live with him defrauding an insurance company, but for him to complain about *their* greed and dishonesty while he did so – the hypocrisy of it turned my stomach.

I mulled over why I felt that hypocrisy was so much worse than simple dishonesty. A simple liar acknowledges, at least to himself, that he's abusing the truth, but a hypocrite is out to deceive himself as well. He wants to believe that what he's doing is good, or at least harmless. He can lose sight of the truth altogether, and when that happens, you're in trouble. Accept as reality a story which is rejected by your hearers, and you lose your ability to communicate with them, or even to understand their point of view. You can slide deeper and deeper into delusion, growing ever more isolated.

I thought, though, of the way Brian and I had talked on the beach, openly and honestly. I thought of his embarrassed, abortive attempt to hug me when I first showed up in Arrivals, of his relief when he jumped out of the car on finding me that night. I thought of his image of a river of our blood, flowing from the remote past, through him to me. My eyes stung again; he wanted to love me. I'd never had a father's love, and he was trying, however clumsily, to give it to me. Should I turn it down? Truth is a precious thing, but love is priceless.

Sleep on it, I told myself. Things may look clearer in the morning.

I slept badly, and just at dawn woke from an unpleasant dream in which I was lost in a shopping mall which was mysteriously running out of air. I lay in bed, muzzy-headed and queasy, and watched the light brighten on the bedroom wall. There was an exceptional clarity and purity to that light; you felt it ought to be illumining paintings by Bonnard or Hopper, transfiguring the mundane into something quintessentially beautiful. It failed, however, to transfigure me, and eventually I got up, went through into the kitchen, and braved the machine to make myself some coffee.

It was about half past six, and nobody else was up. I presumed that Sharon had returned to the house after I went to bed, though I hadn't heard her come in. She would sleep late, and go in to work that afternoon.

I supposed that she would be required to work that weekend too. Brian had said that her television company lumped a weekend in with the evening shift. I wondered how Brian had expected that to affect our tour of the state. Had Sharon been intending to take time off work, or had he meant the expedition to be a father-daughter outing?

Maybe he'd never really believed in it at all. It had certainly never been so much of a priority that he'd booked anything ahead. I didn't really blame him for canceling the tour, given the chaos he'd been dealing with in his lab and the dicey deceits he'd been spinning in response, but I hated the way he'd lied about it, insisting that it would still go ahead – always after he'd sorted out just one more problem.

On the other hand, perhaps he'd really intended for it to go ahead, and had genuinely believed that he could salvage it, once x and y had been cleared up at work. The truth was, I still didn't know what to think of him.

Perhaps the real truth was that I'd wanted him to be a fantasy father, someone perfect, who could somehow magic away all the dissatisfactions of my childhood. I'd been telling myself not to expect too much; I'd warned him that it might not work, but some seven-year-old part of my soul had carried on dreaming. Maybe it was time to grow up. The world is imperfect, and sometimes it has no good choice on offer. Sometimes all you can do is pick whatever seems to be the lesser evil.

There was an Auden poem which had haunted me for the last year, the way Marvell had haunted my father:

The desires of the heart are as crooked as corkscrews,
Not to be born is the best for man;
The second-best is a formal order,
The dance's pattern; dance while you can!

I'd read it to Steve once. He'd hated it. I'd known he would: there was nothing crooked about *his* heart.

I took my coffee into the lounge, but there was no *LA Times* to read: whoever normally picked it up, hadn't. I went on out on to the deck and drank the brew looking up at the mountainside. There were birds singing in the bushes, and a hawk turning in lazy circles high up in the cloudless sky. The natural world never seems second-best: in its way, it's as perfect and merciless as mathematics. Why is the human world so different?

I'd finished the coffee when Brian came out on to the deck behind me. He cleared his throat. 'Good morning.'

'Good morning,' I replied, and got warily to my feet.

He cleared his throat again. 'You feeling any better this morning?'

'Uh . . . yeah.' I met his eyes. 'I'll stay a bit longer. If that's OK.'

He began to smile, slowly at first, then more widely, his whole face lighting. 'It's more than OK. I'm very glad.'

'Right,' I said, looking away. 'Um. Roberto Hernandez wanted me to get back to him. About the photos of the skin cell cultures. I'd prefer it if you talked to him.'

There was a moment's silence, and then Brian said,

'What's the score on those pictures? Has he told his office about them?'

'No,' I said coldly. 'He admires you. He wants to believe there's an innocent explanation. Maybe he'll swallow your story that it's just the best way to tell your investors the truth. But if you want him to believe that, you should be the one to tell him, because I won't.'

There was another silence, and then Brian said, 'All right. I suppose I should be grateful for your forebearance. I'd prefer not to talk to him at his office. Do you have his cell-phone number?'

I provided the phone number.

I left Brian to take himself to his lab, and said that I would do some walking, and do it from the house. I borrowed Sharon's white sun hat, filled an old coke bottle with water and packed it in a day bag, slathered on the sun cream and set out. I still didn't want to take the hiking trail from behind the house, but I decided that it would be OK to take it from the carpark down the road.

The trail actually continued on the other side of the road, into an area I hadn't explored before. I followed it for some miles, pausing occasionally to drink some water and fan myself with the sun hat. The countryside was, as ever, beautiful, in a dry foreign way: rocky mountains, the gray-green chaparral, the scent of sage in the hot sun, occasional clumps of trees where a gully provided a little additional moisture. There were birds, lizards and ground squirrels, but I met no other hikers. The solitude and the heat were mesmerizing, and it was easy to let my mind rest, to float in the present world of sensation, and let the pain inside me slowly die down.

Eventually I came to Nojoqui Falls – a thin trickle of water running down a vertical rock face. Here there were people: fat women in shorts and halter tops; skinny teenagers in baseball caps, determined children paddling in the stream. When I went on a little, I could see why. Just along from the falls was a huge country park, equipped with picnic tables and a recreation ground. It had a large carpark, so that the citizens of Santa Barbara county could enjoy a pleasant day out in the country without straining themselves to get there.

I was in no mood to relish company. I refilled my water bottle at a tap, splashed more water over my head and face, and started back. By then the sun was fierce and white at the zenith, and the day was the hottest I'd encountered since my arrival. I plodded back along the trail. I hadn't noticed that it was mostly downhill on the way there, but now the fact that it was mostly uphill made itself felt with increasing force. I paused more and more frequently, and started rationing my sips of water. When I reached the carpark on Brian's road, I felt queasy and light-headed, and wondered if I were getting sunstroke.

The eucalyptus trees in the carpark provided the first decent shade for miles, and I sat down in it with a groan. If I put my hand up a couple inches from my face I could feel the heat coming off me like an oven. I poured the last of my lukewarm water into my palm and splashed it over my face and neck.

I was still sitting there, recovering, when Curtis Langford walked down the trail from the direction of Brian's house. He had a pair of binoculars slung around his neck and he was carrying a water bottle. He stopped abruptly when he saw me. I got slowly to my feet, hoping I didn't have to make a dash for it. I realized, too late, that one of the cars in the little lot was the dusty old van in which I'd ridden to the Botanic Gardens.

'What are you doing here?' demanded Langford in amazement.

'What are *you* doing here?' I replied. 'I thought the police warned you to stay away!'

He shrugged, face set. '*You* saw to that, didn't you?'

'Yeah, well, I didn't tell them about the gun,' I said sharply. 'I didn't tell them about you ordering me around while I was in my underwear, or about you going into the house and searching it and trying to break into the computer. All I told them was that you'd turned up, that we talked, and that you went away again. You ought to be *grateful*, not angry!'

He gave me a puzzled look. 'I can't figure you out,' he complained. 'Sometimes I think you're with the enemy; sometimes I think you could almost be on our side.'

'I'm not on your side *or* Brian's,' I told him, with a shudder. 'I told you before, I think the whole debate is stupid.'

Langford took a couple of steps closer. He didn't seem to be angry or violent, so I stood my ground.

'You ought to be on our side,' Langford said. 'Your father wanted to *kill* you before you were born. Unless that was a lie.'

'It wasn't a lie. I just don't find it as unforgiveable as you do.'

He looked at me in utter astonishment.

'I'm not saying I want to die!' I told him impatiently. 'But sometimes I wish I'd never been born. You know, I think the point where I really disagree with you pro-lifers is on your insistence that life in itself is an absolute good. I don't think it is. I think being alive, being a human being, is *hard*, and most people are very bad at it. Oh, there are wonderful bits, but I think most people, if they kept an honest balance sheet, would conclude that the pain and the frustration and the grief outweigh the happiness. I don't think you should bring a child into the world unless you're willing to do your utmost to see that the poor thing gets at least *some* good out of the experience. To bring it into the world and abandon it is just wicked.'

'You think it would be better for it not to *exist?*' he demanded indignantly.

'Yeah, I do!' I shot back – and was vaguely appalled at myself.

He shook his head. 'I'm sorry for you.'

'Oh yeah?' I said, stung. 'You know something else? There's a lot more Biblical support for my view of the world than there is for yours. Job and Jeremiah both say it's better never to be born, and curse the day they were, and the New Testament says the prince of this world is the devil. Your belief that life is just this wonderful privilege and we shouldn't deny it to anybody, doesn't come from your religion. I don't know where it does come from. Have *you* really had such a wonderful time all your life? Beating up your girlfriend and going to prison for it is your idea of fun, is it?'

He gave me a look of disquiet and took a step backward. 'How do you know about that?'

'The police, of course,' I said, with contempt. 'They showed me your mugshot when they wanted me to identify you.'

'Well, let me tell you, Miss Smart-ass, you don't know anything about it!' he exclaimed hotly. 'Cindy murdered our baby! I told her I was willing to look after it, but she went ahead and *killed* him! You surprised I lost my temper?'

'All I can say,' I shot back, 'is that *I* wouldn't trust you to look after a baby, either! Not if you hit people whenever you lose your temper!' Then I bit my lip: that was provoking him to lose his temper with me again.

He didn't, though. He glared angrily, but didn't move.

'What are you doing here, anyway?' I asked, when I was confident he wasn't going to attack me. 'Were you spying on Brian's house?'

He glowered – yes, he had been.

'Why?' I asked, in exasperation. 'What do you think you're going to get from it?'

'He accused me of stealing that stuff, the elixir,' said Langford sullenly. 'I need to find out what really happened to it.'

'How're you going to find that out by watching Brian's house? And I told you before, I'm not sure it even *existed*!'

'It did,' Langford replied at once. 'I thought about it, after you said that yesterday, and I'm sure it was in the freezer when we took out the stem cells. There was a lot of stuff in there. Since we didn't take it, it must still have been there after we left.'

'Then maybe somebody at the lab destroyed it. Brian said they threw out all the things that were left in the freezer, because the power had been off and they couldn't be sure whether or not they'd been contaminated. Maybe whoever destroyed it didn't make a note of it, or used a wrong procedure and didn't want to admit it, so there's no record of what happened to it. It wasn't that big a deal to Brian: he could always make more.' I studied Langford a moment. 'Look, I told you before, it's not even true that Brian accused you of stealing it. He just said he didn't know what had happened to it. I really wouldn't worry about getting charged with grand larceny, or whatever it was.'

'It's missing!' objected Langford, as though I were being stupid. 'I was there; I have a criminal record. If I can't find out what really happened to it, they're gonna pin it on me!'

'They can't pin it on you without any evidence! Everybody knows that sometimes things just get lost.'

'Things worth millions of dollars?' Langford asked sarcastically.

'It was only worth millions if it was delivered in good condition to the right person. Otherwise it was just medical waste. Who offered you money for it, anyway?'

'I don't know who he was,' said Langford. 'I already told the police that. He was just somebody on the internet. He got in touch after we completed the mission and said that if I had the stuff he'd give me five hundred bucks for it.'

'Just five hundred?' I asked in surprise.

Langford nodded ruefully. 'He said it would've been a couple thousand if we'd kept it frozen, but he'd still give me five hundred for it if I could freeze it again right away. I didn't have any idea how much the stuff was really worth – not until the police told me.' He shrugged. 'Five hundred bucks – it seemed worth going back to look and see whether we'd dropped it.' He went to his van and leaned heavily against it. 'And I was wrong about that, wasn't I? If I hadn't gone back to search, and if you hadn't met me while I was doing it, there's no way they could've pinned it on me. I would've been OK.'

'If you hadn't broken into the lab, you would've been OK,' I pointed out.

'Yeah, and the baby-murderers and butchers would flourish,' he said defiantly. 'I can't stand by and watch that.'

'Your side has been *winning* recently, in this country!' I protested. 'By peaceful, legal means. Breaking into Brian's lab was just stupid. All it did was make you look bad.'

He looked at me for a long minute, more sad than angry. 'I'm no good at petitions and talking,' he told me. 'When I'm angry about something, I need to *do* something about it.' He looked away. 'Maybe it is dumb, but I don't have a smart mouth.'

The way I did. I hardened my heart. He was justifying his abuse of his girlfriend. He'd wanted to 'do something' about her, too.

'Why were you waiting for me, anyway?' he went on.

'I wasn't!' I exclaimed, startled. 'I was just sitting down in the shade. I walked to Nojoqui Falls, and it was hot coming back.'

'Oh.' He blinked at me. 'To Nojoqui Falls, huh? Nice place.'

'Yeah.'

'Course, it's best in the spring, when there's a lot of water in the stream.'

'It was pretty, anyway.' I couldn't believe we were having a conversation about parks.

'So . . . you weren't waiting to talk to me or anything?'

I shook my head. 'Look, to be perfectly frank, if I'd known you were going to turn up, I would've run.'

He looked surprised at that, then, peculiarly, he grinned. 'I guess I deserved that. Hey, I'll run you back to your dad's place, if you like!'

'No thanks.'

He unlocked his car, got in, and drove off without further comment. I sat under the trees a bit longer, wondering how long he'd been watching the house and why he'd given up for the day. Had he burgled the house, or planted a bomb? Or had it just got too hot to sit up on a mountainside staring at the back of an empty house through a pair of binoculars?

I discovered that, while I was a bit nervous about the first possibilities, I found the other one more likely. Curtis Langford was a monster, but he was a clumsy, stupid one. Or maybe I only thought that because I'd faced him down.

Eight

When I got back to the house it was about two thirty, and there was no one home. Sharon had, presumably, already headed off to work. I was still feeling queasy and the headache was worse, but I made myself look around the place carefully before I went in. Nothing had been disturbed: the dry-country garden grew in fragrant disarray, and the swimming pool glowed sapphire blue in the sunlight. None of the windows had been broken, nobody had forced the doors. Langford really hadn't done anything more than watch.

I went into the house, locking the door again behind me, then had a long drink of water and a cold shower before lying down on my bed. I'd missed lunch, but I wasn't hungry. Too much climbing in the heat, I told myself. I should've remembered I wasn't used to it.

I fell asleep, and woke to the sound of voices. They were men's voices, indistinct, from another room. I got to my feet and went out into the corridor. The voices seemed to be coming from the kitchen. I padded on, into the kitchen, and found that they were in fact coming from Brian's study, just beyond it. One of the speakers was Brian; the other was Roberto Hernandez.

'I don't see how you get round the problem of rejection,' Roberto was saying.

'You haven't been listening!' exclaimed Brian impatiently. 'At this stage, the stem cells have fused with the

141

patient's own skin cells. All the surface markers are "self". Look.'

'Oh!' Roberto's voice was delighted. 'Oh, that's *elegant*! That's the surface?'

I took a few more steps and reached the study door. Brian, glancing up from the lit screen of his computer, noticed me and smiled. 'Alison! You're up. You were sound asleep when I got home.'

Roberto tore his eyes away from the prickly tennis ball on the screen. 'Alison!' he said, smiling at me. 'Hi!'

'Hi,' I said, and took another step forward. 'What are you doing?'

'I'm explaining some of my research to Roberto,' said Brian, as though it were the most natural thing in the world.

I looked quickly at Roberto. He smiled again.

'Oh,' I said helplessly. 'Um. What about the photos you were worried about?'

Roberto shrugged. 'They're not worth mentioning, compared to what your father's been telling me.'

Brian had been listening to this keenly, and now he said, ever so casually, 'Did you bring them?'

'I think they're still at home,' said Roberto.

'I'd appreciate it if you'd return them to me,' Brian told him. 'They are the property of Greenall Research, after all. We might be able to use them.'

'I was handed them by the police,' replied Roberto. 'I don't know whether I'm allowed to just hand them back to you. They might be evidence.'

Brian looked at him warily. 'Maybe I should ask the police to return them, then.'

There was a pause. 'Maybe,' Roberto agreed reluctantly. Then he smiled at me again; it seemed to require an effort. 'Anyway, Alison, good to see you. You OK? You look a bit pale.'

'I caught the sun a bit,' I mumbled. 'I think I had a touch of heat stroke.'

'Oh, you'd better sit down, then!' said Brian concernedly. 'Have a cold drink.' He quit the program on the computer.

Roberto made an inarticulate noise of protest. Brian looked at him, and their eyes held a minute.

'I think you've seen most of it,' Brian said, and shut the computer down.

In the kitchen he poured out three glasses of orange juice and added ice, and we took them out on to the deck. It was early evening: I'd slept for about three hours. I glanced up at the shadowy hillside above us and wondered if Curtis Langford was again sitting there somewhere, watching.

Roberto was full of molecular biology questions, which he asked eagerly and Brian answered tersely. Mention of a professor at UCLA revealed that Brian had agreed to provide an introduction. I listened, sipping my orange juice, saying nothing. I wondered to what extent either man was aware that Brian had purchased Roberto's silence. Both of them would undoubtedly reject any such allegation. And yet . . . that byplay about who kept control of the photographs, that meeting of the eyes when Brian switched off the computer, at some point the dealings between them must have become almost explicit.

I was not surprised that Brian had offered Roberto an inducement for his silence. I was surprised, though, that Roberto had solicited one. That reluctance to hand over the incriminating pictures, though, had held no hint of innocent hero worship.

At last the conversation dried up. 'Did you get to Nojoqui Falls?' Brian asked me.

'Yeah,' I said. 'It was good. It was a bit of a climb coming back, though, and the sun was fierce. I think I overdid it.'

'Should've warned you,' said Brian contritely. 'At least you don't seem to have got sunburned.'

'Sunblock,' I informed him, 'and Sharon's sun hat.'

'That's good,' said Roberto. 'People with your sort of skin really need to watch it when it comes to the sun.'

'I know that, thanks.'

'My mother always tried to tan,' said Brian meditatively. 'She was the same skin type as us – Connaught Irish, same red hair – but we'd go on beach holidays when I was young, and she'd put on tanning lotion and hope. It was bad enough when it was somewhere like Brighton, but when we started going on package holidays to Corfu, it was terrible. End of the first day, she'd be the colour of a lobster and barely able to move.' He met my eyes. 'She died of melanoma. I don't know if Claire ever mentioned that to you.'

I swallowed. I thought of how he'd sworn that, as far as he was concerned, his research was intended to save lives. I believed him now. 'Uh, no. She just told me that my gran on your side died of cancer before she ever met you.'

'The year I was seventeen. Came back from holiday with a sunburned mole on her shoulder and was dead six weeks later.'

'God!'

'Yes.' Brian nodded. 'Yes, it changed everything.'

Roberto had listened to this with obvious discomfort; now he cleared his throat and asked, 'Is that what made you go into molecular biology?'

Brian gave him a look I couldn't interpret. 'No. It made me resolve to become a doctor. I stuck med school for a year before I admitted to myself that I'd be absolutely hopeless.' He sloshed the orange juice in his glass, making the ice clink. 'I don't have either the patience or the compassion. Molecular biology was a substitute.'

'Your research will do more for melanoma than any doctor could,' said Roberto piously.

Brian shot him another look, this time one of real dislike. 'It's still a substitute. I hope what you said is true, but it's still a substitute. Thought for feeling; abstract for concrete.' He turned his eyes soberly to me. 'Is philosophy ever a substitute?'

'I suppose it can be,' I said. 'For belief.'

'Ah!' Brian nodded as though I'd confirmed something he'd suspected.

'For religious belief?' asked Roberto. 'Then it's a good thing, isn't it?'

'For all belief,' I admitted, half-unwillingly. 'Belief in God, belief in science, belief in humanity . . . even belief in evil. Instead of committing yourself, you ask questions, and analyze what, exactly, is being believed, or even what *precisely* it means to believe. There are philosophers who believe passionately, but I guess I'm not one of them.'

'Science isn't a matter of belief,' objected Roberto.

'Oh, it is!' I told him. 'It starts off with the assumption that the world is intelligible and that humans can understand it – which is a pretty whopping great assumption to make. You can't prove even that the universe *exists*, let alone that we can make sense of it.'

'Of course it exists,' said Roberto impatiently. '*And* it's consistent. You can repeat experiments, and get the same results.'

'How do you know?'

'You just . . . just do it twice!'

'How do you know that what you read about the first trial was right, or, if you conducted it yourself, that what you remember was right? How do you know that your sources aren't lying, or that you weren't hallucinating?'

He stared at me. 'This is stupid!'

'All right, try a different example. Prove to me that there's such a country as Mongolia.'

'Mongolia? Of course there is!'

'How do you know? Have you ever been there?'

'Well, no . . . but . . . but lots of other people have!'

'Anyone you know personally?' He shook his head. 'Then you're relying on what you've read, on second-hand accounts. Haven't you ever encountered a situation where information you got second-hand from books and popular accounts turned out to be *wrong*?'

'Well, yes, of course! But it's not the same!'

Brian gave a snort of amusement.

'What's different, then?' I asked.

'The . . . the accounts. There are lots of different *sorts* of account in lots of different sorts of media, all consistent with one another.'

'How do you know they aren't all just citing each other? That's what happens with common fallacies, isn't it? It's like the Eskimos having forty or sixty or a hundred different words for snow: that's a factoid that crops up in all sorts of different sources, but apparently it all goes back to one guy in the nineteen thirties or something, and he got it wrong.'

'It's wrong?' asked Roberto in surprise.

'Yeah. Apparently they only have four root words for snow. Or so I've read. Now, I believe the guy who said there were only four words, because he knew about the other versions while they didn't know about him – in other words, because his story is more *complete*. I'm still taking what he said on faith, though, because *I* don't speak Inuit: I have no first-hand knowledge. If I did what you say I should do, and simply checked how many different sources claim that Eskimos have lots of words for snow, there's no doubt I'd have to plump for the fallacy. Can you prove that the existence of Mongolia isn't a factoid like that?'

He was irritated, at a loss. 'This is ridiculous!'

'Well, how do you expect to prove that you have an accurate picture of the workings of the universe when you can't even prove the existence of Mongolia?'

Brian laughed. 'What my daughter's saying,' he told Roberto, 'is that science, like everything else, relies on faith and trust. We have faith in what we were taught at university; we trust that what our colleagues say in journals is the truth. By and large it is – but sometimes it isn't. Sometimes someone comes along and and says, "objects of different mass fall at the same speed!" or "species change and evolve over time!", and a whole orthodoxy is overturned.'

'But science accommodates that,' Roberto said irritably. 'It *responds* to evidence.'

'I don't dispute it. But from the viewpoint of a philosopher – or, for that matter, a mathematician – all our evidence is merely a catalogue of empirical observations, none of which, individually, can be proven. The universe we think we know is really an image we've constructed inside our own heads. We believe in countries we've never visited, in people we've never met – and in theories other people have developed from experiments we ourselves never conducted. We believe in them because they're part of our world view, and we have faith in the system that provided us with that world view. Like you, I believe that our faith isn't misplaced, but I agree with my daughter, it *is* faith. It's not knowledge.'

Roberto had that look – only too familiar to me – of someone who completely disagrees, but can't think of any killer objections. He finished his orange juice with a gulp. 'Well, that may be very *philosophical*,' he said contemptuously, 'but how much has it got to do with the real world?'

'Try to define "real",' I suggested. 'You'll find it isn't as easy as it looks.'

He paused, looking at me uneasily, then shook his head. 'Um. It's getting late. Would you and your father like to go out to dinner?'

He didn't take ideas seriously: to him, anything outside his own system of beliefs was, at best, ridiculous, and at worst, malign.

He took bribes.

We hadn't even got on to animal experiments yet.

'No, thanks,' I told him. 'I'd really like to take it easy this evening.'

He accepted that with, I thought, relief, and got up to say goodbye.

'That *was* pretty philosophical,' I told Brian, when Roberto had gone. 'Specially that bit about living in the image of the world we've constructed inside our heads. I didn't know you were interested.'

'Oh, that's philosophy as discussed by drunken under-graduates,' Brian said dismissively. 'I used to do a lot of that.' He grinned at me. 'You didn't seem as keen on Mr Hernandez as I expected you to be.'

'I've gone off him,' I confessed.

'Good,' said Brian. He did not elaborate why it was good, and I didn't ask him.

We had a light supper out of the fridge, and sat in front of the television to watch Sharon present the local news. She looked, as always, poised and confident and beautiful. Her hair shone in the light and her golden tan glowed. 'How did you meet Sharon?' I asked, watching her.

'Oh, she was with a production company that was doing a feature on the California biotech industry,' replied Brian. 'She came to interview me, and I asked her out to dinner.' He smiled. 'I thought she was out of my league, but that it was worth a try. It'll be ten years next February.' The smile widened. 'February the fourteenth. That got me points for romanticism.'

His marriage to Sharon had lasted about twice as long as the one to my mother. I thought for a while about that time span. 'Did Sharon ever want kids?' I asked at last. She would've been young enough.

His smile vanished. 'Television is a cut-throat business. Apparently, if you don't have a secure foothold, getting pregnant is a good way to lose your job.' He made a face. 'Sharon used to hope she could make it up to the national level – maybe not in news, but in some speciality field. For a long time she was always trying for some national job or other. She never got one. I don't really know why not: she's good, and she had the experience and the recommendations. I suppose she was always just the wrong flavour for the month, or something. Anyway, she never felt she could risk getting pregnant *just then*.

'Eventually she sort of gave up and decided that she wanted kids anyway – and we found we'd left it too late. There were problems, and solving them would've needed a lot of medical intervention. She couldn't face that.'

'I'm sorry,' I said quietly.

He looked away from the television, met my eyes. 'The funny thing is, I think I minded more than she did. It was partly because I *did* remember you. I wanted to do the whole father thing again, and get it right this time. I missed my chance, though, and it didn't come round again. Sharon and I, we both missed our chance.' He shook his head. 'I'd always thought I'd have as many second chances as I wanted, and suddenly they'd all run out.'

For some reason, I thought of Steve. I'd often been aware that I was annoying him, but somehow I'd always assumed that we could make it up. I'd thought, yes, that I could have as many second chances as I wanted – and then the chances ran out.

'So you started to hear "Time's winged chariot" at your back?' I asked at last.

'I suppose so,' he said sadly. 'I certainly felt I should stop putting things off. Make things up with the daughter I'd never forgotten. It took a while, though, to work up the nerve.'

'I'm glad you did,' I said impulsively – then looked away, wondering if I meant it and not wanting to see how he reacted.

The local news ended just then, and there was a commercial break. American breaks have many more ads than English ones, and the ads themselves are phenomenally stupid: the term 'gross insult to the brain' springs to mind. I gathered up the supper plates. 'Would you like some ice cream?' I asked Brian.

'Ice cream?' Brian repeated, as though it was some unheard-of delicacy. 'I don't often eat that. What sort have we got?'

'Burgundy Cherry Chocolate and . . . something else, I forget what.'

'I'll have the something else, probably, depending on what it is. That cherry stuff is a bit over the top, if you ask me.'

'It's *completely* over the top!' I told him. 'That's what makes it so gorgeous.'

I took the plates off into the kitchen, put them in the dishwasher, and had a look in the freezer. The other ice cream said it was raspberry ripple. I relayed this to Brian, who said he'd have that, then.

When I pulled at the carton, though, it clunked. Puzzled, I dug it out from under the frozen peas. It was a big cardboard tub that held a gallon, so it needed a bit of pulling. Whatever it held, it wasn't ice cream: I could feel things shifting inside it. I set it down on the kitchen counter and opened it.

The contents were five small black plastic boxes.

I stared at them numbly for a long moment. My first conscious feeling was of rage, because Brian had lied about this, too. Hard on the heels of emotion, though, came thought: if Brian had stashed these here, why had he actually *asked* for raspberry ripple? Could he really have forgotten where he'd put them so completely that he didn't even *worry*? It didn't seem likely.

If Brian hadn't hidden the boxes, then . . . Sharon. The possibility brought a spasm of dread.

'Brian!' I called. My voice came out as a whisper, so I picked my head up and shouted it. 'Brian!'

There was a pause, and then he hurried in, surprised and alarmed. He saw the open carton and its contents and suddenly stopped, frowning.

'That's . . .' he began, and changed it to: 'What're *those* doing here?'

'Sharon,' I said quickly. 'I mean, I don't know, but is it possible that Sharon . . . thought she could use the serum? That when your lab was scrapping things after the break-in . . . she stole it?'

Brian's eyes widened. 'No,' he whispered. 'No! No, she's not that stupid!'

'She thought it *worked*,' I pointed out. 'You told her so.'

'But it hasn't had any clinical trials! She *knows* it hasn't!' Ignoring his own argument, he staggered forward and hurriedly opened one of the little boxes. As he'd told the police, it held four small stoppered test tubes of a faintly pinkish ice. He opened the next box: four more test tubes. The third . . . one full tube and three empty ones.

'Oh, my God!' whispered Brian again. He carefully closed the box, then stood with his hands on the counter, staring down at it. 'Oh, my God!'

151

I opened the remaining two boxes: the test tubes in both were empty. I thought of Sharon's youthful glow in front of the cameras that evening, and how I'd noticed her fresh look when I got back from the camping trip. 'Now therefore, while the youthful hue/Sits on your skin like morning dew . . . Now let us sport us while we may.'

'It causes *cancer*!' I said, appalled.

'How could she be so *stupid*?' Brian shouted it, suddenly, painfully. He banged his fists down on the counter, looking wildly around the kitchen as though he expected to find someone who could give him an answer. 'She *knew* it hadn't been approved for use yet!'

I closed the little boxes again, then shut the ice cream carton. I put it back in the freezer, not so much to preserve it as to get it out of sight. 'Is it the serum?' I asked. I knew it was, of course, but I still hoped.

'Yes,' said Brian, suddenly quiet again. 'And she did come over to the lab, after the break-in, while we were arguing whether or not to throw out the things that were left in the freezer.' He closed his eyes. 'She's been worried about her job. Clinical trials . . . take time.'

'If she did take it . . .' I stopped, my throat felt tight. Some people might call this divine retribution, but why should Sharon be the one to suffer because Brian had lied? 'If she did,' I tried again, 'is there . . . can you give her an antidote or something?'

'The antidote is what I was trying to develop in the first place,' Brian said wretchedly. 'The closest thing I have to an antidote is in the freezer.'

'Maybe it won't hurt her,' I said, after a silence. 'Maybe it'll even *work*.'

We didn't phone Sharon at work: there was nothing to be gained by it. Instead we waited in the lounge. We tried to watch television for a while, but the ads got on my nerves, and I asked Brian if I could put it off. Then we tried to read; I don't know about Brian, but I couldn't concentrate. I went to the computer and checked my email, but apart from deleting all the spam I couldn't deal with anything, and I shut the machine down again.

At last, at about half past eleven, we heard the car in the drive. Brian jumped to his feet and went into the hall, and a moment later the door opened and Sharon breezed in. I hadn't actually seen her for two days, and I think that even if I hadn't been primed to look for changes, I would've noticed something. The over-tanned, parched look had gone from her skin: she was as fresh and golden as a teenager. She stopped when she saw us – Brian in the hall, me in the entrance to the lounge – and stared in surprise and apprehension.

'What's the matter?' she asked.

'Sharon,' said Brian breathlessly, 'Sharon, did you take the serum? Did you *use* it?'

She gave a guilty flinch. 'Oh. You found it.' She set down her handbag and rubbed her mouth nervously. 'I'm sorry. I should've told you. It's just . . . I went over to the lab, after the break-in, and you and Dave were talking about just throwing it away, and it seemed such a criminal waste. I couldn't see how it could've thawed enough to hurt, not in such a short time, and it didn't look to me like it'd thawed at all. But there it was, ready to be dumped, and everybody was running around and arguing about what had been damaged, and I thought I should just take it home before it thawed out.'

'But have you *used* it?' Brian demanded in anguish.

She set her teeth. 'All right. Yes.'

'Oh, God, *why?*' cried Brian in dismay. 'You *knew* it hadn't been passed safe yet!'

'It's all right for *you!*' replied Sharon, suddenly angry.

'Nobody cares what *you* look like; you can get as wrinkly and fat as you like, and it won't affect your job or your earnings or the *respect* you get. But I was on the edge, Brian, I was going to be past it very soon! And I know you said there'd be clinical trails next year, but you know as well as I do that "next year" really means "sometime in the next *five* years" – and then they probably wouldn't accept your wife as a subject, or I might get the placebo or something. I'd be fifty-something before I could be sure of getting the stuff, and it'd be too late, do you understand? As it is . . .' She held out her hands. 'As it is, look! Look at me!' She ran her fingers over the smooth skin of her face. 'It *works,* Brian!' she said, now urgent with delight. 'Your stuff really *works*! You said it would, and it does!'

He stared at her speechlessly.

'I know, I broke the rules,' she told him, apologetically now. 'I'm sorry. But I'll tell the police and the FDA that I took the serum without your knowledge. They can't blame you for that, can they?'

'Sharon,' he said wretchedly – then stopped.

'Oh, look!' she protested. 'Honestly, it isn't a *crime* to take an unlicensed medicine!'

'It wasn't safe,' I told her, since it seemed Brian couldn't bring himself to admit it.

'I know it hasn't been *proved* safe,' Sharon said dismissively. 'But there's no reason to think it's dangerous.'

'But there is,' I said.

She looked from me to Brian, puzzled.

'Fifteen per cent of the skin cell cultures treated with the serum developed lesions,' said Brian miserably. 'I would never, *ever* have given it to any patient at this stage – let alone to you.'

Sharon stared at him, still more puzzled than alarmed. 'But you *said* . . .'

'For the *investors*!' Brian cried. 'I said lots of things for the *investors*. It was . . . they don't understand science, OK? You have to exaggerate a bit if you want to keep getting funded. I never meant anyone to *use* the stuff until it was safe!'

Sharon began to frown. 'You're saying you know for sure it's *not* safe?'

'It's very dangerous,' Brian finally admitted. 'It would never have been passed as fit for human use, not at this stage. Oh, darling, *why* did you do such a stupid thing?'

Sharon looked down at her hands again. 'But it's working!'

'I pray to God it *stops* working!' exclaimed Brian, his voice cracking. 'Now, before it hurts you!'

'What are you saying?' demanded Sharon, frightened now.

'It works *too well*!' Brian told her. 'It fuses with your own skin cells' DNA, and sometimes it corrupts the coding instead of correcting it. When it does that . . . it can cause cancer.'

'Cancer!' exclaimed Sharon. 'But . . . but . . . it's supposed to be a *cure*!'

Brian stared at her for a long moment in intense distress. 'It was supposed to be a cure when it was *finished*,' he told her. 'And it won't be finished for a couple more years, at least.'

Sharon looked at her hands again, frightened now.

'You should never, ever have touched it!' said Brian. 'God knows what it'll do!'

'I'm sorry,' Sharon said, in a small voice. 'I'm sorry.'

Brian said nothing for a long minute. Then he went forward and put his arms around her, pulling her close, tenderly, protectively. 'It'll be all right,' he whispered. 'It was only a minority of the cells in culture . . . and cells in living skin are probably going to be more robust. Don't worry, darling, there's every reason to trust that it will be all right. Just . . . don't take any more. Please. We'll make an appointment with your doctor tomorrow.'

Nine

Sharon did make a doctor's appointment next morning. It was a culture shock for me: she rang up at eight a.m. and got an appointment for half past ten. I suppose that's what you get when you have very expensive private medicine and top-rate insurance.

Everyone was subdued over breakfast, Sharon anxious and apologetic, Brian nervous and miserable. I thought Brian should be the apologetic one, but I didn't say so, because he was wretched enough as it was.

After breakfast we killed time with coffee and newspapers, all of us uncomfortable and ill at ease. At last Brian and Sharon set off for the doctor's, early.

I wandered around the house, not sure what to do with myself. It was Wednesday; in precisely a week I'd be headed back to England. For two weeks I'd been trying to treat my visit as a holiday, but there seemed little point in carrying on the pretense. I couldn't even resent it any more. The things which had happened since the break-in at Brian's lab could not just be set aside to let me play tourist.

I wasn't really part of those events, though. I'd been an observer, and, in part, a critic – watching and pronouncing judgement. Now I felt like an intruder.

I went out on to the deck and looked up the mountain-side. Then I went and found the house key Brian had left for me, locked up the house, and picked my way up the faint track through the prickly chaparral.

Nobody was on the hiking trail when I reached it, and, as far as I could tell, nobody was sitting in the scrub of the slope, peering down at the house through binoculars. Disappointed, I walked along to the right, as I had the first time, until I reached the gully with the live oaks.

It was another very hot day, and I'd neglected to put on the sunblock before setting out. I made my way into the shade with relief. To my surprise and pleasure there was a stream in the heart of the wood: a trickle of clear water snaking over the rocks and forming tea-coloured pools in eroded hollows of stone. I sat down on a boulder where the path crossed it. Midges danced over the surface of the water and a bird was singing; there were no other sounds.

I wondered what I thought I was doing. Had I really come up here hoping to meet Curtis Langford? What had I meant to say to him? 'It's OK, you don't need to worry, we found the serum, it was frozen all along, and right now it's just down there in the empty house, to which I have the key'?

Yeah, right. So why had I wanted to talk to him?

Because Brian and Sharon both had been perfectly willing to let him take the blame for things he hadn't done. He was a self-righteous pig with a nasty temper and some peculiar ideas, but that was no justification for sending him to prison for a crime he hadn't committed. He was owed something in compensation. What was more, he'd given me truths which I couldn't have learned any other way; in return I was bound to give him at least enough truth to set his mind at rest. I admitted, too, that if I'd succeeded in talking to him, it would've made me feel less of a helpless onlooker.

I sat on the rock for perhaps a quarter of an hour, then decided that it would be a lot more comfortable back at Brian's. I got up, then paused to climb down over the rocks and trail my fingers in the water.

Something buzzed loudly, close by to my left. I looked round and saw the snake. It was coiled up in a space between two rocks, about three feet from my left hand. It had a blunt, ugly nose, and its thick body was marked with a diamond pattern in cream and brown. As I stared, it shifted, and I could see the vertical slit pupils of its yellow eyes.

Very, very slowly, not breathing, I drew my hand away from it. It made the buzzing noise again, and this time I saw the rattle, half tucked under one of the coils. My heart thudded in my throat: so there really *were* rattlesnakes!

What happened when one bit you? Were you paralysed, or did it just hurt a lot? Like a bee-sting, twenty bee-stings, a hundred bee-stings? How likely were you to die? Maybe life was more grief than joy, but, oh, when I looked at that snake I knew that I didn't want to die!

I took a crouched step back; the snake lifted its head a little, but did not otherwise move. I took another step back. The snake stayed poised. Its raised head was motionless as a dried branch, but I was aware of the muscles holding it steady, too powerful to waver, ready to strike. Another step; another. I straightened, drawing a deep, deep breath, took another step back and reached the path. The snake suddenly turned its head away and glided, smooth as water, off between the rocks. I glimpsed it once, oozing its way over a bare patch of earth, and then it was gone.

Wow! I thought, stupidly. Now that the snake was safely gone, I was elated. I was alive! I had run into a primeval danger, and escaped unscathed!

Of course, I told myself, the snake had no reason to attack a human. It couldn't eat anything so large. It would bite to defend itself, but it tried to warn its enemies off first, sounding that useful rattle. It was not a malevolent thing – just a dangerous one.

I started back along the path happy and excited. I couldn't help feeling that the rattlesnake was a good omen for

Sharon: sometimes disaster appears right in front of you, but doesn't strike.

I was looking for the track back to the house when somebody shouted, 'Hey!' I looked up sharply, and there, after all, was Curtis Langford, walking along the trail toward me. I noticed that he had the binoculars and the insulated water bottle again, ready for a few more hours' spying. I stopped. Now that I was actually facing the man, it struck me that coming to look for him had been a very stupid thing to do.

I had no choice, though, except to carry on with plan A. 'Hi,' I said, to his suspicious expression. 'This time I *was* looking for you.'

He was surprised, pleased, and, at the same time, even more suspicious than before. 'What do you want?' he demanded bluntly.

'I wanted to tell you that they found the serum! It was just mislaid in another freezer; it was never really missing at all. You're in no danger: nobody can charge you with having stolen it!'

I'd expected him to be relieved, but he frowned at me wordlessly for a long time. 'I can't figure you out,' he said at last, as he had before. 'You haven't even told the police I've been coming here, have you?'

'No,' I admitted. He was still frowning suspiciously, so I added, 'I've had a lot else on my mind. Brian was already blaming you for things you hadn't done, too, so it didn't seem fair to get you into worse trouble.'

This seemed to puzzle him even more. He looked at me for a long moment with an expression I couldn't interpret, then finally blurted out, 'Do you . . . *like* me?'

Dangerous word, *like*, with far too many shades of meaning. I knew, though, exactly which meaning Curtis Langford intended. I had *liked* Roberto, when I first met him.

'Good *God*, no!' I exclaimed in horror. I almost added, 'I wouldn't touch you with a barge pole!', but I thought better of it. I knew he had a nasty temper, and the vehemence of my denial had obviously hurt and offended him.

'So why are you being *nice* to me?' he demanded, angrily now.

'Does somebody have to be in love with you to be nice?' I asked in disgust.

'In my experience, people aren't nice unless they have a reason,' he replied at once. 'If they're Christians, it's because they know that's how God wants them to be. Otherwise, it's usually because they want something.' He scowled at me, the offense growing. 'I can't figure out what *you* want, but I bet there's something.'

I don't like the taste of that brand of ethics at all: it assumes that the ground state of the human heart is pure and unadulterated selfishness, and the only reason to care about anyone or anything else is fear of retribution. 'Maybe I want to be good,' I told him. 'I may not be as nice as I should be, but I do try to be honest and fair. You don't have to be religious to want to be good.'

'Or maybe you're trying to trick me,' said Langford in a low voice.

Perhaps I should have been frightened at that, but I was too disgusted. I raised my eyebrows. 'Why should I? What could I conceivably get out of it?'

'It would let you feel superior!' he exploded. 'You could go back and *laugh* about it! Yes, and laugh about *me,* you bitch, about how I was stupid enough to start to like *you!*'

God! I backed off several steps hurriedly. 'I'm not trying to trick you,' I told him, now working to keep my voice level and calm. 'And I wouldn't laugh at you. Just because you're not my type doesn't mean I'm going to be foul to you! I came up here hoping to give you some good news.

I thought it would stop you from worrying, and let you go home. If you don't believe me . . . well, it's still true.'

The anger in his face eased. 'Oh. You thought it would make me go away.'

Now, obviously, it made sense to him. Now, too, he suspected I was lying. Probably he'd decide that he needed to watch the house even more carefully.

I gave up. The trouble was, I hadn't spotted the track back to the house, which meant it must be beyond him, and I didn't know how to get past. He was standing in the middle of the trail, full of righteous belligerence.

'Why *have* you been coming up here, anyway?' I asked in exasperation. 'What do you think you're going to *see*?'

He smirked. 'What are you afraid I'll see?'

'There *isn't* anything to see! Except me and Sharon in the swimming pool, and, I admit, I hate the thought of you sitting up here with your binoculars ogling us!'

'I'm not some peeping Tom!' he said indignantly. 'I'm just trying not to get shafted by the police! If I keep watching long enough, I'll learn something about your father. Maybe I'll see some clue as to where the serum is. If what you say is true, then maybe I'll see something to *prove* that it's true. I'm not going to believe it just because you say so!'

'Have it your way! If you *want* to sit here cooking in the sun and worrying about something that isn't going to happen, I can't stop you. Look, can I get past you?'

He hesitated, then moved over to the side of the path. I edged forward; when I was about to pass him, he shot out his hand and caught my upper arm. I froze. His palm was rough against my skin, and his fingers were frighteningly strong.

'If you were telling the truth,' he said slowly and seriously, his blue eyes inches from my own, 'thank you.' He let go.

I stumbled on a few steps, saw the track ahead of me, and hurried over to it. I paused, looking back. Langford hadn't moved. I forced my way hurriedly downslope through the chaparral. When I next looked back, he was nowhere to be seen.

I got back to the house, got myself a drink of water, and thought about phoning the police. I wasn't sure, though, that Langford's spying was even illegal. Presumably the police had warned him to stay away from Brian's house, but Langford hadn't actually approached the house again. It seemed unlikely that there was any sort of injunction in force to ban him from a hiking trail on what was, after all, public land. Brian hadn't applied for one, and I doubted that the police would've slapped it on without being asked. Maybe I should phone the police anyway, though, just to let them know what was going on.

The trouble was, I really didn't want to be the one to tell the police about the serum. I assumed Brian would inform them, but I wasn't sure exactly how much he would say. Sharon had kept her mouth firmly shut while the police searched for evidence that Langford had stolen the stuff; presumably she could get in trouble for that. I didn't want her to get in trouble with the police, not with the nightmare she already had hanging over her, but if they asked me something directly, I didn't want to lie. If I told Brian that Langford was watching the house, and let him discuss the situation with the police, then I very much doubted that the police would get the whole truth.

I noted with disgust that I was willing for Brian to lie, if it spared me from having to do so. That was probably worse than telling lies myself, but, even so, I didn't want to lie to the police. I might get caught. Yes, sure enough, my selfish fear of retribution outweighed my abstract ethics! I still didn't think that's all there is to the heart, but there's no doubt it's a part of it.

163

In some people more than others. Steve was generous to a fault. Maybe I was more like Brian.

I hoped Brian would at least tell Sharon's doctor the truth. No, I was sure he would; the medical details would be vitally important. Anyway, he probably felt it would be perfectly safe to do so. The doctor wouldn't tell the police because he wouldn't know that the police might be interested.

I went into the kitchen and made myself another cup of coffee, then sat down with it in the lounge. The deck was washed in brilliant sunlight, and the mountain rose behind it, but I had no inclination to go outside. I had, I admitted again, been stupid to go looking for the Monster of the Mountain. I'd known he could be violent, and I'd had the sense to be afraid of him before, but the last couple of encounters had dulled the edge of that fear. I suppose it was because he'd responded to reason.

I should be fair, he hadn't really threatened me. It was just that the thought of having the Monster in love with me was alarming in the extreme. He seemed just the sort to turn into a stalker. I hoped I'd managed to dissuade him in time. I consoled myself with the thought that in another week I'd be home.

It was nearly noon when I finished my coffee, and I had nothing to do. Now that I thought of it, neither Brian nor Sharon had indicated that they intended to return to the house after the doctor's appointment. I checked the terrace: both cars were gone. Presumably they intended to go off to their different places of work after they'd spoken to the doctor.

I couldn't imagine how Sharon could cheerfully present the local news while her skin fermented the possibility of cancer, but presumably she intended to. Now that I thought of it, I could see that she'd want to conceal everything from her employers. From all she'd said of them, they would have no interest in retaining the services of a newscaster in ill health. No, she'd keep quiet about what she'd done. People would undoubtedly notice her lustrous new look, but she would attribute it to a new skin cream or a new brand of make-up. She would smile and accept the compliments, then appear on air to discuss the crime report or a new hotel development. I shivered: that would take more fortitude and self-control than I was ever likely to possess.

Anyway, it looked like I was stuck at the house. I thought about phoning Brian and asking for a lift some-where, but it seemed incredibly self-centered to harass him just now. I would simply have to amuse myself for a few hours.

I could go for a walk, but it was too hot, and I didn't want to meet the Monster again. I could read, but I didn't fancy historical romances or thrillers. I could watch tele-vision, if I could stomach the American ads.

I went to Sharon's computer and switched it on. My email was singularly unsatisfying. There was a brief note from Mum, saying she and Matt were just heading off, see you when we get back, hope all's well; there was a round-robin from a friend about her journey across Australia; there was a note about a philosophy conference and one about an animal rights petition; there was spam. I was deleting the latter, click, click, click, when I real-ized that an email I'd just excised had the address 'rh3@fda'. I undeleted and opened it.

Hi, Alison,

I hope you don't mind me emailing you. I noticed your address on your dad's computer the other night. You seemed sort of upset with me last night, and I thought it might be easier to contact you this way.

I don't know why you were upset. Maybe you think there's something dishonest about keeping quiet about those photos? There wasn't. Your dad's research is real and it's getting results. I was very, very impressed with what he showed me. Nobody's getting cheated; in fact, his investors are going to make a lot of money one day, and if I had any cash I'd invest in his company myself.

I know you're probably busy, but I really enjoyed going out with you, and I was hoping we could manage it at least once more before you go back to England. I'm coming up to SB Friday afternoon, if that's any good.

Hope you can make it!

I frowned at the email for a while. If Roberto had phoned I would probably have just brushed him off; replying to an email required a bit more deliberation. I would have to say either that I really didn't want to see him again, or that, yes, I'd see him on Friday.

There was no possibility of even a holiday romance now, but presumably he knew that, since he'd commented on how soon I was going home. It seemed likely that all he really wanted was something to do on Friday evening. Dinner with even a semi-girlfriend would be a pleasanter way to end his afternoon's business in Santa Barbara than driving straight back to LA. Refusing to see him at all felt churlish. After all, I'd been eager enough at first, and he'd never even been rude, let alone unpleasant. I stared at the screen, feeling a bit put-upon. I didn't really want to see Roberto again, but I would feel rude if I didn't.

I clicked *reply*, and wrote:

Hi, Roberto,
    I don't know whether Brian has any plans for Friday. If he doesn't, it would be nice to meet up. I'll get back to you. Alison

I told myself that by Friday I'd probably welcome the date. I was going to get very bored if I had to suffer another two days of doing not much of anything around the house. Moreover, if I decided I *really* couldn't face an evening with the man, I could lie, and say that Brian had plans. Reassured, I hit *send*, and watched the message disappear out into the net.

That left me with the unsatisfactory contents of my inbox. I stared glumly at the open-envelope icons, wishing that there was something – anything – from Steve.

Dammit, it had been a month now, I should be getting over it. Instead, the loss seemed to be bigger every time I looked at it. When I *had* Steve, I used to laugh at him, sometimes, or cringe, but now that he was gone, all I could think about was his warmth, his intelligence, his kindness, his . . . oh, God, how I missed him!

Maybe – radical thought – *I* should email *him*. He was the one who'd broken the relationship off, though; I was the one who wanted him back. If I pursued him . . . well, first it was undignified, and second it was pathetic, and third it might well be irritating and offensive. He didn't want me any more. I should come to terms with it.

I quit Outlook Express and mooched off to the kitchen. I'd bake something, I decided, a nice surprise for Sharon when she got back.

Brian returned at about five. He stopped in the entrance hall, sniffing and looking surprised. 'What's that smell?' he asked.

'Muesli coffee cake,' I said proudly. 'The recipe was on one of the packets. I wanted to make something nice for Sharon. I know she's not here for supper, but I figured she could have it for breakfast.'

'She never eats cake,' replied Brian. 'Her figure.' Registering my look, he added quickly, 'She'll be touched by the thought, though, and I *love* cake. I hardly ever get it, either.' He smiled at me.

We went through into the lounge. 'What did Sharon's doctor say?' I asked anxiously.

'That right now she's perfectly healthy,' he said, hopefully. 'We've agreed that she'll go in for check-ups at least once a week, until we're sure that there aren't going to be any adverse effects. You want to open a bottle of wine and sit outside?'

I'd been smiling, but at this I stopped. 'You know that guy Curtis Langford? He's been sitting up on the hillside watching the house. I don't know if he's gone yet.'

This brought a shocked stare. 'What?'

'I met him. When I went up there for a walk.' I didn't want to confuse things by mentioning the previous meeting. 'He says he's afraid of being charged with grand larceny for stealing the serum, so he's spying on us to find out what really happened to it. I told him it had turned up and that nobody was going charge him, but I think he thought I was lying just to make him go away.'

Brian was outraged. 'This is intolerable! Where is he?'

'I don't know whether or not he's still there. I couldn't see him from the house.'

Brian strode over to the picture window and flung it open. As he started out of the house, I realized that he meant to go up and deal with Langford personally. 'No!' I exclaimed in horror. 'You mustn't! You mustn't go near him!'

He paused, regarding me with indignant surprise. '*You* talked to him!'

'Yeah, but he doesn't have anything much against *me*. He thinks *you're* an evil Nazi who experiments on babies, and that you're trying to send him to prison for something he didn't do. He has a nasty temper and I really, truly don't think you should go anywhere near him!'

Brian scowled. Then he went back into the house, though without closing the picture window. He went into the bedroom he shared with Sharon and came back a moment later with a gun.

I gaped at the thing in astonished horror, wondering remotely where that had been when Langford searched the house. 'Oh, no!' I protested. 'Oh, no, that's just asking for trouble!'

'I'm not going to be a prisoner in my own house!' Brian declared angrily. 'Don't worry, though.' He slipped the gun into his jacket pocket. 'See? I'll just ask him to leave. I won't even take it out, unless he turns nasty.'

'Going up there with it at all is just *asking* for disaster!' I objected. It was only too easy to imagine Langford threatening Brian, and Brian shooting him. I was cold with panic at the thought. 'Phone the police, for God's sake! They're *paid* to deal with this sort of thing!'

'I've had enough of this Langford character,' said Brian mulishly. 'He breaks into my lab, he invades my property and scares you and tries to poison your mind, and now he's spying on me!' He marched out on to the deck, then down past the swimming pool and up the slope.

I ran after him, terrified, praying that Langford had already left his watching post. About halfway to the hiking trail, I realized that I should've gone back into the house and phoned the police, but by then it was too late.

Except that it wasn't. Brian marched all the way to the hiking trail and stopped, looking around furiously. The hillside lay open and empty, shadowed by the bulk of the mountain between it and the lowering sun. Langford was nowhere in evidence. He must have gone home to eat his supper.

'Where did you meet him?' asked Brian.

'About here,' I told him, my heart slowing again. First I'd escaped a rattlesnake; now it was a shooting. 'Maybe a little that way.' I pointed along the trail upslope. 'I guess he's gone home.'

Brian grunted resentfully. He strode up the path a few paces, then paused, turned, and waded into the chaparral. Following him, I could see the broken twigs which showed that somebody else had recently done the same. After descending about fifty yards, Brian gave an exclamation of satisfaction. There on a sort of hillock, snuggled between a rock outcrop and a sagebush, was a kind of den. A bit of fabric that looked like old upholstery provided a place to sit that was free of prickly bits of branch, and an old umbrella was tucked under it, ready to provide a bit of shade. I went over to the spot and, sure enough, found I had a good view of the house.

'The bastard!' said Brian vehemently.

'Yeah, well, he's not here now,' I pointed out, devoutly relieved that he wasn't. 'So we should go back and phone the police.'

He scowled, but stamped back up to the hiking trail, then back down the track. I heaved a sigh of relief when we climbed back on to the deck.

Back in the lounge Brian paused, frowning at me. 'Why didn't *you* phone the police,' he demanded, 'when you met him?'

'I didn't know what to say if they asked about the serum,' I informed him.

Brian's look of puzzled indignation faded to mere disgruntlement. 'Oh,' he conceded. 'I see your point.'

He telephoned the police. I went and fetched the bottle of wine he'd suggested before blowing up – I certainly wanted it now. As I rummaged in the kitchen for a corkscrew, I could hear fragments of his conversation: '. . . I don't know. No, not directly; that's not the *point*! He's a violent criminal! . . . I don't know! The National Forest, I suppose . . . Why can't you lock him up?'

No mention of the serum at all; presumably he was happy for the police to carry on believing it had been stolen. It was too much. I went into the lounge, clutching the wine bottle, and said, 'You should tell them you found the serum. You should let them know that.'

Brian grimaced, but said, 'Oh, yes, another thing. We've accounted for the missing serum . . . No, it seems not, after all. It was mislaid. Procedures weren't followed because of the confusion, and nobody realized where it had got to . . . Well, *I* never said it was! It was that FDA man, Hernandez, who was bent on making a drama out of a crisis . . . I *am* telling you! . . . No, we only just found out! . . . Thank you. Yes. No! How can you say that? No, it isn't, it's the next thing to terrorism! . . . Well, ye-es . . . but they do! Not in this case, I grant you, but . . . I totally disagree!'

There was a long silence, and finally Brian asked angrily, 'What about this man Langford? . . . No, he's a violent criminal, and he's hanging around my house spying on me! All right. *Thank* you.'

He set the phone down. 'That was a great idea!' he remarked bitterly. 'Apparently if the serum isn't missing, the whole break-in isn't much of a crime, as far as the police are concerned. It doesn't merit a detective or a lot of police time, and they're going to, quote, "reallocate their resources to more urgent cases". They're basically going to stop investigating altogether!'

'Well, nothing was stolen!' I protested. 'Except the stem cells and your pictures, and you know what happened to them. So what was left to investigate?'

Brian grimaced. 'Who was trying to buy the serum. How far up the pro-life organization the decision to carry out the attack went, and who else was involved. Lots of things. I suppose you don't think they're important!'

I set my teeth. 'I didn't say that. But I don't think it

was fair, or even a good idea, to let the police go on investigating the theft of the serum. I mean, what if they found out that Sharon took it? You want her to be charged with wasting police time, or something?'

That gave him pause. After a moment he nodded reluctantly. Then he sighed, sat down, and rubbed the back of his neck. 'You're right,' he said quietly. 'Sorry.' He looked up at me soberly. 'Sorry. I just . . . it's just it's been a very rough couple of weeks.'

'Yeah,' I agreed. After a moment I added, 'You want some of this wine?'

'I think I'll opt for something stronger,' he replied.

I had some of the wine; he had a gin and tonic. We had supper, an *ad hoc* curry concocted by me from all the odds and ends I could find. Brian remarked with surprise that it wasn't bad.

When it was finished we went into the lounge. There was an awkward silence, and we looked at one another warily.

'Would you like to watch a movie?' Brian offered at last. 'I have a lot of them.'

I don't know why I hadn't spotted them before. Sure, they were in a cupboard in his bedroom, but there *were* a lot – hundreds, in fact, on a turntable so there'd be space for them, VHS at the back, DVDs in front, all neatly shelved by director's surname. Many of them were off some internet 'vintage film club' or other, though there were plenty of freelance purchases as well. There were old Ealing comedies and Golden Age Hollywood flicks; there were Japanese samurai and French Art House pictures; there were oddities from small independent companies and mega-blockbuster hits.

'Oh, wow!' I said, drooling a bit and running a finger along a shelf.

'I like movies,' Brian explained. 'You fancy anything in particular?'

'You must've been collecting these for *years*!'

'Yes,' he admitted, smiling sheepishly. 'I've *always* liked movies.'

I laughed and asked which were his Top Ten. His list was pretty eclectic, though with a bias toward crime: *Citizen Kane*, *The Godfather*, *Day for Night*, *Taxi Driver*, *Psycho*, *The Leopard*, *Casablanca*, *Frankenstein*, *Kind Hearts and Coronets*, and, oh, he didn't know, maybe *Kill Bill* or *Pulp Fiction* or . . . or, no, no, he should throw out *Frankenstein* in favour of *The Third Man*. No, he decided, that wasn't right, *Frankenstein* ought to be on the list, and *The Maltese Falcon*, and really he needed a Top Twenty. No, a Top Fifty!

We talked movies. Brian discussing Tarantino or Bogart was a much warmer, more animated man. He smiled, and his eyes lit up; he waved his hands in the air and laughed. For the first time I could see why my mother had married him.

Eventually he convinced me that I really ought to see some Kurosawa, since I liked Sergio Leone, and we went into the lounge with an old VHS cartridge of *Yojimbo*.

When Sharon came in we were watching *A Fistful of Dollars*, for comparison, and eating popcorn.

'Hello!' she said, setting down her handbag in the hall. 'You two having fun?'

Brian paused the tape and got up to kiss her. 'She likes Clint Eastwood!' he informed her triumphantly.

'In that picture? Of course she does,' replied Sharon, smiling. 'She's female.' She turned the smile toward me. 'Don't let him show you his gangster pictures, though. He has some horribly gory ones.'

Brian grinned at me. 'Sharon prefers rom-coms.'

'And romances,' she agreed. 'Brian just fidgets through those. Last time we watched *Gone with the Wind* he went out to get a beer during the burning of Atlanta.'

'I didn't think it would have changed much since the first time we watched it together!'

'Huh! You have the soul of a scientist, that's your problem!'

'I thought my problem was being male.'

'That too.' Sharon sat down on the sofa. Brian settled beside her and put an arm around her, and she kissed him.

'You doing OK?' he asked her tenderly.

She nodded, but did not elaborate. 'You have an OK day, Alison?' she asked me.

'Sort of quiet,' I told her. 'I made you a muesli cake for breakfast, but Brian says you don't eat cake.'

She gave me a surprised smile. 'Oh, that's sweet! I'll make an exception. I could do with some cake to cheer me up.'

'We could have some now!' suggested Brian, pleased.

So the three of us sat on the sofa, eating muesli cake and watching *A Fistful of Dollars*. Sharon and Brian sat close together, exchanging comments about the film, holding hands. I wondered if Brian and Mum had ever sat together like that, before I arrived to wreck their marriage. It was an odd thing to think about and made me feel uncomfortable, so of course I poked at the thought until the film ended and we all said goodnight.

Ten

The following morning, Brian again offered to drop me off somewhere. I suggested that I drop *him* off, and borrow the car, but he said he didn't think the insurance would cover it.

'Sharon's did, the other day,' I told him.

'I don't think it can have,' he replied. 'Sharon may have thought so, but she's not used to the differences between English and American insurance practice.'

He didn't offer to rent a car for me again, either. I didn't really fancy any of the local attractions, but, once again, I felt ashamed to harrass him. I accepted a lift to Santa Barbara, and Brian promised to pick me up again at about five.

I was heartily sick of the town by two: sick of the sun, of the heat, of the crowds of tourists, of the way everything I wanted to do cost money. Luckily I came across the public library, and it was well stocked. I spent most of the afternoon in it, reading in air-conditioned quiet.

Brian phoned at about five to say he would be late. I was tired of reading by then, and I fumed. When he eventually turned up, at quarter to six, he got a pretty frosty reception.

'I'm *sorry*!' he said, after one glance at my face. 'It's just it's been another hellish day.'

'You should've postponed this whole enterprise,' I

told him coldly, climbing into the car. 'Right after the break-in, you should have emailed me and said there'd been a disaster, and fixed a date in late August instead.'

'I didn't think you'd come if I postponed it,' he replied. 'You weren't exactly enthusiastic to begin with. Look, I'm *sorry*! I kept thinking I could manage to deliver, but the fact is, I can't.'

'Yeah,' I agreed bitterly.

There was a moment of silence. 'Look,' he said at last. 'Let's go out to dinner. There's a health-food place on Anacapa which should be good for vegetarians.'

Food and a cold lager had a predictable effect on my temper, and Brian and I managed to talk pleasantly enough over the meal, about American and British politics mostly.

When we started back to the house, Brian admitted, 'I have pretty much neglected you the last couple of days. I'm sorry.'

'It's understandable,' I replied, much mollified. 'You're stressed-out and worried about Sharon.'

'Yes,' he agreed. After a moment he added angrily, '*Damn* those pro-lifers!'

It seemed to me that he was heaping rather more blame on the pro-lifers than they actually deserved. Some of his troubles were undoubtedly the result of his own lies, but if he now felt that lying had been a mistake, he hadn't said so. I kept the thought to myself, though. He'd said he was sorry; I shouldn't respond with criticism.

'We'll get away at the weekend,' he said. 'Fly up to San Francisco again, maybe drive up to Napa or Yosemite. We could all do with a break.'

'Doesn't Sharon have to work?'

Brian was silent a moment. Obviously he didn't want to leave Sharon to fend for herself while her health was so uncertain. 'She was planning to take some time off,' he said at last. 'Originally she was going to take all of last week and half of this one. But her boss wasn't really happy about it, and she decided that she would just come and join us for a couple of days at a stretch. After the break-in . . . I think in some ways she was relieved that she didn't need to take time off. I don't know how things stand now. She must *need* a break, and they certainly *owe* her one. I tried to discuss it with her this morning, and she agreed that she would see if she could get away for the weekend. I hope she can.'

I was in bed before Sharon returned that night, more from boredom than because I was sleepy. The following morning, however, Brian informed me happily that Sharon had managed to get the weekend off. He seemed surprised about it, and I suspected that he hadn't expected her to try very hard to get away. Probably there was some history there. I remembered what he'd said about her postponing children in favour of the next step up the career ladder; yeah, I could bet she'd been reluctant to take holidays.

'I'll see if I can get some flights for this afternoon,' Brian went on eagerly. 'And a car. We can drive up toward Napa, stop somewhere en route. It'll give us a couple of days.'

'Napa?' I asked. I would've preferred Yosemite.

'Sharon loves Napa. You'll like it, too – beautiful country, very fine wine.'

I told myself I shouldn't complain. A weekend in the Napa valley was undoubtedly better than one in Slough.

Brian got on the phone about the flight to San Francisco. I remembered the dinner I'd agreed with Roberto, and with a quiver of guilty relief, went to the computer to cancel it. I composed a polite apology and explanation and sent it off, then got out my borrowed phone and sent a brief text message to the same effect. Then I sat a minute, staring at the computer screen. The possibility of emailing Steve again presented itself.

Undignified – yes. But . . . what if he regretted breaking up, but couldn't bring himself to say so? What if we were *both* keeping quiet because we'd have to sacrifice some pride to speak? It was a dangerously seductive thought. I tried to quash it; it was what I wanted to be true, which meant it was probably false.

But it *might* be true. We'd had no contact since our acrimonious split. Probably he was enjoying his freedom, possibly he'd found somebody else, but it *might* be true that he regretted having dumped me.

I should look at this rationally. What did I stand to lose, and what might I gain? I risked making a fool of myself and making Steve cringe a bit, but I might gain . . . well, *Steve*. The love of my life, maybe. I hadn't lived much of my life, so maybe he wasn't – but it felt like that. It felt like that more and more as the days went by.

I bit my lip, cursing myself. Then I clicked on 'New Message' and typed in Steve's email address.

Hi,

I hope it doesn't offend you to have me emailing you. Probably it's a bad idea, but I think I need at least to say that I'm sorry. There were lots of times when I knew I was being smart for the sake of it, and annoying you, or even hurting you, and I went on and did it anyway. I just always thought we could make up, and now it's too late, and I regret it.

I hope you're OK, and that you got that research job. I'm visiting my long-lost father in California and having a very strange time. Brian, my father, badly wants to make things up with me, but it's hard to cancel out a whole life's experience, and he's not as honest as he could be. It's also been really weird. His lab was broken into a couple of days before I arrived – I don't remember if I ever told you he has a medical research company? – and the consequences have dominated everything since I got here. Brian is in the middle of developing a serum to repair genetic damage to skin, and for a while it looked like the prototype serum had been stolen. It would be worth a lot of money, so the police were investigating hard. They arrested one of the people who broke in – it was a pro-life group that did it, because Brian uses stem cells. They let this guy out on bail, though, and he's been sitting up on the hill behind the house watching us through binoculars. He says he wants to find out what really happened to the serum, to clear himself of the suspicion of having stolen it. Yesterday, I was afraid that Brian was going to go up there and confront him and that somebody would get killed, but luckily he'd gone home when Brian got there. Now the missing serum has turned up, not stolen after all, so I hope our pro-lifer has gone away.

Actually, it's all been pretty stressful and there's been nobody to talk to about it, which I suppose is why I'm dumping all this on you. Sorry. I didn't intend to, when I started; it's just I've been thinking of you a lot, and realizing all the things I did wrong. Brian told me that he knows he failed as a father. He says he always thought he'd get a second chance, but then a couple of years ago he realized that he wouldn't. That's why he invited me here: to try to patch up what he got wrong, even though he knows it's too late, because it's that or no fatherhood at all. Maybe that's what I'm doing, too. Probably we'll have lots of other chances at true love, you and I, but there's something in me that says, no, I'll never find someone that good again. Oh, I'll probably fall in love and marry eventually, the way people do, but it'd be settling for second-best. I don't want to. So much of life is a compromise, a choice between greater and lesser evils, a question of making the best of a bad deal. Just occasionally we get a chance at something truly excellent and glorious – and we blow it, mostly, because we don't see it for what it is until it's too late.

I'm sorry. I don't mean to whine at you. It's just that it's been a rough few weeks, and I miss you. Please answer this, if only to tell me, sorry, but it really is over.

I stared at what I'd written, cringing. It was shambolic, it was only marginally coherent, and it was much too honest. I should start again from the beginning . . . only I knew that if I did that, I'd lose my nerve.

I hit 'Send', and then immediately wished I hadn't.

Brian tapped on the door, then came in. 'We can't get a flight this afternoon,' he told me apologetically. 'I just double-checked with Sharon, and she says she has to work this evening. I booked us on one tomorrow morning instead.'

'Oh!' I wondered if I should cancel my cancellation of dinner with Roberto. It seemed like a lot of bother, though, for something I didn't really want to do anyway.

'I . . . could still take today off, if you like,' Brian offered hesitantly. 'We could go down to LA or something.'

This, I hadn't expected, and I was surprised and pleased. 'Yeah, I'd like that!' I said. 'Getty Museum?'

'You're on,' Brian agreed at once.

It was a good day. The Getty Center is on the north side of LA, so it was a manageable drive. We arrived about noon, looked around for an hour or so, ate lunch, and looked around some more, then relaxed by wandering around the gardens. We didn't see more than about a tenth of the collection: the place is huge. What we saw was enough, though, to flood the imagination and over-power the brain in a sea of form and colour, and when we left we were arguing happily about whether modern art was or was not a degeneration from the traditions of the past.

We arrived back at the house at about half past six, having decided not to stop off for supper but to carry on and eat at home. Brian pulled the big car into the drive and out on to the terrace, then stared in surprise at the dusty blue Honda already parked there.

'Isn't that Hernandez's car?' he asked me, as he switched off the engine.

I stared at it, thinking guiltily that I should have phoned and made sure I *spoke* to him, instead of just emailing and texting. 'Uh, yeah, it looks like it,' I agreed. 'He'd asked me out to supper tonight, but I'd emailed him to say I couldn't. I guess he didn't get the message.'

'Oh.' Brian looked at the blue car with distaste. 'So *are* you going to go out with him, or tell him to go away? Where is he, anyway?'

He got out of the car without waiting for an answer; I followed. I supposed that Roberto must have gone round the back of the house to wait for me, but as we approached the front door, it opened, and Roberto himself looked out at us.

It was hard to say who was more surprised. Roberto's jaw dropped; Brian recoiled with a start.

'What are you doing in my house?' demanded Brian, more puzzled than indignant.

'Ah. Ah,' replied Roberto, a look of near panic on his face. 'Ai . . . I came in through the back. Someone broke in.'

'What?'

'Somebody broke in round the back of your house,' said Roberto. 'I-I went in to see what the damage was.' He was breathing hard and sweating.

Brian pushed his way through the door, and Roberto

181

fell back. Brian hurried through the house to the lounge, where, sure enough, someone had cut a neat circle of glass out of the picture window and dismantled the lock.

'That *bastard*!' exclaimed Brian. He stooped to examine the lock, then glared up the hill behind the house. 'That son of a bitch!'

'It was like that when I got here,' said Roberto, blinking. 'But there wasn't anybody here.' After a moment he added, 'Maybe they left when they heard me arrive.'

I felt a sudden, almost visceral, conviction that he was lying. He hadn't expected us to turn up. He'd been shocked; he hadn't known what to say. He'd seized on the idea that 'someone had broken in' with relief. *He* had broken in; he *had* got my message, and had believed that we were safely away for the weekend.

Even as I thought it, I queried it. So Roberto had looked shocked when we turned up. How was he supposed to look, arriving to meet me, and finding nobody at home and the place marked by a recent break-in? Of course he was alarmed! Why should I think he was responsible?

Because I could imagine him breaking in to steal the details of what he'd seen on Brian's computer the other night, that was why. He knew the information was there, he might have glimpsed the password – and he wanted it, badly.

Now that I thought of it, that offer on the pro-life websites was suspicious. It had been posted the day after the lab was broken into – a quick response. Presumably the break-in had featured in some kind of police report, but, given that Brian hadn't published much for years, how many people would've known that he was working on an 'elixir' and that it was near complete? *Maybe* there were foreign pharmaceutical companies which kept track of all the small Californian bio-tech firms, and watched for news on the ones that were most interesting, but it seemed more likely that they'd concentrate their attention on the big boys. The FDA, however, which licensed the research, they'd know who was doing the really hot stuff. They'd probably know, too, which companies would be in the market for secrets. Roberto was, by his own admission, dissatisfied with his job, and had been forced to abandon his plans for a career in research because of shortage of money. He'd been hanging about Brian ever since the break-in, loudly worrying what had happened to the serum and doing his best to track it down.

He'd been hanging around Brian's daughter, too, if it came to that. At the start I'd felt he was interested in me solely because he was interested in Brian, and now that I thought about it, I couldn't see why I'd changed my mind.

I drew in a deep, shocked breath, and Roberto's gaze flew to me warily. Our eyes met, and I was *certain* – and then he looked away again, and I wasn't.

Brian, at any rate, had no doubts: as far as he was concerned, this was the work of Curtis Langford. 'What time did you arrive?' he asked Roberto impatiently.

'Uh . . . about half an hour ago?' said Roberto. 'Maybe twenty minutes? I rang the doorbell, and after no one answered I went round the back, to see if anyone was there. Then I saw this, so I went in to see if there was anything I could do.'

There was nothing incredible in what he said, but I didn't trust it. My heart was beating hard, and I was torn between a furious desire to denounce him – and the fear of the mortifying embarrassment if I'd got it wrong.

'Damn!' Brian grimaced angrily. He glared up the hillside. 'He'll be well away. We'd better phone the police.' He started for the phone, then paused, sweeping the room with his eyes. 'Better check first whether anything's missing.'

The computer from Brian's study, disconnected from its monitor, was sitting in the hall; on the way to the lounge we'd walked right past it without noticing. Brian swore, and at once picked it up and carried it back to his study. He set it down tenderly on the desk, then glanced around the small room. 'Probably the stupid git couldn't have got into it anyway,' he consoled himself. 'But I'm glad he didn't have the opportunity to try. That *bastard!* The police just *left* him there!'

'You don't know that it was Langford,' I pointed out.

Brian turned on me, his face flushing. 'What *is* this with Langford? Why do you keep defending him?'

'I'm not defending him!' I protested. 'I just don't think there's any reason to keep blaming him for things he didn't do!'

'Of *course* it was Langford!' Brian was almost shouting. 'The son of a bitch has been sitting up there, spying on us, *waiting* for a time when nobody was home. You want to believe that we just *coincidentally* get burgled when we go out for the day? He had a buyer for the serum. Look at the way he went for the computer!'

'Who's Langford?' asked Roberto confusedly.

'The pro-lifer who broke into my lab,' replied Brian. 'He's been sitting up on the hillside spying on us. I phoned the police about it, but they said that as long as he isn't trespassing, he isn't breaking the law, and I'd have to apply for an injunction. This is what we pay taxes for! Alison, go check that we've still got the serum!'

Roberto stared in consternation. 'The serum?'

'We found it,' Brian said shortly. 'The police know, which is why they've ceased to give a damn about us. Alison, go on! I'm going to phone that bastard Kermode.'

He picked up the phone in his study, then set it down, dug out his wallet, and began searching through the cards in it, presumably for something with the relevant police phone number. He glanced up and waved me impatiently out toward the kitchen, so I went, unhappily.

Roberto followed me. I gave him a hard look, but he wouldn't directly meet my eyes.

'You found the serum?' he asked.

'Yeah,' I admitted, not knowing what else to say. 'It was just mislaid.'

'What, it's here? In that freezer?' He stared at the fridge in amazement.

'Yeah. Just for now.'

He made a move toward it, then checked himself. 'Your father said to check that it's still there,' he reminded me.

I didn't move. 'What were you doing here?'

He hesitated. 'I came to see you. We agreed to go out to dinner, remember?'

'I cancelled.'

'Oh? When? I've been out of my office since yesterday afternoon and I haven't checked my email.'

'I sent a text as well.'

'Oh. Well, I forgot my phone. I left it in the charger.'

'That *is* a coincidence, isn't it!'

'What are you implying?' he demanded, his voice edged with what might have been either anger or hysteria.

'I just think it's a bit strange,' I said in a low voice. 'When I cancelled, we hadn't fixed a time or a place to meet, but you didn't try to get in touch about it. When Brian and I turned up, you didn't ask where we'd been or why I wasn't here.'

There was a moment's silence. His face was flushed and sweating. I felt a surge of triumph: I'd caught him.

'We'd said dinner,' he replied, just a bit too late. 'I assumed I'd pick you up here. And I would've phoned, but, like I said, I left my phone on the charger. And, and you'd been *burgled*! How could you expect me to ignore that?'

Oh, he made perfect sense – except he'd been much too worried, and just that bit too slow, and he'd given me too much detail. If he'd really been innocent, he would've come back at me with indignation rather than carefully set out his excuse for each individual point I'd raised – or so it seemed to me, anyway.

'I don't believe you,' I told him flatly, in a low voice. 'I'm going to ask the police to check whose fingerprints are on the lock and the computer.'

In retrospect, it was an incredibly stupid thing to say – a *criminally* stupid thing. Brian and I had turned up unexpectedly and caught Roberto in the very act of stealing the computer. All his excuses had been spun in a desperate attempt to ward off exposure. For me to push him was equivalent to trying to grab that rattlesnake.

Roberto lashed out abruptly, backhanded me across the face and sent me staggering back against the kitchen counter. When I picked my head up, I saw that he'd taken a gun out of his pocket.

I put my hands up, seeing with terrified clarity just how stupid I'd been. Roberto caught my wrist, pointed the gun at my head, and dragged me back into Brian's study. 'Put the phone down,' he ordered Brian.

Brian, phone to ear, stared stupidly.

'Put it down!' ordered Roberto. 'Put it down, or she gets it!'

Brian set the phone down. 'I don't . . .' he began.

'Shut up!' Roberto dragged me a couple of steps nearer, picked up the phone, and checked that it was off. 'Had you phoned the police?' he demanded. 'Did you get through?'

'They put me on hold,' Brian replied numbly. 'What is . . .'

'It's him,' I told Brian wretchedly. 'It wasn't Langford, it was him.'

Brian's stunned expression gave way slowly to understanding. 'Shit,' he whispered.

Roberto's hand on my wrist was trembling. I thought about pulling away from him and trying to snatch the gun. I didn't think he'd actually shoot – he'd always been so polite, so *friendly*! And yet I wasn't quite sure, and the gun might go off even if he didn't deliberately pull the trigger. He was scared, and I was somehow certain that his gun, unlike Langford's, was loaded.

'Look,' I said instead, unsteadily, 'where is this going to go? You don't want to shoot us. You can't hold us here.'

'Shut up!' Roberto commanded.

'But, look, you're only making it worse! You haven't actually *done* anything yet. If you . . .'

He shook me so hard my teeth rattled. 'I said shut up!'

'Let her go!' said Brian. He was pale and breathless. 'Please, let her go!'

'You shut up, too!' Roberto stood still a moment, breathing hard. Then he tugged at my arm and began to back out of the study. 'Get up!' he ordered Brian. 'And put your hands on top of your head.'

Brian obediently got to his feet and linked his hands behind his head.

'Now,' Roberto said grimly, 'where's the basement?'

'There isn't one,' replied Brian. The gun wavered toward him briefly and he said, desperately, 'The house doesn't have a basement! It's all on one level! What is it you want? Somewhere to lock us up?'

'Yes,' said Roberto, staring at him wildly.

'The broom cupboard has a bolt on the outside of the door,' Brian said. 'It's the only room in the house you can lock from the outside.'

'Where is it?'

It was off the entrance hall, next to the kitchen. Roberto marched us there, then watched as Brian carefully removed a vacuum cleaner and a laundry basket to make space in it. He jerked the gun to indicate that we were both to go in.

We had to squash against one another uncomfortably to fit. About the only thing that could be said for the cupboard was that it wasn't under the stairs, like Mum's, so we could stand upright. Roberto began to close the door, then flung it open again and demanded our mobile phones. Brian had to edge out into the hall to dig his out of his pocket, but he did so.

'Mine's in my handbag,' I told Roberto.

It was the truth, but he gave me a stare that made me flinch, his eyes white-ringed behind the specs, the pupils shrunken with hysteria.

'I put it down when I came in!' I protested desperately. 'In, in the lounge, I think. It's a black canvas bag, and the phone's in a pocket on the outside!'

Roberto jerked the gun to make Brian get into the cupboard, then closed and bolted the door. He marched me into the lounge, where my bag had indeed been tossed on to the sofa. I picked it up and showed him the phone.

'Put your hands above your head, then!' Roberto ordered.

I did as he said.

'Now, turn around – slowly!'

I obeyed. I don't know if he was looking for a second phone or a concealed weapon, but of course I had nothing so useful.

'All right.' Roberto drew a deep breath. 'All right, you can join your father.'

We marched back into the hall. Brian flinched when the door opened, then looked relieved. I edged in next to him, the door shut, and the bolt scraped home. The darkness wasn't total: a little light seeped in around the edges of the door. It wasn't enough to see by, but it at least gave the darkness some shape. It was hot, though, and the air was thick, smelling of furniture polish and dust. Brian's elbow was digging into my ribs, and a shelf pressed painfully against the small of my back. I wriggled forward a little.

'I'm sorry,' Brian whispered. 'I should have . . . when we saw him, I should have realized. I shouldn't have been so fixated on Langford.'

'I shouldn't have pushed at him,' I admitted miserably. 'If I'd just kept my mouth shut . . .'

There was a thump, and the sound of the house door opening.

'He's taking the computer,' guessed Brian. I could feel him tense.

I reckoned we could force the door if we had to: the bolt hadn't looked to be very strong. Remembering Roberto's white-rimmed eyes, I didn't feel inclined to try it immediately, though.

'If we try to stop him, he might shoot,' I whispered urgently. 'If we just let him leave, there's a good chance the police will get him.'

'Yes,' agreed Brian. He did not relax, though; the muscles pressing against mine were rigid with tension. He listened for the sounds of a thief driving off with his life's work.

There was the sound of a car door closing, but no sound of an engine. Brian twisted awkwardly. I realized that he was putting his ear against the door, so I crouched a little and copied him. The door of the house closed again, and then footsteps went past us into the kitchen. I could hear someone moving about, and then the scrape of things being moved out of the freezer. The serum, of course. There was every reason to think Roberto knew of a buyer for it; now he knew it was here, safely frozen, naturally he'd take it.

There was a series of thumps and rattles I couldn't iden-tify. 'Ice,' Brian whispered. 'I think he's getting ice to pack round it.'

Footsteps, and the door opening again. Then the car door again, opening, closing – but still no engine. Once more the house door closed, and the footsteps came back past the cupboard where we were trapped.

'Now what?' I asked, sick-scared.

'I don't know,' Brian admitted. 'Maybe he's searching for the encryption key.'

I hadn't even focussed on the fact that his data was encrypted as well as password-protected. 'Is it in the house?' I asked.

'Not in a form he could use,' replied Brian. 'I do have something written down, but I very much doubt he'd know what it was, even if he found it.'

'So he can't get at the data even if he has the computer?'

'Shouldn't think so. His buyer might be able to decrypt it, though, if he gets it to them. It was a pretty basic encryption program.'

'Oh.' I wondered what Roberto planned to do. Sell the computer and the serum in a hurry, and then move to South America with the proceeds? It seemed a fairly drastic solution to the problem of what to do if caught red-handed stealing scientific secrets. It meant sacrificing his career hopes as well as his home and family. Even if he got a good price for Brian's secrets, even if he had relatives in South America, even if he expected to come back, eventually, with a different name – it still seemed worse, really, than just enduring a conviction for attempted burglary. A first offence was unlikely to carry a severe penalty, after all. There was a substantial risk, too, that he'd get caught before he was able to sell the computer. He was an intelligent man: he must be able to see that as soon as Brian and I raised the alarm, his buyer would vanish.

The thumps from elsewhere in the house had stopped. There was a long silence. Brian's arm, pressed against mine, was damp with sweat, and I could hear the rush of blood in my ears.

Then the footsteps came back. They stopped. The bolt rasped back, and the door opened slowly. Roberto took a step back, then another, levelling the gun at us. His face was pale, and he looked at us as though he were in pain.

Brian stared at the gun in his hand. He frowned. 'That's *my* gun,' he said.

Roberto only nodded. I understood, finally, that the real solution to his problem was to murder the witnesses. If the police found two bodies, shot with the gun which had been in the house, their first assumption would be that it had been a domestic murder. Once they noticed that the serum and the computer were missing, they might blame Curtis Langford – but why should they suspect the helpful Roberto Hernandez? As far as they were concerned, there was no reason to believe he'd been here at all.

Eleven

I panicked. It was terror, not thought, that sent me leaping toward Roberto, screaming at the top of my lungs. Perhaps that was why I survived: Roberto had expected us to be thinking too hard to actually *do* anything. He was an intellectual himself, not an impulsive criminal; he'd been having to work himself up to the deed, perhaps reminding himself of the consequences if he failed. He'd found the gun in my father's room, and must have stood there for a couple of minutes, holding it, nerving himself. Everything had been very quiet when he opened the door of the broom cupboard. The explosion of animal violence took him by surprise.

I crashed into him, clawing at his face with one hand, trying to hit the gun with the other. He instinctively brought his hands up. The gun went off with a deafening *bang*, and something stung my shoulder. Roberto grabbed my hands, and for a moment we wrestled, face to face. I'd knocked his specs off, and the marks of my fingernails were red across his cheek. He still had the gun in his right hand, and I twisted my fingers in his grasp, trying to grab it. It went off again, this time firing straight up. Brian was suddenly beside me, also trying to seize the gun. Roberto bellowed and shoved me backwards with a convulsive thrust; I tripped over the vacuum cleaner and sat down gracelessly on the hard tiles of the floor. Brian was still clinging to Roberto's gun-hand, clinging with both hands, trying to prise those clutching fingers loose; Roberto wildly tried to shake him off. I kicked frantically at Roberto's legs and he staggered. The gun went off again, this time striking splinters from the floor tiles. Roberto hacked at Brian with his free hand, hit him in the chest, then in the face. Brian made a wheezing sound and lost his grip on the gun just as I succeeded in getting back to my feet.

Roberto staggered back three paces and pointed the gun at me.

'No!' Brian exclaimed, and stepped between us, just as the gun went off.

I screamed and caught Brian as the impact threw him into my arms, then staggered to my knees under his weight. Part of me was aware of Roberto standing over us, gun in hand, gaping – but he seemed all at once unimportant, a person in a city I'd visited once, nothing to do with the present. Brian looked up at me, his eyes wide and astonished. He opened his mouth, but no sound came out.

'Brian,' I said, and then, for the first time, 'Dad!'

He caught my hand.

'Drop it!' ordered a new voice.

I looked up, away from my father's face, and saw Curtis Langford standing in the entrance to the lounge, his gun pointed firmly at Roberto. Roberto gaped at him. I looked away, back at my father. I tried to see where the bullet had hit him. There was no crimson blotch of the Hollywood variety, only a small red flower, black-centered, in the middle of his chest. My heart rose. Surely a little thing like that wouldn't kill him? He seemed, though, to be having trouble breathing.

'I said, drop it, you faggot!' Langford repeated. Without waiting for Roberto to obey, he strode forward, eyes full of cold menace.

Roberto dropped the gun. Langford hit him across the face, then stooped and picked up the weapon. Roberto made no attempt to strike back, merely stood bent, hands to his nose.

'You better phone 911,' Langford advised me, with satisfaction. 'I'll take care of this asshole.'

I nodded, worked my hand out of Brian's grasp, then patted his shoulder. 'I'm going to phone an ambulance,' I told him, my voice choked and unfamiliar. 'Hang on.'

About ten minutes later we heard the sirens screaming closer and closer up the road and finally halting, nerve-janglingly loud, on the terrace. I went to the door and found myself facing two guns while a police car flashed lights madly in my eyes.

'Where's the ambulance?' I demanded.

The two officers looked alarmed. 'Didn't you phone about an armed robbery?' asked one.

'Yeah, for an *ambulance*!' I shouted. I'd been sitting with Brian, holding his hand and trying to make him comfortable while he struggled to breathe. I'd been trying to stay calm, but the appearance of more guns instead of paramedics with oxygen had me on the edge of hysterical tears. 'My father's been *shot,* he doesn't need your fucking guns, he needs an ambulance!' I flung the door open.

The police came in quietly, and stared concernedly at Brian, who was still sitting on the floor of the hall, since he wasn't able to stand and I hadn't wanted to move him. I'd fetched cushions from the lounge; I'd wanted him to lie down on them, but he'd indicated that it was easier to breathe if he sat up. He was sitting now, wedged upright against the wall, his head back. His eyes seemed to focus for a moment on the police, then his attention returned inward, to his own silent struggle for life. I sat down next to him and put an arm around his shoulders to help keep him from slumping over, and he caught my hand again. There was more blood on his chest now, seeping down the front of his shirt, and his lips and nostrils were flecked with red. He was breathing in quick, shallow, painful gasps. One of the policemen began muttering into his radio about casualties, and I caught the helpful word, 'ambulance'.

'In here!' called Langford triumphantly, from the lounge. 'I've got the perpetrator!'

He'd tied Roberto's hands with the flex from the table lamp, and had him sitting on the floor. Roberto had said nothing since Langford's arrival, and when the police came in he looked up at them quickly, with relief. The police began asking Langford what had happened. I listened with half my attention. Langford's story was rambling, excited, and only marginally coherent: he'd seen Roberto arrive, noticed him breaking in; the police had to understand, he, Curtis Langford, had been watching this house for days, because that bastard Kermode had tried to shaft him over the theft of a wonder drug from Brian's lab, he'd known all along that somebody else had set him up, but Kermode wouldn't listen, he had Kermode's number somewhere . . . anyway, he'd come down the hill, and he'd heard the shots, and . . .

The ambulance finally arrived and I stopped listening.

I went in the ambulance with Brian as it rushed him to hospital. The paramedics gave him oxygen and painkillers and debated an emergency operation 'to clear the lungs'. They decided to wait until they reached the hospital, and to rush him into surgery there. They asked me about his health insurance policy, and I had to admit that I didn't know anything more about it than the fact of its existence. I told them to phone Sharon, which they did.

One of the paramedics asked to look at my shoulder. It had been grazed by Roberto's first bullet, but until he mentioned it, I hadn't noticed. I'd been aware that my left hand was sticky with blood, but I'd thought it was Brian's. Now I found there was a long painful streak on my left shoulder, gluing my T-shirt to the skin. The paramedic cleaned it and taped on a large wodge of bandage. He told me I should get it looked at again, it would probably need a couple of stitches. I nodded distractedly and held Brian's hand.

When we arrived at the hospital it was like a scene from *Casualty*: the ambulance pulled up, siren howling and lights flashing; the paramedics rushed the stretcher straight on to the waiting trolley, and the trolley clattered madly along the corridors. Brian, his face half-hidden by the oxygen mask, held my hand the whole time. His grasp was weak and dry against my sweating palm.

We arrived in a pre-op room where the surgeons were suiting up. An anaesthetist appeared and asked me if Brian was allergic to something-or-other; I said I didn't know. The anaesthetist checked some records on a computer, then came back, readying the syringe.

I kept tight hold of my father's hand while they gave him the anaesthetic. His eyes, above the oxygen mask, held mine with a look of desperate urgency, until the drug took hold and they closed. When the medics began to take the trolley into the operating theatre, I tried to follow, still holding Brian's now-limp hand. A nurse had to tell me to let go. Gently she directed me to a room where I could wait.

The waiting room was nightmarishly ordinary: a green-carpeted lounge with deep leather chairs and some side-tables piled with magazines. A television mounted on the wall was blatting away, showing imbecilic ads for cars and fast food. A middle-aged couple sat opposite it, watching with blank faces; another woman was curled up in a corner staring at nothing.

I sat down slowly, taking a seat directly underneath the television so that I wouldn't have to look at it. I felt as though my whole existence were a bubble that was stretched thin and fading, about to burst in the dry air. The woman of the couple stopped looking at the television and stared at my left arm, and I glanced down and saw that it was still covered with blood, now dry and beginning to flake. I looked away from her.

'What happened to you?' asked the woman, awed.

'My father was shot,' I told her. 'They're operating now.'

'God!' she exclaimed.

Above my head, the television began to advertize Coca-Cola. I couldn't bear it, and I covered my face with my bloodstained hands. If the woman said anything else, I missed it.

Sharon arrived a few minutes later. When she saw me she ran over and grabbed me by the arms. 'What happened?' she shrieked. 'They said Brian's been *shot*! Where is he? What happened?'

I burst into tears. Sharon shook me violently. 'What happened?'

'They're operating,' I managed to say. 'It was Roberto Hernandez. We got back . . .' Everything seemed to dissolve, and all I could see was Brian crying 'No!' and stepping between me and the bullet. Words lost all meaning: the universe became a jumble of fragments, which no logic of cause or sequence could piece together. I turned away from Sharon, curled my head into the chair, and wept.

Sharon shook herself loose and went to question the hospital staff. It took a while – I think they asked her all the questions about insurance and medical history which I hadn't been able to answer – but after a bit she came and sat down next to me. The television was still blatting, and I was still trying to stop crying. Sharon wasn't crying. She was very, very quiet.

A little while later a police interviewer turned up, asking for me. 'I'm sorry to trouble you at a bad time,' he said smoothly, 'but there are just a couple of points we need to clear up at once.' I gulped and nodded, and he handed me a tissue to blow my nose.

He did at least show me into a different room for it, one mercifully without a television. Sharon came along to listen. Her fresh, youthful face was like a mask, and her eyes stared out from behind it, old and full of terror.

The room was some sort of office, and there weren't enough chairs for all of us. The police interviewer fussed around, sending someone out to fetch a folding chair, asking us if we wanted coffee, then getting his assistant to fetch cups of water before finally getting down to business. I don't think I made much sense at first, but as the questions proceeded – patient, reasonable, methodical – I managed to get control of myself. It was a dialectic, giving meaning to the jumble of experience: this had happened, and then that; people had acted, and others had reacted to them. Gradually I began to give more-or-less coherent answers, and the sense of being adrift in pure chaos receded.

The interviewer was particularly concerned about Curtis Langford. It was obvious that the police were inclined to view him as a perpetrator rather than a rescuer. I repeatedly had to tell him that no, Langford had not been present at the house when Brian and I arrived there, that he had only appeared after the shooting started. Yes, I'd known he was watching the house. I'd met him up on the hiking trail, I said, and I'd told Brian, and Brian had telephoned to complain about it. Langford, though, I said again, had not been involved in the shooting; in fact he'd appeared just in time to prevent Roberto Hernandez from killing us both. Roberto Hernandez, I insisted, was the guilty party. We'd interrupted him in the middle of a burglary; he probably still had Brian's computer and the serum in his car.

We were still in the middle of this when one of the surgeons came to the door and stood there a moment, his green surgical mask dangling from one pale hand. There was blood on his sleeve. 'Mrs Greenall?' he said.

We all turned toward him, the messenger who had come to bring us news of life and death.

'I'm Sharon Greenall,' Sharon told him, her voice low and hoarse.

'Mrs Greenall,' the surgeon repeated. He took a deep breath and came into the room, and the police interviewer got to his feet and offered him his chair. 'We can finish this later,' the policeman murmured, closing his notebook and switching off the cassette recorder.

'Mrs Greenall,' said the surgeon for the third time – and, with a glance at me, 'Miss Greenall? I am very sorry to have to tell you that Dr Greenall has just passed away on the operating table.'

Afterwards I wondered at how quietly we received this news. I was too exhausted to have another fit of hysterics, and all I wanted was to curl up and be miserable. Sharon simply sat with a frozen face, her hands clutching one another in her lap, and asked for the medical details.

It seemed that the bullet had gone through Brian's right lung and lodged in a rib. A branch of the pulmonary vein had been severed, causing heavy internal bleeding. His thoracic cavity had filled with blood, compressing his lungs. He'd arrived at the hospital, however, before he'd actually drowned in his own blood, but the shock and the blood loss had stressed his heart and starved the muscles of oxygen. When the surgeons operated to drain his lung and stitch the vein, his heart stopped. They'd tried to start it again, but hadn't been able to. They were extremely sorry for our tragic loss.

Sharon asked to see the body. I wasn't sure I wanted to, but I followed when the surgeon led her along more hospital corridors. They hadn't moved him down to the morgue yet: he was still on the operating table, a blood-stained sheet over his face. A nurse was cleaning the room when we came in.

Sharon pulled back the sheet and looked at her husband's face. The blood around his mouth and nose was still there, but otherwise he looked peaceful. Sharon stroked his cheek and smoothed back the graying hair. She traced the curve of his ear, his chin; she took his hand in both of hers and bent to kiss him. Then she began, silently, to cry.

The police claimed me again for about another hour after that. I had to finish telling them what happened, and then they sent a policewoman with me to get another doctor to look at the graze on my shoulder. It was Evidence now, and they were annoyed with the paramedics in the ambulance who'd cleaned it. The policewoman even took a picture of it, which was a bit surreal.

Sharon, who'd stayed with the body for a bit, turned up while they were doing this. When the doctor started fixing the cut up again with surgical tape, she picked up my T-shirt, then dropped it hurriedly. It was the PETA shirt I'd worn on the flight over, and the 'Wear Your Own Damned Fur' slogan was now thickly splashed with crusted blood.

'It's mine,' I told her. 'Not Brian's.' Then I looked down at the horrid thing and had doubts. The gore on the left was certainly mine, but there were smears on the right and the hem as well. I remembered holding Brian upright while he struggled to breath, and my skin crawled. 'Maybe some of it is Brian's,' I admitted. I knew suddenly that I couldn't touch that shirt again, let alone put it on.

'You can't put it back on,' Sharon said in horror. She turned to the policewoman who'd photographed the graze. 'Get her something else to wear!' she ordered angrily. 'She can't put that back on!'

The policewoman didn't argue. She went away and came back with a blue T-shirt emblazoned with 'Santa

Barbara Police Department' on the chest, and I eased it on over my bandages.

The police suggested that we stay the night in a hotel, telling us that they needed to examine 'the murder scene' and that it would be easier for everyone if we let them finish doing so before we went back to the house. Sharon accepted the suggestion. It was late by then, nearly midnight, and we were both in shock. The hospital gave us sedatives. Sharon said very little else, except to correct a nurse who referred to me as her daughter.

The police booked the hotel for us. It was a plain, clean place only a few blocks from the hospital. I slept very soundly, thanks to the sedative, but woke disoriented and confused by the strange room. When I remembered where I was, I felt a stab of intense homesickness. I longed to be back in my own bed in my own messy, book-piled room, and to hear my mother clattering about downstairs in the kitchen. I wished I'd never come to California, and that the last few weeks had never happened. I felt sick and stiff; my shoulder was horribly sore, my head ached and my eyes felt sandpapered. I had no idea how I would get through the day.

I picked my head up and saw Sharon lying in the twin bed next to me. Her eyes were wide open and she was staring at the ceiling.

Guilt twisted my stomach so hard I thought I would be sick. Again I saw Brian stepping in front of the bullet.

'I'm sorry,' I told her quietly.

She looked over at me, slowly, as though it required a great effort to move her head.

'I . . . I shouldn't have pushed Roberto Hernandez,' I confessed wretchedly. I don't know why I couldn't name my real crime. 'I shouldn't have let him know I suspected him. If I'd let him go on thinking Langford was going to get the blame for the break-in, Brian would still be alive.'

'Oh.' Sharon wrinkled her nose as though she hadn't thought about this, and that now she had, she didn't like the smell of it. 'Don't worry about it,' she said at last. 'There are a lot of things that could've made a difference. Brian could've phoned 911 instead of trying to get hold of Detective Kermode – or he could've got *through*, instead of being put on hold. Your friend Langford could've come in sooner, or the bullet could've been half an inch to the side, or the ambulance might've been faster, or the medical team just a bit more sensitive to the dangers. For that matter, you and Brian could've stopped for supper on the way back from LA, and missed the whole thing. You have to leave the "might-have-beens" alone, or they'll drive you crazy.' Her voice hardened. 'Brian died because Roberto Hernandez shot him. It was deliberate, premeditated murder. Obviously, when you pushed the bastard you didn't believe he'd be willing to do that. *I* wouldn't have believed it, and *I* never liked him.'

'You always knew better than to trust him,' I ventured.

'I know his type,' she replied. 'Manipulative sons of bitches who think they know it all and are entitled to whatever they want.' She sighed. 'I was dumb at your age, though. I fell for a couple of them myself.'

There was a silence. My real guilt continued to press against my heart. 'I'm sorry,' I managed at last, in a small voice. 'I'm sorry I . . .' I swallowed. 'I'm sorry Brian died instead of me.'

She looked at me for a long minute. Then she sat up and ran her hands through her tangled hair. '*He* wouldn't be,' she said, wearily but with great certainty. 'It would've been worse for him the other way round. Much worse.' She met my eyes again. 'Alison, you were his future: if you'd died and he'd lived, he'd have felt he was just waiting to be buried.' She pulled her hair back and sat there a moment, resting her hands on the back of her head. 'I've been thinking a lot since . . . since Brian told me about that serum. You know the Buddhist story, about the Prince Siddhartha when he was young? His father wanted to protect him, so he didn't allow him to meet anyone who was old or sick. He gave him a fantasy palace to live in, where everything was beautiful and everyone was young and healthy, and nobody ever died. But one day the prince rode out from that palace, and he saw a diseased cripple, and an old man, and a corpse waiting for burial, and he realized that he'd been living in a stupid fairytale. So he set out to look for enlightenment.

'I've been thinking how modern Western culture, maybe particularly in California, is that fantasy palace. We sweep age and disease and death out of sight and pretend it only happens because somebody's been careless – and that it will never happen to us. It will, though. We can deny it all we like, and we can use creams and dyes and plastic surgery and magical anti-aging serums, but it'll still get us in the end. We'll still get old, and we'll all still die. Brian went sooner, God knows, much sooner than he should have, but what really matters is, he had a *life* first. He had people he loved who loved him, and he did work that had real value, and he died knowing he'd saved his daughter's life. There are *lots* of people who don't have it that good.'

I said nothing. My sore eyes started to sting again, and I mopped them with the bedsheet.

'At least I had ten good years with him,' Sharon added at last. 'You never really got to know him at all, did you?'

'No,' I admitted thickly.

'One of the nurses said you held his hand, though, right up until they took him into the theatre. I envy you that, but I'm glad somebody was there for him.'

I gave up, hauled the bedspread around my good shoulder, and went to the bathroom to find a tissue.

When I came back into the room, Sharon was on her

feet, tall and dignified, sombre even in her underclothes. She'd slept in her shirt, which was now badly crumpled, but her cotton skirt was draped neatly over the back of a chair. She stepped into it and pulled it on, then looked at me in my bedspread. 'You have to get dressed,' she said gently. 'The only way to get through it is to go on.'

The police arrived during breakfast, wanting to talk to me some more. Sharon excused herself and went off to begin arrangements for the funeral. I went to the police station to give a formal statement.

Detective Kermode met me at the station, looking rumpled and weary and also, disquietingly, angry. I realized soon after we started that I had a dilemma: should I lie, or tell the truth? Kermode wanted to know about the serum: when it had turned up, where it had turned up, and whether Roberto had known it was in the house. He also wanted to know what Roberto had expected to find on the computer. The answers incriminated Sharon and exposed Brian.

I told the truth anyway. In part it was because I was worried about what Roberto might have been saying: *he* had no reason to suppress the truth. In part I was simply too tired to try to lie my way round the difficulty. I told Kermode all about Brian's suppression of the serum's problems, Roberto's tacit blackmail, and Sharon's theft and abuse of the wonder drug. I admitted that she'd misled the police, but I begged Kermode not to charge her with anything because of it. Kermode listened to me with a disturbed expression.

When I finished, his first question was, 'Is she all right? Has this stuff hurt her?'

I liked him much better for that. 'So far she's OK,' I replied. 'Brian took her straight to her doctor, and she's supposed to get check-ups once a week.'

Kermode let out his breath through his nose and shook his head. 'Jesus!' he muttered. 'The world just gets weirder all the time.' He checked a notepad, then looked up at me again and asked, 'What about Curtis Langford?'

'What about him?' I asked. 'He saved my life yesterday.'

Kermode gave me a stiff look. 'What was your relationship with him?'

'What do you mean?' I asked warily. I thought he must've found out that I'd met Langford a couple more times than I'd mentioned.

Kermode sighed resignedly. 'Were you *romantically involved* with Curtis Langford?'

'Good God, no! *Yuck!*' The detective looked surprised and sceptical, so I went on, 'He's a foul-tempered, ignorant *yob*. He put his last girlfriend into hospital, you told me so yourself! I wouldn't touch him with a barge pole!'

This seemed to please him. 'Langford's fingerprints are on the computer,' he said. 'Can you explain that?'

I hesitated – then, again, told the truth. I told him about every one of my meetings with Langford. 'I didn't . . . want to make a big deal of it,' I finished. 'At first it was because I just didn't want the hassle, and then it was because I . . . I felt bad.' I realized that I was going to strike another blow against my father's reputation, but I couldn't help it. I was committed now to the truth. 'Brian was blaming him for things he hadn't done, things that would've come up in court, and affected his sentence. He let Langford take the blame for destroying all the skin cultures and the lab records, when really he must've wrecked them himself to hide the evidence that there were problems with the serum, and he exaggerated the damage to the lab so he could claim more off the insurance. And . . . and Langford didn't really do any harm. The one time he came down to the house, he *didn't* hurt me. He scared me, and I didn't want him coming back, but still, what I

205

said before was all perfectly true: he didn't hurt me and he did go away when I asked – in the end, anyway. He said the gun he had wasn't even loaded.'

Kermode nodded. 'It wasn't loaded yesterday, either,' he told me quietly. 'Apparently he's afraid of his own temper, so he never takes a loaded gun into a situation where he might be tempted to use it. He charged in to rescue you from an armed murderer with an empty gun.' He looked at me thoughtfully. 'Your considered opinion of him is *yuck,* is it, Miss Greenall?'

I could feel my face heating.

'He'll be disappointed,' said Kermode. '*He* thinks he's going to get the girl, now that he's rescued her.'

My face went hotter. 'Look, I . . . I'm sorry about the "yuck" comment. Obviously there's more to him than that. But still, I don't want anything to do with a man who beats up his girlfriends.'

'Good attitude,' said Kermode, with satisfaction. 'Wish more girls felt like that. It would make a lot less work for us.'

Looking more cheerful now, he went over my statement with me, and I clarified a couple of points and signed it.

'Thank you, Miss Greenall,' said Kermode, putting it in a file. He closed the file and rested his hands on it. 'I have to warn you: Roberto Hernandez is claiming that Langford shot your father. He says that you are romantically involved with Mr Langford, and are lying to protect him.'

My jaw dropped. 'That's . . . that's *outrageous*! How can he . . .'

Kermode raised a hand for me to stop. 'I think he'll change his story before he goes to court. We got some good evidence, stuff he'd have a lot of trouble explaining away. We got swabs off his hands when we arrested him: we can prove he fired a gun and Langford didn't, and we got his phone and his computer records—'

'He put the serum and the computer in his *car!*' I interrupted furiously. 'How does he explain *that*?'

'He says your father loaned them to him to look at over the weekend,' Kermode replied evenly. 'Now, I think his defense lawyer will advise him to change his story. The version he's trying now would never stand up in court. Still, it's pretty clear that you are going to be the key witness for the prosecution and that Hernandez and his defence are going to try to discredit you. You need to be prepared for that.'

'He's a *liar*! A foul, self-serving slimy *murdering* liar!'

'Yeah,' agreed Kermode. 'So you're going to have to expect him to tell lies. I think you're going to be a good witness, Miss Greenall, a real star, and I think any jury that listens to you will know who to believe. I'm relieved to hear that there's nothing between you and Mr Langford, though; that makes things much clearer.'

'Oh,' I said weakly. I hadn't thought about a trial. I suppose I'd vaguely assumed that there would be one, but the prospect had been remote, and if I'd thought of it at all it was as a formality: justice would be done. Now I could see that it would be a bitter ordeal that would dominate my whole life for . . . how long? Months? Years?

Another horrible thought struck me: did California have the death penalty? I was opposed to the death penalty, even for Roberto Hernandez. Though a life sentence in a California prison would probably be *worse* . . .

This was going to be unspeakable. I'd woken up not knowing how I could get through the day – and today was only the beginning.

'I gather you're only over here from England for a visit,' Kermode continued. 'When are you due to go back?'

'Wednesday,' I said faintly. 'My flight's on Wednesday.'

I suddenly remembered that Brian had booked us flights to San Francisco on Saturday morning . . . this very morning. It seemed somehow a monstrous impossibility that he could be booking a holiday one day, and lying in a hospital morgue the next. I remembered some Bible story, about a man who was planning what to do with his bumper harvest: 'And God said to him, you fool, this very night your life will be demanded from you. Then whose will these things be?'

'In the midst of life, we are in death': old words, but suddenly they felt meaningful and terrifying. The whole world became a soap bubble, one that could burst without warning. Sharon had claimed that Brian's life was meaningful, because he had loved and been loved, because his work had value, because he had died saving me. What meaning would *my* life have?

Kermode was still talking, telling me that it would be better if I didn't go home Wednesday, that I ought to stay at least another week, and meet with the prosecutor. He added that then I could go home, and they would fly me back to Santa Barbara for the trial.

'When will that be?' I asked weakly.

Kermode shook his head. 'Look, we haven't formally *charged* the guy yet; no way do we have a date for the trial! Sometime early next year, I hope.' He looked at my face, then got up and came round his desk. 'Here,' he said. 'You can sit quietly in the staff room for a bit. I'll have somebody fetch you some coffee.'

Twelve

Sharon met me at the police station in the middle of the afternoon. She'd apparently been there a couple of hours before I saw her, giving her own statement to the police.

When we met she gave me a look of weary fellow-feeling. My conscience struck me, and my face went red. I almost blurted out that I'd told the police all about how she'd stolen the serum, but I was ashamed to. Besides, I didn't want to have a confrontation in the police station.

We went out to her red sports car, and she drove back to the house. The police had finished there now, but the entrance hall was still littered with dust and tapes from their investigation, and there was a guard posted on the drive. We made some sandwiches in the kitchen – neither of us had had any lunch – and took them out on to the deck.

The mountain hadn't changed: it stood gray-green, dry, fragrant of sagebrush and juniper and dust. The swimming pool shimmered blue beside the dry-country garden, and a bird sang in the bushes. Everything was as perfect and beautiful as ever, unconcerned with the breaking of hearts, and hence a balm to them.

'The police said I should stay here another week,' I told Sharon.

She looked surprised and pleased. 'That would be good.'

That hurt. I'd got Brian killed, then blackened his name and told on her to the police, and she still wanted me in the house? I bit my lip. 'Don't you . . . I thought maybe you'd want to go stay with your family.'

'Maybe in a little while,' said Sharon. 'Not . . . quite yet.' She sighed. 'My mother's eighty. She thought I was finally settled: she's not going to handle this very well. I can barely face *phoning* her with such bad news, and staying with her would be much worse. I'd have to reassure her all the time about how well I'm coping, and I can't. I just can't. My brother . . . well, I couldn't cope with his wife, either, not yet.' She gave me a forced smile. 'I'd like it if you stayed. I'd prefer it if I could stay in my own house, but I really don't want to be alone here just yet.'

I mumbled something embarrassed. 'I told the police about the serum,' I admitted at last. 'I'm sorry. I hope—'

'Yeah, so did I,' she interrupted. 'There wasn't any point in keeping our mouths shut now. Don't worry. Brian was the one who wanted the problems kept quiet, not me.'

That threw me. I don't know why I'd expected her to keep quiet; it actually made sense that she'd want to come clean, now that Brian was dead and she needed medical surveillance.

'I hope they don't . . .' I began. I trailed off shamefacedly, then managed to finish, 'That is, I know it could make trouble for you, and I'm very sorry.'

'Oh, I think the police are smarter than that,' Sharon said dismissively. 'Harrass a grieving widow – particularly a grieving widow who's a newscaster? Make a big fuss about a minor obstruction to their inquiry, when *they* pulled their investigator off the case just before the victim got murdered? They won't bother me, don't worry!'

Put like that, I could see they wouldn't. I sighed in relief. Then the memory of what Kermode had said came back with shameful clarity, another reason for her not to welcome me. 'I, uh, I should warn you,' I told Sharon unhappily. 'Apparently Roberto Hernandez is claiming that Curtis Langford shot Brian, and that I'm lying about it because I'm in love with the guy.'

Sharon raised her eyebrows in disgust. '*Curtis Langford?*'

'The pro-lifer,' I explained, remembering that she'd never met him and hadn't even been around most of the times he was discussed. 'I'm *not*; I think he's repulsive! But I thought you should know what Roberto was saying before you invite me to stay here.'

'Oh, look!' exclaimed Sharon dismissively. 'I *know* you're not in love with some stupid pro-lifer. A girl like you could fall for a creep or a jerk, maybe, but he'd have to be a *smart* creep or jerk, and from all I've heard this Langford character is just a dumb redneck. Roberto Hernandez is a liar. We already *knew* that; we have to *expect* him to lie!'

I thought of protesting that not all pro-lifers are stupid, but it would be a pointless contradiction, since Langford was, and Sharon's assessment of my minimum requirement in a man was undoubtedly correct.

'Thanks, then,' I said helplessly. 'I'll stay on another week. I suppose I'd better phone the airline, and see about changing the flight.'

Sharon nodded. 'If they give you any hassle, you can probably refer them to the police. I think I have a card somewhere, with a reference number.'

It seemed to me utterly bizarre that Sharon and I were sitting on the deck eating sandwiches and discussing how to deal with the airline, when Brian was dead. It seemed incredible that life should just go on like that. A husband and father dies; we take time off work, rearrange our travel plans, hold a funeral – and go back to normal.

I supposed that, really, people dying *was* normal. It happens all the time, after all. It just hadn't touched me before.

'You'd better phone your family, too,' Sharon added, after a silence. 'Let them know you won't be back for another week.' She winced, and added reluctantly, 'You probably should invite your mother to the funeral. She's entitled.'

I looked at my watch: half past three. Half past eleven, in England. 'It's too late,' I said wearily. 'And anyway, I think my mother will be in the Dordogne by now.' I wondered how I could reach her: I had no idea of the address. Could I send an emergency message through last-minute.com? Was it really an emergency, though?

She was never going to come to the funeral, not all the way to California. 'I'll send an email,' I said vaguely.

I didn't get up to do it, though. 'Normal life' felt like it was on the top of a very steep hill, one I was far too tired to climb. I wanted to lie down and do nothing at all for a long time.

The phone rang. Sharon heaved herself out of her deckchair and went to answer it. She came back frowning. '*LA Times*,' she informed me. 'Wanting comment.' She grimaced. 'It'll be in the news tomorrow. SBCTV already know, and now the papers have it, and all Brian's colleagues will want to know whether it's true – those that haven't heard already, that is. God.' She pulled her hair back, frowning. 'God, I ought to contact the guys at the lab. They think Brian's gone to Napa for the weekend!'

'I think they'll understand it if you don't,' I offered.

She sighed raggedly. 'Maybe they will. We should have some wine and try to relax while we can. Tomorrow's going to be hell.'

The following day was a Sunday, and, for Sharon, it was certainly hell. The phone began ringing before either of us was out of bed, mostly with condolences, sometimes with inquiries. Eventually Sharon switched it off. She went to the computer, instead, and sent out an email. She had appointed the following Saturday for the funeral – a date carefully chosen to allow the police to finish with the body – and she began inviting people to attend. I found a notebook for her so she could jot down who she'd invited and who'd said they would definitely come.

I couldn't phone the airline, because the phone was switched off, and I couldn't email, because Sharon was using the computer. I did some house-cleaning, figuring that I should at least try to be useful, and then I borrowed the car – taking a risk on the insurance – and bought some things for supper. I suppose it wasn't hellish, but it was certainly boring and stressful.

While at the shops I picked up the *LA Times* and a local paper, the *Santa Barbara News-Press* and read them back at the house. They both had stories about Brian's murder, and the *LA Times* also carried a long obituary. It felt peculiar, to read what some stranger had to say about my father, and learn all sorts of things I hadn't known. It seemed Brian's work had won awards from the National Science Foundation, that he'd been a member of an advisory panel on biotech research funding, that he'd had papers published in all the top journals – and had also penned a history of mad scientists on celluloid.

It also felt odd to be mentioned next to Sharon at the end: 'Dr Greenall leaves behind a wife, Sharon, and a daughter, Alison.' Anyone reading that would assume Sharon was my mother.

By the middle of the afternoon, Sharon had had enough. She switched off the computer and went to lie down. I at once went into her study and switched it on again, to send my own email.

I clicked on 'New Mail' and wrote Mum a terse statement

about what had happened, relaying Sharon's invitation to the funeral. I sent it, then checked lastminute.com for an email address and wrote them a note of explanation and a plea; I attached the email I'd sent my mother, and sent that, too. Then, more out of habit than anything else, I checked my inbox.

There was an email from Steve.

I stared at it for a long time. As long as it was unopened, I could hope. Once opened, though, there'd be no more room for hope or dread: I would know, irrevocably. If it contained what I feared . . .

I quit the program, leaving the email there, untouched, and I shut the computer down. I simply didn't want to have to cope with a rejection now, on top of everything else. I would open it later, when I felt stronger.

I went out of the house and walked up the hillside, slowly because of the heat. Langford wasn't there, of course; finally I had the hiking trail safely to myself. I followed it to the gully where I'd seen the rattlesnake. There was no sign of the snake now, though there were lots of birds and a ground squirrel which greeted my arrival with a peculiar alarm-call, a sort of *plonk* more like a machine than an animal. I splashed some water over my face and arms and thought about following the trail deeper into the mountains. I hadn't put on any sunblock, though, or brought along any water; it seemed better to postpone the hike, as I'd postponed the email, until I'd had time to prepare myself. I sat on a rock for a while, then went back to the house to fix some supper for Sharon and myself.

The following day, Monday, brought the first condolence cards for Sharon, some official letters from the police and some life insurance forms – and a letter for me. It was written in a rounded scrawl in black pen on some paper headed 'Santa Barbara Police Department', and it said:

Dear Alison,

It's weird calling you that, I only learned you're name when the police told it to me. I'm sorry about your Dad, even tho he was a baby butcher. Maybe I shoulden say that to you. But he was. Still he was your Dad, so I'm sorry, and I hope he repented at the end and is with God now.

The police have locked me up again, but Det. Kermode says they're gonna let me out. He says this Hernandez guy, who killed youre Dad, he says he's saying I killed him. But he says the police know it isn't true and are gonna letting me out soon as they charge the other guy. I know you told them the truth, about how I saved you. I would really like to meet up with you when I get out, because I think your a really smart girl, and pretty, too, and I would really like to get together with you. I know your probly upset now, with your Dad dead and everything, but you can call or send me a letter when you have time.

Love, Curtis Langford.

He added his phone and address.

I showed the letter to Sharon. She pursed her lips and gave a slight contemptuous snort. 'Trailer park,' she said, indicating the address.

'He did save my life,' I said unhappily. I was ashamed that I felt so embarrassed and repelled at the thought of Langford as a suitor. So he didn't know the difference between 'your' and 'you're'; he was brave and idealistic. Yes, his particular ideals justified breaking into medical research laboratories, but I knew at least one animal rights activist who'd done the same, and, while I didn't agree with it, it didn't make me cringe the way Langford did. I could tell myself that the problem was simply that I didn't *share* his beliefs and his ideals – but I knew perfectly well that if he'd been, say, an academic theologian, it wouldn't matter so much. It was true that he was violent, but if I was absolutely honest with myself, if he'd been brilliant as well, I would've been willing to overlook it, at least for a while.

What it boiled down to was class and education. Sharon had spotted that at once. She seemed comfortable about it. I wasn't, but I wasn't going to go out with Curtis Langford any more than she would've.

'I'm a snob,' I confessed unhappily.

'So write him a nice letter,' said Sharon. 'Thank him for saving your life, tell him he's a hero – and tell him you've got a boyfriend back in England, and you're going home to him next week.'

That seemed to tempt fate. 'I don't have a boyfriend,' I said hastily.

'*He* doesn't have to know that.'

So I wrote Curtis Langford a letter. I drafted it on the computer, so that I could get it right before sending it, but I copied it out longhand, to make it look less impersonal.

Dear Curtis,

First, thank you very much for saving my life. You were incredibly brave, charging into the house like that, particularly since – as the police told me – your gun was empty. I have no doubt at all that if you hadn't come, Roberto Hernandez would've shot me as well as Brian, and I'm in your debt forever.

I'm afraid there's no possibility of us getting together, though. I have a boyfriend back in England: his name is Steven Marlow, we've been together for about a year and a half, and I'm very much in love with him. I'm going home to him next week. I'm sorry. I think, though, that even if I were free, it wouldn't have worked. You've noticed that I have a smart mouth. To be perfectly honest, I don't have much more control over it than you do over your temper. I do argue and twist people's words all the time, just because I can. I think the combination of my tongue and your temper would've been a complete disaster for both of us.

There's also the problem that Hernandez is apparently claiming that I'm lying about who shot Brian, because I'm in love with you and want to protect you. For us to get together would make it look as though that could be true. I think it would be much wiser for us to go our separate ways.

I am, though, deeply grateful for what you did: you're a real hero! I hope your friends and your family appreciate you, and that you're able to claim the happiness you deserve.

With sincere gratitude and all good wishes,
Alison Greenall

I felt better after writing this. I might be a snob, but the bit about my tongue and his temper being a bad combination was absolutely true.

I folded the letter and went to ask Sharon for an envelope.

I found her in the lounge, notebook and pencil on the coffee table in front of her, thoughtfully rubbing her upper arm. There was something unsettling about her expression, so I didn't immediately blurt out my request; instead, I came and sat down next to her and looked a question at her.

She met my look with one of acknowledgement and moved her hand, though she kept it on her arm. Her slim fingers framed a scaly red mole on the top of her arm, just down from the shoulder.

I looked at the mark, then looked back up into her calm, resigned eyes. 'Oh, no!' I whispered. 'Is it . . .' I swallowed. 'I mean, have you had a doctor look at it?'

'I'll take it to the doctor,' she said quietly. 'It could be nothing. But look.' She turned her arm and pointed to another red dot, just emerging a couple of inches below the first; she turned and showed me another one on the other shoulder. 'All places that caught the sun,' she pointed out. 'It's what Brian was afraid of.'

I swallowed again. 'But . . . but maybe the serum . . . is his lab . . .? That is, can someone else finish his work and . . .?'

She sighed. 'I'm sure someone *will* finish his work. He had a terrific reputation at the sharp end of the biotech industry, and I expect we'll get offers for Greenall Research Inc. within days. I doubt, though, that they'll keep the lab *here*. Whoever buys it will take the patents and the research notes and move it to their own company. The research will certainly go on, but it'll be disrupted, and I won't have any priority on access to it. I don't think it'll be successful in time for me.' She shook her head, then looked thoughtfully out the window. 'I think I'm relieved, in a way. I don't want to live forever, now that Brian's dead.'

She noticed my stricken look and smiled weakly. 'I'm being gloomy. Even if this is . . . *cancer* . . . well, most skin cancers aren't very dangerous. You take them out, and stitch them up, and all's well. In a way, I'd like it if this was something deadly like melanoma, because right now I feel like dying dramatically – but actually it's much more likely that they can just cut this blotch out and I'll be all right again, provided I have regular check-ups and stay out of the sun. Probably in a week or two I'll be glad it isn't anything fatal.'

'Oh, Sharon!' I exclaimed, horrified. 'I'm sorry, I'm so, so sorry!'

'Hush,' she said gently, and hugged me. Despite her brave words, she was trembling, so I hugged her the way I would my own mother, and told her again that I was sorry, so sorry that she was hurt.

*　　*　　*

I didn't manage to get my letter to Langford posted until the evening. When I finally did ask for an envelope, Sharon asked if she could see it 'just out of curiosity', so I let her look at it. She raised her eyebrows.

'Steven Marlow?' she asked.

My face went hot. 'He's . . . he did history at Oxford. We were living together. We had a terrible row just a couple of weeks before I came over here, and he walked out. It was my fault, for arguing too much.'

'I *see*,' said Sharon, as though she did.

'I emailed him,' I blurted out. 'Just the other day. Before Brian . . . before he was shot. And he's emailed me back, but I'm afraid to open it.'

'Oh!' she said, and began to smile – faintly, but with the ghost of her usual gentle amusement. 'Are you afraid it's bad news?'

I nodded.

'It might be good news,' Sharon pointed out. 'He might be glad to make up.'

'There's so many horrible things happening now,' I said, 'I don't think I could cope with another one.' Then I was ashamed of myself. She had faced that lesion on her shoulder: surely I could face an email from Steve.

'If you don't answer it, he may decide you're not serious. Do you want me to come give you moral support while you look at it?'

I drew in a deep breath and let it out again. 'No, thanks,' I told her. 'I'd rather look at it in private. But I'll do it.'

She held up her hands, fingers crossed.

Hi,

    You have the most incredible sense of timing. I got the research job, and I was wishing you were here, so I could tell you about it, and we could go out and celebrate (and then come back and celebrate some more in bed!) and bang I get your email!

I started thinking I'd made a mistake a couple of weeks ago. Oh, sure, you piss me off, regularly, but, my God, all the girls I've met since have seemed vapid. I started telling myself that if only you could understand how maddening it is to have someone pulling your ideas apart all the time . . . and then I wondered how good my ideas would've been, if I hadn't had you dismantling them. I went over my thesis, and I ticked every paragraph which I'd recast because of things you'd said, and you know what? There were more ticked paragraphs than unticked ones.

Then I started thinking of all the relationships I've had, and I started realizing that I never wanted to work at them. I wanted everything to be all sweetness and light, all the time – and human beings aren't like that; life isn't like that. Anything worthwhile takes work; anything beautiful has to be maintained. What we had was bigger and richer than anything I had before, but I wanted it to just be a warm bath I could lie back in. That was a big mistake, and yes, I'm sorry too.

Something truly excellent and glorious, that we don't recognize for what it is, until too late? That describes you, Alison, and if you hadn't emailed me, I would've emailed you. I miss you like crazy and I want you back, OK? Tell me when your flight gets into Heathrow, and I'll be at the airport to meet you.

All my love, Steve